HER PAST RETURNS

Her Hidden Heritage Series Book 1

Gynn Laine Stone

Dedicated to my good friends who believed in me and helped in various ways with this process. From simply encouraging words, helping me with my indecisiveness and actually helping with edit and input. I could not have done it without you all.

Yesterday is history.
Tomorrow is a mystery.
Today is a gift.

ELEANOR ROOSEVELT

CONTENTS

PROLOGUE

Six years ago I thought I'd experienced the worst loss I would face in my life when my mother died. I was wrong, so very wrong. Barely two years after I lost my mother, my grandmother died, and that was even worse. While her death itself was horrible, the worst part was that I lost my entire family with it. No, they didn't die. They merely turned their backs on me. The only family I still have left outside my home is my father who stepped in after my bio-dad bailed, Daniel Wagner, and my brother DJ. While, a few cousins and aunts still speak to me for the kids. No one else does unless left without a choice. I'd understand if I had done something to deserve it, but I didn't. The reality I suppose is I never really measured up and my grandma just prevented them from turning on me sooner.

Of course, I have my close friends Vivika, Sarafina, Maggie, and Lisa who are more like family than the majority of my blood ever was. This of course means instead of just one niece I have two nieces and two nephews. Maggie's in-laws are amazing even if her husband is a tool and has adopted us as family. Maggie's and Vivi's dads even seem to care more than most of my family. So while I don't have much in the way of blood relatives I do have plenty of loved ones. Whoever said *Blood was thicker than water* was very very wrong.

Maybe it's better that way. Maybe a burden, a burden I didn't see has been lifted. Maybe life will be better now. Once the pain lifts, possibly I will find the silver lining in the loss. After all, it's only been a short time. Growing up in a tight-knit family would surely take longer than a couple of measly years to recover from such abrupt isolation, would it not? As hard as it is on me, it pales in comparison to how hard it is on the children.

I think deep down I always knew my family didn't care much for me. I mean there were definitely signs to it, and I'm not a stupid person. I think I just didn't want to see it or believe it. After all, I was raised to believe family is the only thing you can always count on. So who can I count on without them? I'm pretty sure I was simply afraid to be alone so I let myself believe the beautiful lie instead of the cruel reality.

I mean come on what family who actually cares can see you do something amazing and then say oh well this person did this so you could have done better? What kind of person who cares can always find something better to do than to be there for your achievements? My Aunt used to always be there but then she seemed to start drinking the Kool-aid too and was only there when she needed me. That change came around when I was about six. So I escaped into fantasies.

This is why I've always believed in Magick, maybe it's a fanciful delusion that allows me to deal with the challenges I've faced in my life, God knows there's been plenty. Maybe it's just a feeling deep down inside my soul that humans can't be the only creatures on earth. Whatever the reason however I've always believed the supernatural are among us, I'm betting they live in hiding to stay safe from humans' insatiable need to dissect and torture everything we discover.

Don't get me wrong I do understand the need to understand the world we live in and the stuff around us. The creatures we live beside are necessary to understand but humans have a disturbing ability to take their curiosity to a whole new disturbing level.

Maybe human cruelty and a lifetime of feeling out of place, among my peers, is why I believe so heavily in the supernatural. Lord knows being bullied one's whole life can damage the psyche. Oh don't get me wrong I wouldn't call myself a victim oh no every one of my bullies paid for the torture they attempted to inflict. It's a huge part of what made me a tougher person, it helped me learn not to care what anyone else ever thought of me.

Most people would always look at my bleach blonde hair, crystalline blue eyes, standing at barely five feet, and mistakenly believe I was an easy mark. They would assume I was sweet and naïve as my appearance and name, Angelika, would suggest I be. Which is part of why I started dying my hair red in hopes that they might stop underestimating me, even though my attempts were in vain. The reality is I can be a cold bitch, of course only to those who deserve it.

The reality of my life is why I agreed to move out here, to practically the middle of nowhere. Sure the housing market sucks, and finally being able to buy a house we wanted to do it quickly. Still I might have pushed more to stay in town if I didn't think this might be good for us. A new start if you will. Done with the apartments and living like sardines. No more feeling sad family that's only minutes away don't come see us. A chance at a brand new beginning.

CHAPTER 1

“Tasia!”I call sticking my head out of the shower curtain. I've been calling that damn child for a good fifteen minutes now to no avail. I swear when kids become teens, they're hearing diminishes. At least when it comes to hearing adults, and sixteen-year-old girls, by far the worst. “Anastasia Laine Abbott!”

Anastasia, my oldest, my mini-me. Tasia is a fiery, sixteen year old with bleach blonde hair. She's taken to dying it all the colors of the rainbow, she stunningly glacier blue eyes at five foot two. She is just like me, including her over-sensitivity. Unlike me, however, she doesn't hide it well. Nor does she handle rejection very well. She's also scared of her own shadow. Her book smarts, however, are off the charts.

“Gah what, mom?”, When she finally answers, it's with an attitude no less.

“Don't you hear the fucking doorbell?” I ask in frustration.

“ Course I do, mom. Aren't you going to answer it?”

“ Suppose I will don't want to inconvenience you now, do I?”

“Whatever mom.”

Guess I will have to get out of the shower to get the door. This had better be important for someone to be ringing relentlessly for so long. I secure my towel around under my arms and head to the door. "I'm coming", I yell. Yet they won't stop the persistent ringing of the damn bell. "Kyra shut up, would you? It's just the door." Damn, dogs barking is almost as annoying as the doorbell. Though I'd never trade her for anything in the world. She's a gorgeous white pitbull wolf mix with a few tan markings. We'd gotten her from a friend whose husband was mistreating her. I yanked the door open and step out, closing it behind me. "You know, generally when no one answers the door, it means they're busy." Yeah, you could say I'm annoyed.

A young man couldn't be more than twenty-five well groomed, with short black hair, with striking emerald eyes looking like a Boy Scout in his light blue polo and slacks staring at me. His mouth hangs open, in obvious shock, "I Um, my apologies, Ma'am. My name is Theodore Russett."

"Well, what do you want? That's so very important then?" I demand.

"Would you like to dress before we speak, ma'am? I'm OK waiting a few minutes while you do so."

"Well, isn't that just so Considerate, of you? No, I'd rather be done with whatever this is so I can finish my shower. So what is it you want?"

"Very well, I'm an Attorney looking for someone it's urgent that I locate them.. Would you happen to know where I can find Angelika Evelyn Tyler? Miss, sorry I didn't catch your name?"

I carefully school my expression. No one has used that name since I was five. That name is attached with my real father, who is, shall we say? Dangerous. Very carefully, I reply. "I didn't give it. You may call me Mrs. Abbott. Why are you looking for Angelika?"

"I'm sorry, but that's a private matter of which I may only

discuss with Miss Tyler."

"Well, then, Sir, I'm sorry, but I have no information to give you. Angelika has a good reason not to easily be found. I can get a message to her if she's interested, but that's all."

He looks me directly in the eyes and I get this strange feeling of pressure in my head as he replies."Mrs. Abbott, this is very important. I must speak with Angelika immediately."

I ignore the strange sensation and hold his gaze. "That's too damn bad unless you tell me what you need, I won't give you anything. Now, if you'll excuse me."

He flinches as he drops his gaze. Then he hands me a business card. "Very well. Please give her my contact information as soon as possible. Explain this is an extremely urgent matter."

I take the card, walk inside, dismissing him and close the door. I see Tasia's rainbow hair at the desk in the corner of the kitchen where she's doing her school work, and of course, listening to music. I walk over, tap her on the shoulder and she jumps damn near ten feet in the air.

"What the hell? Mom, don't do that." She shrieks.

Any other time I would have laughed, but the man using that name has me spooked. "Tasia, please pay attention. I don't want you answering the door for a while, OK?"

"Mom, you just got mad at me for not answering it."

"I know that I'm now asking you not to. I'll be taking your brother and sister to the bus for a while as well."

"Mom, are you OK? What's wrong?"

"Everything's fine. I'm sure. I'm just being paranoid. I'm going to finish my shower. Take Kyra outback, please."

I escape to my room before I begin shaking. No one should know that name except my father. Maybe his family saying they even know of my existence. My sperm donor, as I call him, was an evil man who committed many atrocities. My mother always feared him finding me, taught me to fear it. It's one of my few fears that has ever ruled my life and choices. I don't even know if it's a rational fear or not. After a few calming breaths, I go to finish my shower and try to forget about the man looking for me. A man that used a name that struck fear into my heart.

Theodore

After I get back in my car, I pick up the phone to call Edward for an update. While I sorely wish I could pass off the job of calling the boss, I can't. So I might as well get it over with now.

"Edward Wulfrik", he answers.

"Hey boss, I went to that address you sent me to. A woman answered, she seems to know Angelika, but she won't give me any information." I tell him.

"Did you press her?"

"Of course I did. I tried applying subtle dominance. It had no effect whatsoever. She was firm."

"You should have pressed her harder. We have to find her immediately before they do. Her life might depend on it."

"Yes Sir, I know how pressing this is. Unfortunately, she wasn't having it. To be honest, I felt difficulty maintaining eye contact. I've never felt that with a human before. She shut me down flat, leaving no room for argument." No way am I going to admit I actually had to break eye contact with a human of all things.

"Are you sure she isn't Angelika? Are you sure she's even human?"

"I'm as sure as I can be. I sense nothing but human from her. That wouldn't be so if she were Angelika, correct?"

"That's true enough. OK, keep an eye on her. If she knows Angelika, she'll reach out, if nothing else to warn her she's being looked for. I'm sure we can track her down that way."

"OK, boss, how long do you want us to keep an eye on her?"

"As long as it takes, as long as it takes."

Angelika

It's been two weeks since the man looking for me came to my door. I can't shake the feeling that I'm being watched, followed. I feel it everywhere I go. At home, the store, hell even in my car, everywhere. I've been having an even more difficult time sleeping than usual, feeling eyes on me twenty-four seven. I'm certain I'm being paranoid that the people I see, whom I could swear are following me are just a figment of my paranoia. Brought on by hearing a name I never thought I'd hear again. Of course, living in a small town probably accounts for seeing the same people all the time more so than anything else.

Tonight is Wednesday night, an unusually cold September night for Arizona. Of course, Jake went to help his mother with yet another unnecessary task that she deemed urgent, so no telling when he'll be home. After all, it's already eight at night and he's still there a good hour's drive away. So, it's just me and the kids. I've decided to use my time trying to finish reading my book, *Iron kissed by Briggs*. I love mouthy female Heroines.

Suddenly I hear a blood-curdling scream, the most ear-piercing scream I've ever heard. It's Tasia, of course, she spooks easily. Probably her siblings teasing her again. However, she's never screamed like that before. I throw my kindle down and start heading for the living room.

"Mom! Mom, come quick." I hear Fy. Well, that's odd. Fy is fearless, nothing scares her. While not the same terror I hear in Tasia's voice, hers is definitely tinged with fear.

Feiry Rayne Abbot is the perfect mix of her dad and me with dark blonde hair, and deep ocean blue eyes at five foot four. She hides her pain so well, so much better than most adults I know. Fy, the fourteen-year-old fearless tomboy who will take the world by storm, no doubt.

I pick up my pace and round the corner to find all three of my kids, wide-eyed, mouths open, pointing to the front window. I look, but I see nothing.

"What is it? What the hell are you staring at?" I Demand. None of them speak. I walk up to Fy and force her to look at me. I ask again, "What is going on, Fy?"

She Blinks a few times and shakes her head clear. "Mom, there was a man. He was licking the window. He had fangs and wild glowing red eyes. Mom, I don't think he was human."

I roll my eyes and start walking towards the door. "Come on, you guys, it was probably just a fucking coyote. Calm the fuck down, will you?" As I put my hand on the door lock, there's a slam at the window. I look over expecting a coyote like I told the kids. Sure enough, there's a man, if you can call it that. Dressed all in black, pasty white skin, completely bald , and glowing red eyes. He's hunched over and looks slightly like *Golem from Lord of the rings* though more demonic. He's literally licking my fucking window with a long pointy tongue and he has fucking fangs. Bloody fucking fangs!

"Well, I'll be a monkeys' fucking uncle. What the flying fuck is that?"

The creature hisses. Then in the eeriest voice, I've ever heard in my life, says, "Little Wolf. Little Wolf come out and plaaaaay."

"No little wolves here, you ugly fucking little creep. Why don't you go fuck your mother and leave us be?" Don't let my words fool you, I'm terrified, literally shaking.

"Now, now. My mother is long dead, little wolf."

"Then dig her up, you little fiend, and leave us be."

"Mom, maybe don't piss off the demon licking our window?" Fy whispers quietly.

"Well, if he needs a safe space, he's at the wrong god damned house," I reply. I turn around, and Tasia is crying silent tears. Remi is in the corner, saying go away over and over. Fy is staring at me like I grew a second head. Suddenly all the power goes out and I look back at the window and the creature is gone.. The kids all scream. Fuck the Breakers. "Alright guys, grab Kyra and Solas, and follow me."

Poor Remi looks completely terrified. Of course, our only boy at twelve years old Remington Wyatt Abbot looks just like his father, Jacob. Remi's brown hair and hazel eyes. He's exceptionally tall for his age. Even though he's extremely sensitive, he was never close to my family, being one of the only boys to be born into it.

They listen immediately, moving faster than I've ever seen. I take them through my room and into my bathroom. "Lock the door. Don't under any circumstances, open it until I or your father come and get you. Got it." The Mutely, nod their heads but say nothing. After closing the door I hear the lock click in place.

I head to the closet and grab my machete. Thankfully, I'm paranoid, so all my doors and windows are already locked. Heading for the front door. I look out the window and don't see the creature anywhere. Granted, at night here it's pitch black, so that doesn't guarantee it's not out there somewhere.

Very alertly, I began to unlock the door to step outside, closing the door behind me, machete in hand. Granted, I'm confident enough with a knife, I have little experience with a long blade. However, with those fangs, I really want to keep some distance. Hopefully, the blade will make it hesitate to do anything at all. I pause on the porch, allowing my eyesight to adjust and trying to see if the creature appears. When it doesn't, I cautiously make my way towards the breaker box off to the side of the house. If I can flip them, the outside lights will turn on, letting me see where the damn thing is. As I cross in front of the garage, I hear something above me. I quickly look up and see the creature dropping towards me. By some miracle, I barely get out of the way.

"Son of a bitch." I mutter under my breath.

I swipe my machete at the creature, the swing clumsy and awkward, but I do manage to slice his arm. Undeterred he lunges at me. I swing around it, but I feel the slice of sharp claws in my shoulder blade as I do. Ignoring the sting I kick out at the creature's knee, dropping it.
Unfortunately, it pops right back up in seconds. We continue trading hits while I'm holding my own, I'm tiring quickly. Meanwhile, the hell-spawned demon seems completely unfazed. It doesn't help that he's fast and impossibly strong. It's probably only been minutes, but it feels like it's been hours. Suddenly, the lights flick on outside. Startled, I stumbled backward and tripped, slicing my calf with the machete as I faltered.

"Fuck!" I hiss in pain, but I refuse to drop I can't I know the second I do I'm dead. Shit, how many more of them are there? Frantically, I look at the creature he's shielding his eyes with, his arms, hissing. What the fuck?

At that moment, something slams into the Red Eyed Devil, knocking it across the yard, where it lands with an audible thump, in a crumpled heap unnaturally still. I moved my eyes to what hit him. There's a man maybe five foot eight, with short spiky blonde hair and unnaturally eerie blue eyes. He's handsome in a dangerous sort of way. Black jeans, boots, and leather jacket reminds me of *Spike from Buffy*. I very slowly get to my feet, keeping my eyes on the stranger. My blade at the ready, "And who the fuck are you?" I ask.

"Now, is that any way to thank your savior, love?" He says amusingly. With probably the sexiest English accent I've ever heard.

"Oh, my sincerest apologies for not bowing at your feet, especially when I have no clue who the fuck you are. Let alone if you're in some way related to that, that demon. So, I ask again. Who are you?" My supposed Hero began laughing, the audacity of the prick. "Are you seriously laughing at me? You spike wannabe?"

He pulls himself together, but his irritating grin remains along with the amusement in his eyes. "Sorry, no, I'm not laughing at you, love. You're just not at all what I was expecting and I was caught off guard. My name is Ian Jacobson, and that was a vampyr, not a demon. As I'm sure you know."

"A vampyr, of course. Why wouldn't it be a vampyr?" I take a few calming breaths. "OK, so what are you doing here? What do you want?"

"Well, love, one of my associates came by looking for Angelika. It was obvious you know her. So, we were told to keep an eye on you in case you contacted her. From what I've seen, you can't help us. Given tonight though, it's a good thing we were watching, I reckon. Probably why he was here too."

I lose it. I start laughing hysterically. I can't help it. Of all the cruel fates, my sperm donor curses me yet again. The man just stares at me it's clear he thinks I've cracked. Maybe he's right. Through my laughter, I look at him. Thankfully my blades are still up since I don't know how he will react when I tell him the truth. "I'm Angelika, you fucking idiots. How the hell have you not found that out? What do you fools want with me? His goal was clear yours, not so much."

"That's not possible." He mumbles in complete and utter confusion.

"Unfortunately it's extremely possible, and sadly my reality. Would you like to see my birth certificate?" I glanced into the window and see Fy. Damn it, I knew she wouldn't stay. I got to wrap this up quickly. I look back at Ian. "Answer me this. Do you and your associates wish me harm?"

"Wish you harm?" He asked, confused.

"Yes, harm, what is your intention with Me."

"What? No, of course not. Why would we wish you harm?"

I hear sirens, of course. The neighbor called the cops. I glanced to where I saw the vampyr drop, only to see that he was gone. Great tonight's not getting any better. "OK, our friend is gone. Please tell me he can't get inside my house?"

"I figured he'd bugger off. That wasn't enough to kill him by any means, I merely wanted him away from you. Of course, he can't get inside without an invitation, which you are very well aware of. Don't worry though, he won't bloody well be back tonight."

What the hell? Why would he think I should know that? The sirens are getting closer. So further discussion will have to wait. "OK, I need to grab my kids. The police will be here any minute. I'm assuming, we keep the species of my attacker to ourselves?"

"I think that would be best, yes."

I start limping towards the house, ignoring the burn in my calf.

"Were you hurt? Did he bite you?"

"Fy, go get Tasia and Remi, then come back out here, please." I turned back to Ian. "No, he didn't bite me." Questions on that later. "I'm good with knives, not as much with long blades. When the lights came on, which I now assume was you, I thought it was more of them. I got startled and started to fall. I sliced my calf when I did."

"But their eyes don't adjust well to the sudden light. Why would you think it was them?"

Before I can tell him how sick of his assumptions that I know everything is, the kids fly out of the house. I drop my blade and take them into my arms.

"Mom, what was that?" Fy demands.

"Mom, are you OK? Mom, are you bleeding? Who is he?" Tasia whispers hysterically.

Remi just stares at Ian shifting slightly behind me. Fy informs me she called her dad and he's on the way. She also is the one who called the cops. As if on cue four cop cars come to a screeching halt in front of my house. All four cops exit their cars and put their hands on their holsters. Only one of the officers began to approach us cautiously.

"Ma'am, I'm officer Reyes. We got a call that a man or a wild animal maybe, had been attacking the residents of this home. Where is it? Or is it him?" She says pointedly, eyeing Ian.

"Yes, there was a man attacking us. This gentleman was nearby and interceded. He managed to chase the creep off."

"So, it was a man, the report said, a man, no, a creature with glowing red eyes. Also, that he was licking your window?" She asked in a questioning voice.

"Yes, I'm pretty sure he was wearing contacts. He definitely was quite insane."

"And you decided to come outside and fight him? Is that your machete?" I look around and one of the officers now is talking to Ian. While another is speaking with the kids, I can't see where the last one is. My calf still stings like a son of a bitch. I start rubbing it. "Ma'am, are you bleeding? Are you hurt? Did the man do that?"

"No, he scratched my shoulder blade, but I almost fell, and when I did the machete cut me."

"Alvarez call EMTs now."

"Already en route should be here soon."

The ambulance rounds the corner just as he replies. "OK, ma'am, we're going to get you into the bus and we'll touch base in the morning. We'll have to get an official statement tomorrow. So we'll need you to come into the station."

"I'll get into the ambulance, but I'm not leaving, nor will my kids be out of my sight until my husband gets here."

"Understandable ma'am."

"Also, I'd like to thank Ian before he leaves."

"Of course, I'll see that he comes over."

A good 20 minutes later, the EMTs were speaking with Reyes. I'm going to need stitches, but we are waiting for Jake to get home. They argued with me about it but in the end, I won. Ian walks up.

"So, I'm told you wanted to thank Me, love."

"No, not really. Look, you said that thing won't come back tonight. However, I'm not as confident. If it comes back, my husband won't know what to do. I can't tell him. He won't believe me, he doesn't believe in this stuff. I was hoping… I was going to ask… um…"

He looks amused. "Wow, this is really hard for you, isn't it? Don't worry, love. We'll stay and watch. Someone will come to see you at the hospital."

"Thanks."

"Interesting…" Just as he begins speaking, Jake runs up, having had to park down the street.

Typically a jealous man, he doesn't even seem to notice Ian. I can tell he's scared, even if he won't admit it to anybody else. Jake is athletically built at six feet, he towers me. He's got the same brown hair and Hazel eyes Remi does. Not classically handsome, but ruggedly so. At least I believe he is.

"Babe, are you OK? What happened? Fy was hard to understand."

"I'm OK. Some crazy guy attacked the house. He flipped the breaker, so I hid the kids and went out to flip them back on. I cut myself. He gave me some scratches and bruises, and I'm gonna have to go get stitches. We were just waiting for you."

"OK, I'll meet you at the hospital."

"No! Stay with the kids."

"But…"

"No, we don't know if he'll be back. I don't want the kids waiting at the hospital or home alone. By the way, this is Ian. He was in the area when the attack happened, and he chased the man off."

Jake turns to Ian. "Thank you for helping my family. I can't express how much I appreciate it."

"My pleasure. Pleased to meet you both. Your wife is very brave. Well, I should be going. I hope you all have a better evening."

The EMT comes back and says we're leaving. I assure Jake I will contact Maggie for a ride home and he says he'll wait up.

As the doctor finishes stitching me up, I realize I'm going to have to call Jake. Neither Maggie nor my dad answered their phones. They must be sleeping.

"Ahem," I look up at the door. Standing there is the man who came to my house a few weeks ago. "So you do in fact know, Angelika."

"Right, I forgot. Ian said someone would be coming by. What did you expect? I had no idea why you were looking for me. The only one who knows that name is the sperm donor responsible for my existence. I'm told he's quite deplorable."

"Well, yes, he is quite that and more. I guess I should have thought of that."

"Right. So why were you looking for me anyway?"

"Well, I'm the executive of your inheritance. Technically also your attorney. But you've had a rough night, so we should discuss this more tomorrow. Ian told me what happened and I would also like you to wait to talk to the police until I'm with you tomorrow. While you were clearly acting in self-defense, police don't always see these things that way. How about I give you a ride home?"

I agreed to all of it, but only because I'm utterly exhausted and too tired to argue. We talked on the way to my house about various topics. If I wish I had another car. What kind? How I grew up. Oddly, the whole conversation is about me and my wants, my past. It seems like he has a more personal attachment. Most of the more personal questions I dodge. He says his goodbyes and tells me he'll be by tomorrow morning to talk. He also urges me to wait for him before I talk to the police, which I'll do 'cause I don't really trust them. I head into the house and find Jake asleep on the couch. If he's out here, he definitely tried to stay up, just couldn't. I wake him up and we head to bed together.

CHAPTER 2

The next day I decided to keep the kids home from school. To be honest, I never want them leaving the house again, but Jake says that's ridiculous. Of course, he didn't see what I saw last night. If he did, maybe he wouldn't feel that way. I'm reluctantly getting ready to go to the police station for my statement. I originally planned on bringing the kids, but my attorney claims he has some solution to avoid dragging them with us.

He's coming to pick me up in a few minutes. I figure if I don't like what he has, he'll just have to wait for them to get ready. As I finish applying my makeup, the doorbell rings, and of course, Kyra immediately starts barking.

"Mom, the door," Fy calls from her room. I thought it best for all the kids to stay in their rooms until I see what Theodore has in mind.

"I hear it, Fy. I'm getting it." I reply, on my way to the door.

I opened the door to see Ian and Theodore standing there with a woman I'd never met but recognized from following me at Walmart a few weeks ago. "I wasn't just being paranoid", I mumble.

"Excuse me." Theodore, asks.

"I thought I was being paranoid when I saw her following me the last few weeks. I guess I wasn't."

"Oh no, Angelika, we do apologize, but I did have people following you. We thought you could lead us to well, you. This is Sierra Travis. You already met Ian, of course."

"Of course. Hello again Ian, and Theodore. Good to meet you, Sierra. Please call me Angel."

"You too." Sierra. says briskly. She doesn't seem to like me much. All well, who cares?

"Only if you call me Theo. May we come in?"

"That depends. Do you need an invite to enter?"

"Pardon," Theo asks in confusion.

Ian snickers. "No Angel. We're not vampyrs. I'm glad to see you looking better."

"The wonders of makeup," I reply as I move aside without issuing an invitation.

"Smart." Ian muses as he enters, trailed by Theo and Sierra.

"So, are you ready to go Angel?" Theo inquires.

"Right after we discussed your solution for not bringing the kids and the other matter."

"Oh, of course. My apologies, I brought Ian and Sierra to stay with the kids. As for the other matter, I thought we could stop for lunch and discuss it. Of course, I have a man bringing pizza for the children, if that's OK with you?" Theo calmly explains

"If the kids are comfortable staying with them, that will work. The lunch and the pizzas are fine too." I turned to Ian and Sierra. "However, I will warn you of three things. My oldest is boy crazy and will have a crush on you, Ian. My kids are a handful and if anything happens to them, what I do to you will make *The Saw* movies look like *Sesame Street*."

"Won't be a problem," Ian replies confidently.

"Kids come here," I yell.

They all come to the living room, Tasia, of course, sneaking glances at Ian, as I knew she would. Fy is guarded and Remi, oblivious as usual.

"Guys I'm going to go with Theo here to the police station. This is Ian and Sierra. They will be staying with you. These are my kids Tasia, Fy, and Remi."

"Mom, we don't need babysitters," Fy says.

"It's fine," Tasia replies.

"Of course, you'd say that there's a guy," Remi says.

"Shut up. You're more into guys than anyone here." Tasia exclaims in irritation.

"All of you shut up. They're not babysitters. They're here to protect you. I want you to behave and be respectful. Got it."

"Yes, mom." They all said.

"OK. I love you guys. I'll be back as soon as I can."

"We love you too."

I hugged each one of them and began heading out. Ian must have noticed my nerves because he says "It will be fine. I promise."

Giving my statement at the police station didn't take much time, but it was a huge pain in the ass. By the time I'm done, I just want to head home and go to bed. Unfortunately, we still have to stop and talk about why Theo is actually in my life in the first place. He picked this nice little restaurant. Kind of a mom-and-pop shop I think called Hot Shots. Never heard of it before. We had to come to downtown phoenix to give my statement. Why I had to come all the way out here for this was beyond me. Considering it's over an hour and a half away from my house. Apparently, they told me that there were a couple of escaped mental patients and they believed that one of them might have been the man at my house. But I know that's not true.

"So, let's get down to business," Theo says.

"OK, so what exactly did I inherit and from who? I know my dad was a lowlife, so it's not like he had anything to leave me." I ask.

"Your inheritance is actually from your grandparents; it was passed to you because your father was determined unfit to inherit. While your father had many other children. They, unfortunately, don't meet the requirements to inherit. Because of that, we've been searching for you. We knew that you came from a specific family background and that you had been sheltered from your father. So, you wouldn't have any of his, bad habits shall we say. While it's been allowed for a few of his other children to take place in the company business and get a small amount of the family fortune. We, unfortunately, can't allow them to inherit the bulk of it because it's clear that they take more after your father than their mothers. This, of course, would be a very bad thing to allow power and that amount of wealth to go to people who may use it for bad purposes. However, they did get plenty of money to compensate."

"So you're telling me that I meet the requirements of inheritance because I'm more moral than my siblings?"

"Essentially yes. There is another factor of course that makes you uniquely more qualified. However, your uncle has asked that it be left for him to explain."

"OK, so you said that they got family money. So what exactly is my inheritance if they already have family money but don't qualify for it?"

"Well, yes, your siblings have inherited some of the family money. You've inherited full control of the company as well as main control of the family assets. Properties and of course the bulk of the family wealth that your father was set to get."

"So what exactly are we talking about here? Couple hundred thousand dollars, a house, what?"

"No, actually your family owns and manages a security firm named Wolfpack Security Insurance. Which is what Ian and Sierra work for. In addition to that, they have four main properties in four different countries. As well as a few Vacation homes, if you will. Quite a few business properties. In addition to such, you will have access to not just a few hundred thousand, but a few hundred million dollars."

I damn near spit out my coffee, choking. After I finished clearing my throat, finally I look at him in a stupor and exclaim. "What?"

"Yeah. So like I said, you're pretty rich. Oh. You basically get to control your sibling's finances as well."

"OK. Do they not have any other children? I swear my mom said my dad had some."

"Oh yes, they had other children, but those children have their own inheritances. You will be inheriting your father's share since he's been disqualified. Currently, your uncle Edward is running the business in your stead. He's searched for you relentlessly. We almost found you a couple of times but then we lost you again. When we finally decided to approach your grandmother once more out of necessity, we found that she had passed. I'm very sorry for that loss by the way."

"OK, so what exactly does this mean and what exactly do I need to do?" I say avoiding the grief discussion.

"Well, the bulk of your inheritance won't be allowed to be yours for at least five years. It would have been yours immediately, but because you're married your family wanted to make sure if that was the case, that you wouldn't be taken advantage of. So, you will be given a certain amount for housing finances, day-to-day life, a lump sum in the beginning, and of course, spending for vacations. You will also have a certain number of finances for private business affairs if you choose to use it. In addition, you'll have a monthly allowance which will be given to you until you reach the five years."

"So wait a minute. My inheritance is basically me being treated like a child?"

"No, of course not. Your grandparents just wanted to make sure that in the event of you being in a relationship at the time that you reach inheritance, you don't get taken advantage of. As such, of course, you can only gain your full inheritance at the end of five years, as long as your husband continues working and contributing during that time, proving he won't be taking advantage of it. That or he can agree to sign over any marital rights to claim your inheritance, in which case after its final and non reversible it'll be released to you. However, in the meantime, I promise you will have substantial money to do whatever you wish."

"OK, so how much of this allowance are we talking about here?"

"Well, in terms of spending money alone every year you'll get two point five million dollars."

Again, I say completely shell-shocked. "Two point five million dollars, Are you serious? What kind of crazy allowance is that?"

"Well, they just wanted to make sure that you were being taken care of, of course. They were very distraught that they couldn't find you a lot sooner. They've been looking for you since you were a child, and had no idea where you went or why your mom left. Your dad said that she just took you and ran. They met you a couple of times and were very fond of you. They were sure being raised with your dad would change that, but obviously, you weren't raised with him, so it doesn't matter. Sadly, though they never met your mother's family or knew where she was from. We tracked them down about Twelve years ago but your grandmother said you'd left the state and wouldn't provide information at all. A couple of years ago was when we'd finally decided to try to go back to her. Your grandparents knew they would be leaving us and wanted dearly to find you first."

That must have been the detective my grandma had told me came looking for me just after we had left for Idaho. "OK, so what exactly do we do now?" I say casually. I'm trying desperately to ignore the talk of dead relatives. I'm not sure I can handle it right now and aside from not wanting to break down in front of Theo I also don't want to make him feel bad. After all, he is only answering my questions.

"Well, I figured that since tomorrow is Friday, we can meet on Monday. I'll come over and we can discuss some of your finances. Have a view of your assets and things like that, and we can go ahead and gradually get you involved in the business. I'll be acting as your liaison and official advisor until you get the hang of things. One other thing, your uncle Edward would really like to meet you."

I'm not altogether sure how I feel about meeting my uncle. In truth, Edward was the one my mom always spoke well of, outside of my grandparents but still...

"I guess we can start on Monday. So, will people still be watching my house in case that weird creature shows up again? I really don't know what to do with it. As for my uncle. Yeah, we can meet. But could I get a couple of weeks to get my feet in the water, before diving into the deep end with family reunions?"

"Of course, I'm sure he'll understand, I'll give him a call and talk to him. Besides this, he has to rearrange his schedule so he can come out here and meet you in person. As for the creature, why do you keep calling it a creature? It's a vampyr, a strigoi to be exact. It's a breed that acts as a guard dog to its masters. You should know that."

"Why should I know that? Outside of Ian telling me last night I would have no idea. Yes, I've always believed vampyrs existed. Werewolves and all the other little funky creatures that we hear about all the time, but I've never actually seen any. You act like this is everyday life for people."

"Never seen or heard about vampyrs in real life? Werewolves? The Fae? What about witches?"

"Yeah, of course, I've heard about it, especially witches. I even know a few and practice a bit myself. Obviously not the ones like on *Charmed* that can freeze time or anything, but no, I mean. Outside of a common belief, and maybe legends and stories never heard of any supernatural creatures actually existing." Well unless you count my ghosties but I'm not going to tell him about those. People always look at me like I'm nuts over them.

"OK, then this explains so much. I'm really sorry. Looks like you have a whole lot to catch up on. Maybe we should figure out how to work that out. How about I take you home and we can talk about that on Monday as well?"

"OK, I suppose that will work. I probably better get back anyway. Jake should be home soon, and he's probably gonna freak out if Ian and Sierra are there."

"OK, no problem. I'll drop you off now."

We pull up in front of the house as we get out, he hands me the keys to the car and informs me that this is mine. I noticed that it's a Chevy Traverse, the same car that we talked about the other night. It's a beautiful baby blue with sparkles, the exact color I wanted. I should have found it odd he shows up with the same car in the same color we were talking about. I tell him that I can't take this but he says it's not a big deal because it came out of my inheritance. He grabs Ian and Sierra and lets me know that they'll be by on Monday so we could talk a little bit better about the details which is good because I have a lot of questions for him starting with how my family is involved with this weird supernatural world.

Theodore

"Edward Wulfrik speaking." He answers on only the second ring.

"Hello, Edward, Theo here. I've been trying to reach you, but you've been unavailable. We've found Angelika, so have the vampyrs."

"What? Is she okay? Was she hurt? What happened?"

"Your niece is fine sir; Ian was nearby when they showed up and he handled it. The vamp took out our guard. The thing is, do you remember the woman who I spoke with a few weeks ago we've been watching in case she contacted Angelika?"

"Yes of course I remember her. What about her? Was she hurt? Of course, that would be regrettable but in the end, only Angelika really matters to us right now." He tell me. His voice filled with regret.

"I know sir, no she wasn't harmed. The thing is, she is actually Angelika."

"Wait, what? You said she was human. How is this even remotely possible?" He peppers me frantically with questions.

"She definitely gave no supernatural traces, in fact, she still doesn't. It's definitely her though I'm not sure why we can't feel it. You met her as a child, are you sure she ever had a

trace?”

“Yes, she definitely did and it was strong. It's part of the reason my parents wanted her to take over in place of her father. We knew even then she'd be stronger than anyone else in our family. We knew what she really was. There's no way that could have gone backward, that kind of power grows, it doesn't recede.”

“Is it possible it's hidden? Or suppressed even? Is it possible she doesn't even know?” I ponder.

“Yes, it's possible, if her shifting's been held off, or if a strong enough witch suppressed her powers from her. I'd heard her great grandmother was a strong witch, there are also rumors that she has more magic on that side than just witchcraft. However, why would anyone hide it?”

“I have no idea, but I have very strong reason to believe someone did. Sir, she has no idea who or what she is. Hell, she doesn't even know the supernatural world exists. When the vampyr attacked her home, she had no idea what it was. She didn't even know it needed an invitation to get inside.”

“ I can halfway see her mother's family wanting to hide her place in the supernatural world from her, but to not even teach her about it? That leaves her severely vulnerable. Why would her family do that to her? What did she do when the Vampyr attacked? Who was it? Was it a group?” He inquires angrily.

“I'm not sure which group it was, even if it was a group, but it was just an underling. She actually tried to fight it thinking it was some kind of demon with a machete of all things. Ian luckily was doing his rounds early, it killed one of our guards we haven't told her about that. He intervened and stopped the attack; he wasn't sure if it was alone so he stayed instead of pursuing. We've amped up our surveillance since then. She finally admitted who she was, she lied because she was worried her father might be behind trying to locate her. For obvious reasons that worried her horribly. I have filled her in on the basics of her inheritance, I also got her a new car already hers was run down she wants to keep it so we'll fix it up. Until then though she shouldn't be driving it around. When we were talking I realized her being obtuse about the vampyrs wasn't just an act, she really doesn't know anything concrete. She says she knows a little about witchcraft but I'm unsure the extent it seems to be more the basic practice knowledge though. She specifically mentioned how they can't freeze time and other such magicks which we both know is not correct.

She was however wearing a necklace that did emit a decent amount of power. I decided to schedule a meeting for Monday to talk to her more after I'd spoken with you of course. I also mentioned to you that she's requested a couple of weeks to adjust before meeting with you. I told her I would speak with you about it?"

"I am eager to see my niece again, however, I do understand her reservations. I'll schedule to come out in about three weeks to meet her in person. I think we should have our physician see her. Tell her it's routine for the company or something like that. Educate her in the supernatural world of course it won't happen in a day or two but give her a crash course. We will need to assign someone to help her more thoroughly. For now, however, I think we should withhold information about what she herself is unless absolutely necessary to tell her. It will probably make this easier for her at least for the time being."

"Of course. I think Ian would be a good fit, he can also act as extra security for her. We've already purchased the house across the street and a few others on the block to make sure she's guarded, she lives in a pretty desolate neighborhood so it shouldn't be too hard to do. As for what she is, may I ask what exactly she is?"

"To be honest outside of our True Alpha and extremely powerful I don't really know. I was hoping we would find out when we located her. You know what her father is, I'm not sure what all she inherited from that genetic mess, but we do know her family is magically descended. We never were sure if we fully pinned down the history but like I said her grandmother was a powerful witch and we know a great grandfather was a shaman. Anything else is just guessing. I will send you a file on what we have, hopefully, the Doc can tell us a little more through his testing."

"Do we even know if she inherited the shifting gene? If she hasn't, can she even be alpha?"

"Technically yes she can. It would be near impossible for her to hold if she has no power at all. We will have to cross that when it comes, I'm still able to hold the position for another couple of years so we will be able to figure it out and prep her before we have to have her step into the role. The worst case maybe we can find a suitable shifter mate for her to help hold her position."

"Sir, she's married. To a human, they have kids together. I don't think she would easily leave him, and him being human, he wouldn't understand our customs and probably won't agree to additional mates."

"Shit! Okay, we still have time. Whoever hid this world from her certainly didn't do her any damn favors. You said she has kids? Do you sense anything in them? What are they like?" His curiosity is evident in his questions.

"I've only seen them once. They're pretty great, from what I can tell. They are her world. The oldest looks just like her mom. To be honest, if we found them when she was younger, we'd have found Angelika a lot sooner. Pictures on the wall of her as a baby she looked just like the ones we had to work with.

However, they're too young I believe to even have powers I'm not sure. Though I didn't sense anything either way."

"Okay, extend the physicals to the whole family. Hell, including the mortal husband might as well find out how good of health he's in while we're at it."

"Certainly. How much of the business do you want to be explained to her?" I inquire.

"Go ahead and explain most of it, just don't tell her yet what kind of employees we have. Let's try and ease her in as much as possible. We will decide how to go about that topic after we hear from the Doc."

"Okay sir, I will check in after I meet with her on Monday."

Angelika

It's Sunday night, movie night with the kids. Fy got to pick tonight so we are watching the new *Halloween*. Which of course means a restricted number is going to call me playing the Halloween theme song because well why wouldn't it? I get up and head to the garage unsure who it is calling me.

"**Hello?**" All I hear is eerie breathing, almost sounds like a creepy 900 call. "**Hello? If you're not going to respond I'm hanging up.**"

"**You're going to die BITCH!**" Says an angry voice.

"**Uh huh, like I haven't heard that one before.**" I reply nonchalantly.

"**I'm going to rip out your entrails and feed them to my dogs. I'm going to feast on your cold dead heart. You're going to die begging me to take mercy on you.**" The voice hisses.

"**Well, that certainly is graphic, no doubt. However, I got to say I'm not all that interested in feeding my entrails to puppies, as**

for my heart it's quite comfortable where it is. Thanks so much for the offer though." I say as cheerily as I can manage. Fuck letting this creep freak me out.

"You smug alpha bitch. What the hell makes you think you have a choice?"

"Well since I'm in charge of my life, I guess I say I do. Goodbye, now thanks for your thoughtful words." I say as I hang up. Might as well finish the movie.

Monday morning Theo calls to see what time I want to meet up. We settled on ten which means he should be here shortly. I'm not sure if it'll just be him or if he's bringing anyone else. I haven't told Jacob about any of this yet while I don't want to hide it I would like to know more before we discuss it. I figure we can go out to dinner tonight and discuss it hopefully Theo won't mind having someone stay with the kids again while we do so. I head out to have a smoke while I wait, I'm less nervous with the kids at school where they are hopefully safe. I figure whoever's at me is watching me at home. Sitting on the porch I hear a car, glance over to see it's Theo pulling up with Ian. They get out and head my way. Of course, Tasia is still here but I have her doing her school work in her room today.

"Hey." I great them.

"Good morning, Love," Ian replies

"Good morning, Angel how are you today?" Theo says.

"I'm okay. I got a strange call last night. A bit threatening something about eating my heart and feeding my insides to puppies. It was quite descriptive." I inform them casually.

"Why didn't you call? Do you have the number? Are you okay?" Ian panics.

"Dude chill, it's fine just a stupid call. No, I didn't get the number because it was blocked. Yeah, I'm totally fine."

"You still really need to let us know when these things happen. It's important for security reasons."

"Ian's right. We really need to know these things." Theo chimes in

"Okay, I'll tell you if it happens again. Like I said I'm not worried I got threatening phone calls well before any of this ever happened. I have a habit of saying what comes to mind not everyone appreciates that." Ian and Theo exchange a concerned look. "What? Why do y'all look like you're afraid the world's about to end?"

Ian looks at me, "We're just wondering if you might have been on someone's radar earlier than we thought."

"I'm sure that's not it. I piss people off with my opinions and vocalizations all the time. Really it's no big deal. So are we going to go inside and talk?" I say as I flick my butt.

"We are yes, but Ian will be staying out here keeping an eye out on things until we're finished."

Ian must have seen that this made me uncomfortable. "No worries love, some things are above my pay grade. I'm completely fine with that. Besides I'm sure you'd like to keep your financial affairs private."

"Okay," I say as I head into the house followed by Theo. I lead him towards the desk in the kitchen that has my main computer and two chairs. "Please sit, sorry we've never gotten a kitchen table. To be honest we've never really eaten in the kitchen. Not very family-oriented I suppose, but we like to watch TV while we eat."

"It's quite all right. So to start off here's a list of your accounts, you're cards, the deeds and keys to your personal properties, as well as some cash to get you started." He says as he hands me a couple of vanilla envelopes stuffed to the rim.

I peer inside them and realize the term some cash is a massive understatement. "Damn that's a lot of cash, and it looks like six credit cards?"

"Well one is a gas card, then you have a personal debit as well as a personal credit card. The others are to pay for things like staff, cleaning services, etc. Your allowance will be automatically sent to your personal debit account, all the cards should be labeled. They also have your pin numbers which of course you can change whenever you like."

"Okay, thanks for that it should make things easier."

"Like I said before you have four main residences in four different countries. They are located in the areas we do the most business Washington, France, Germany, and Ireland. You also have sixteen vacation properties but only one is located in Arizona. They are technically located in major territories associated with the business, but we can discuss that later."

What the fuck? "Twenty properties? Seriously?"

"Of course. Your family was very well established. As I said before you will be able to purchase or even build if you so desire additional properties for either your residence or business. There will be some limitations to how many for the first five years, but after that, you do what you want. Immediately we would like to get you the main residence and up to two vacation properties. Locations, build, etc. will be entirely up to you. In addition, we can make improvements on this property or even solely do that if you prefer. Though we would prefer your main residence be a bit more security friendly than this one is."

"Where exactly is the vacation property in Arizona? Also, are there any in Idaho, or Florida?"

"Well, it's up by lake Mead actually. As for Idaho, you do not currently have one. None were built there because that's where a business rival is located however, I'm sure we can figure something out if you'd like. Though yes you do have one in Florida." The way he says business rival gives me a brief pause. Almost as if he was about to say a different term but I let it slide.

"Okay, I would actually like one in Arizona up north. Payson, maybe Flagstaff? One in or around Elk City, Idaho would be amazing as well if possible. Do I have any more in the US already?"

"I think we can arrange something for both actually I will have them looked into. You do have a few more in the states yes."

"Thank you. I actually have a realtor I'd prefer if it's an option. As for this house, there are a few improvements I would like mainly in extending my property. Though I'm not sure that's possible."

"What exactly did you have in mind?"

"Well ideally, I would like to have the entire land of this block. Though I know there are already a couple of houses and one more being built but I'd prefer not to have any actual next-door neighbors. Of course, some yard work and basics like painting and anything that needs fixing obviously. I'd also like this yard extended but not fully with a gate connecting to the rest and a second house, slightly bigger on it."

"I can definitely look into that I'm pretty sure I can make it happen. So do you want to stay living on this property then?"

"Temporarily yes however eventually I'd like to have my own house built I've actually made plans for it already. It has kind of been my dream home for a while." I get up and grab the plans out of my cabinet in the corner. "Here you go. This is the more detailed idea obviously I don't expect it to end up anywhere close to that."

He takes the plans and is looking through them with extreme thoughtfulness. When he's finished, he looks at me with astonishment. "You created this? Is this a tunnel system underground?"

"Yeah, I started working on it years ago. The property has pretty much everything I would ever want. It also has an expansive underground bunker system, in case anything weird ever happened. I really don't like most people."

"These are incredible. I think I need to have you design my home. We have a construction company we work with; I'll have them look this over and get back to me. Then I'll let you know what we can do about it."

"That would be great, thank you."

"Now to the business part of this discussion. So as I explained, You run a security company. The company does everything from body guarding to government contracting. The main headquarters are in Washington, though you can work out of the branch here to start then we can decide if we want to relocate the main branch, relocate you, or have you work remotely." He hands me two more Vanilla envelopes. "Here are all the papers for your review, as well as the keys for all the buildings, and a business charge card which should be with the rest. Additionally, the company has its own insurance as well as private physicians. We would like to get you and your family in for a full workup. When would be good for you, the sooner the better?"

"We can do whenever. So about this whole supernatural topic."

"Oh yes, almost forgot that one. So pretty much everything you've heard about in legends really does exist. You will be taught how to deal with these threats as well as be given proper education on the topic. Your uncle has requested I find someone to teach you, I believe Ian would be best for this job. He will also be able to act as added security. We already have people shadowing your family discretely of course. Additionally, your uncle said he'd like to set up a meeting with you in about three weeks."

"Okay, that sounds great thank you."

"No problem. Well, I better be heading out now. Have a good day, Angel."

Over the next week, Ian had been coming over every day to work with my knowledge of the supernatural world. They seem to think I should have been being taught this information my whole life, and it seems they have been. Somehow, I doubt most people raise their kids to be prepared for a supernatural attack, because of that I can't shake the feeling there's more going on that they haven't told me. I feel like they're still keeping secrets from me. I know most if not all the people I've come in contact with work for the company I suppose I now own so I'm curious if maybe that's the link. From what I can tell it seems as though most of these people's families have worked with the company for a few generations if not more. It would also make sense seeing as how I haven't really had much to do with the company yet outside of the brief explanation Theo gave me, nothing more has come up. I've planned to talk more to Theo about it but Ian told me he's currently out of town on business but has plans to check back in as soon as he's back in town.

So far, the lessons with Ian have been similar to what I'd assume one would learn in school if the subject was taught. Mostly history, basic knowledge of strengths and weaknesses, that sort of thing. Considering the point in my being better prepared to handle supernatural threats that's pretty expected, what's not however expected is that I haven't been taught about vampyrs at all yet. It seems odd to me since vampyrs have been the only threat to come up against me thus far, I would think that would be where we'd start.

However no, I've been learning about Were creatures while Ian has been teaching me about various types of Weres which is not something I'd ever thought I'd say, we've mostly focused on Werewolves. Personally, I've always believed in the supernatural. I told Theo I knew some about witches and have always believed they existed, that was the basic extent of my knowledge. Well, I guess unless you include ghosts, I do have some experience with them but I'm not sure that counts so much as supernatural so I've never bothered mentioning it to either Ian or Theo. Besides, I don't want them to think I'm completely nutty. Ian did tell me that in a few weeks they want to do more hands-on teaching he didn't exactly explain but it sounds like he means teaching me to defend myself which might be a good thing. Besides it would be more fun than learning about how the different Were species came to be, or how Werebirds call themselves flocks, while Werecats preferred pride, and of course, Werewolves went with packs. Let alone the different hierarchy in the groups, seriously why would someone need to know the difference between a Luna or an Alpha unless you're a Werewolf yourself? Though of course, that said it was interesting to find out that Weres have a self-governing system, and that there are more in our society than I ever would have thought.

Truth be told, even in my beliefs I always imagined small groups hiding and living in caves away from the blood-thirsty humans who would no doubt dissect them if they ever knew they existed. I have asked Ian why any of this was important and his simple response was *'it's easier to defend against something when you understand how it works than when you don't'* I suppose that is true. Still, I feel there's more to it than he's explained to me. Later today we'll be going to the new doctor, well myself and the kids will I still haven't told Jake yet. Not sure why I just haven't, we did go out to dinner to talk but the words never came out I plan on trying again this weekend. Until the kids get home though we're killing the time with yet another lesson.

"So, what's on the schedule for today teach?"

"Today I thought we'd talk about the aging of Weres. Now we've already talked about the difference in types of Weres. Those bitten stop aging at the age they are when bitten saying that's over age eighteen. Though biting one younger is a capital offense. As such if you see an old Were you can almost guarantee that they're bitten, that said there are a few reasons that can cause a born were to be older. For the most part, born Weres tend to begin aging more slowly once they hit age seventeen at which point most shift. Some things can stall the shifting but generally if a Were has not shifted by the time they reach forty they never will. A Were that's never shifted will still develop the other advantages but they will continue to age, however still much more slowly than a human. An unshifted Were can still live much longer the oldest we have in recorded history was 240 years old. A Were who shifts before they turn forty becomes immortal, and won't die of natural causes. Even if a Were doesn't shift at seventeen they will still begin showing symptoms of their changing physiology."

He pauses before continuing. "Usually no later than forty a Were stops aging entirely of course this is not always true. The third type of Were we have is a hybrid that unfortunately we have no definitive information about. Unfortunately, their mixed blood can do many unpredictable things to how their shift comes about. Of course, there are different species like we've discussed but for the most part, they all age the same."

"Okay, so depending on which type of Were they are they will age differently. I know you said Weres and shifters aren't the same but do they age the same?"

"There are similarities such as aging slower and living longer, however, no for shifters they are able to shift from the time of birth. They reach the age of maturity at age Twenty-five and should never look any older than that. Additionally, a shifter can't be made through a bite, while there are other ways to create a shifter they aren't as easy as biting them. We will get more into that when we move onto that race."

"Okay, so most Weres are immortal and look young. Got it."

"Correct, due to this fact Were families tend to be large and have many members in it. They also tend not to rush into creating offspring since they have so long to do so. This is actually good because it allows more time for Weres to try and find their mates."

"Their mates? Like in stories those are real?"

"You'll find grains of truth in most stories you've read. Yes, mates are true, there's only one mate a Were male will ever have, strong females however will sometimes have more than one. Granted if a male's mate dies or rejects them there is still a chance to find another, but as long as both live, and the female doesn't reject him, from the time they meet she's the only one he'd be able to be with. Trying to be with anyone else will essentially tear him apart. Even after he is rejected, he will never fully be able to be with another a part of him will always be with his mate. Some rejected males fall into a deep depression or even go crazy and become obsessed. The same is true for the weaker females of course, but strong females can have multiple mates at the same time and very few males would balk at being in her harem. Typically, the stronger the female the more mates she could potentially have. Most supernatural species have their own form of mates, and the different Weres can have different rules where mates are concerned but this is the most common."

"What if they never find their mates?"

"While it's said that living without finding one's mate leaves them never being fully fulfilled, all hope is not lost. They can decide to take a chosen mate, many try to hold out because if this route is taken it can be horrible if their partner's true mate is found later. However, there have been instances where the couple has simply added the mate to their relationship though it can be dangerous."

"Why dangerous?"

"Well, a true mate tends not to feel jealousy over another of their mate's true mate. Some kind of design I imagine. However, a mate that is chosen is more like an interloper, these situations have turned deadly."

"Oh, that's awful"

Our lesson continued for some time after that. Explaining how the births worked and all that other fun sex education stuff. One thing that struck me as strange however apparently Were females tended to have something physical that lessened the chances of getting pregnant or carrying to term outside of a mated match. It made me wonder how common it was to have children of other races. After all, he did mention hybrids didn't, he?

Ian

We'd been here waiting for the Doc to see Angel and her kids for almost an hour now and still no Doc. He's never late. What is going on with him?
"Love, I'm going to go see what's taking the Doc so long."

"Okay, thanks."

I get up the counter and Gloria his receptionist/nurse tells me to go talk to the Doc alone first. So after letting Angel know I would be right back I show myself in.

"What's up Doc? It's been forever."

"I'm sorry Ian, I would have rescheduled or made better arrangements if I'd known it take this long." Doc Ugokwe says.

"It's cool Doc just see them now when you're not busy."

"No, you don't understand. If I'd known I'd have had another Doctor here. I just didn't think, I don't see how. Then Edward said she can't know, but how will she understand if I can't explain?"

"What the bloody hell are you going on about Doc?"

"Your Angelika. I didn't pay much attention to the name it wasn't until I was heading out to get her that I realized. Now I just don't know what to do."

"Okay, Doc going to need a little more than that. Again what the Bloody hell are you going on about?"

"Oh, right. Of course, sorry. Okay so that girl, she was a patient of mine. It was just over six years ago that she came in. It was so bad she was barely getting around anymore on anything but the force of will alone. Seriously I was amazed she was able to stand. So, I performed spinal surgery on her."

"Okay so you were her Doctor, so what?"

"You don't understand. I didn't know who she was, what she was. She has a ton of metal forcing her spine to stay straight."

"That's certainly interesting and all. Doesn't explain why you're hiding like a beat down puppy?"

"With the metal in her back, she can't shift. Well, she could but it probably hurt her so bad she'd die, or possibly be paralyzed. I could take it out, but if you guys are wrong and she can't ever shift she'd become paralyzed in a few years. I can't explain why I'm here for a physician's appointment, or explain anything without her knowing who she is."

"Well, bullocks! Okay, so what do we do it's going to look suspicious if I take her home. Not to mention how would you not know what she is? You had to run tests, how didn't it show up?"

"Well, I have another Doctor on the way in. Not sure what's taking him so long but damn he needs to hurry. As for the rest. I really don't know how we didn't find out. I run those tests with all my patience to be safe. I know stuff like mental and pins can harm the abilities to shift or make shifting dangerous. I know I didn't review all her notes myself but for the ones I didn't my lab assistant did. They're both pack so they know the drills."

"Okay, hopefully, he gets here soon. Who was your lab assistant?"

"Daryl and Tala, we're the two I had around that time. Oh, there's Dr. Smith now." The doc informs me.

CHAPTER 3

Angelika

It's a week from Halloween, finally. It's literally my favorite holiday of all time. The kids and I decided to go shopping for costumes, sadly we got distracted and completely forgot. Fy instantly found her costume, pennywise of course. Tasia went straight for Harley Quinn. Remi however is still searching trying to decide between two different five nights of Freddy characters or Darth Vader. While he's making up his mind I decide to wander looking for a costume for myself. I find this amazing witch costume that's sort of a cross between Celine from Underworld and the blonde Sanderson sister. Dark, dangerous, but sexy and old-fashioned all rolled into one. Remi finally decided on Freddy and I figured, what the hell, and grabbed the witch costume. We pay and head home.

As we pull up there's a package on the stoop. I guess Tasia's *Amazon* order came in. She fly's up the porch and grabs the box going straight inside trampling Fy who just managed to unlock the door.

"Hey! Watch it!" Fy yells

"Sorry, I want to try on my new outfit." Tasia hollers back running into their room.

I head to the kitchen to grab a drink. The security on shift right now don't really invade my space so they never came in and since Fy ran to the backyard with Kyra, Tasia ran to her room and Remi hopped on the game I can decompress a little. I truly hate shopping with other people, they never move at my speed so I'm either waiting on them or being rushed. As I pop open my can of 7-up I hear a blood-curling scream from Tasia so I drop the soda and fly towards the sound. I slam into her room and she's still just screaming. Luna and Theia the girls' cats are in the corner of the bed hissing, backs arched and hair sticking straight up. I walk over and the box Tasia grabbed is opened and she's just pointing at it crying now, thankfully she stopped screaming. I open the box and look inside I can't even tell what the thing use to be, but now it's a mess of gore. I'm thinking some kind of animal because you can see bits of fur in all the blood and guts but it's smashed beyond all recognition. It looks like it's been run through a blender a few times and on the inside flap of the box in what appears to be blood the words *you're next bitch* are written. I spin around to get someone from security but I see Sierra heading my way already.

"Is everything all right? The guards heard screaming?" She asks concern evident in her voice.

"No, I really think we should call Ian and Theo." She gives me a doubtful look as if I'm overreacting. "Just look in the box. Tasia, go in my room and take your brother and sister with you. I'm sure they're in the hall."

She numbly nods and heads out. Sierra tentatively peers into the box. "Oh my lord, what is that?"

"Your guess is as good as mine. It's definitely some kind of animal. I can't tell what and to be honest I don't want to look much closer."

"No I suppose you wouldn't I'll take that outside and call Ian and Theo. I'm sure they'll come running." She says the last bit with a tinge of irritation not sure what her issue is she's not liked me from the beginning.

I will have to address it at some point but right now I need to check on Tasia. So I head to my room. "Tas, honey are you okay?"

"No mom I'm not okay. How could I be okay? Who would do that? Why would somebody do that?"

"I don't know sweetie but we will find out. I'm so sorry you had to see that."

"It's not your fault, it's just ugh. Can I go take a bath? Then wash my sheets?"

"Of course sweetie."

After she leaves Fy looks at me. "Mom, what happened? What was in that box?"

"Something that shouldn't have been."

"You're not going to tell me more are you?"

"No, I'm not. Sorry but it's bad enough she saw it."

"It has to do with the guards hanging around, doesn't it? There's something big you aren't telling us isn't there? Just tell me, are we safe mom?" Fy asks starring directly into my eyes.

"Fy no matter what else happens you will always be as safe as I can make you without putting you in a bubble. Anyone who hurts you or even tries will regret it for the very short amount of life they have left after I get ahold of them. Sadly, that's the best promise I can offer."

She studies me for a few minutes. "Okay, mom." She says as she heads out. Remi just gives me a hug and follows her. A few seconds later there's a knock at the front door. Fy looks at me as I head to it, she turns to Remi. "Hey let's go play Xbox in your room Rem." I mouth a thank you and open the door.

"Love, are you okay? We came as soon as Sierra called." Ian asks instantly as soon as I open the door.

"I'm fine it's Tasia who might not be." I reply.

"Angel I think we need to increase security. It would probably be best if we keep one guard in the house." Theo points out.

"Great, I'm going to have to talk to Jake now. I guess I can't keep putting it off."

We talk a little bit longer before they take off. We were able to purchase the rest of the land on my block. We demolished all but the house on the opposite corner, that one I liked better than the rest and had more space.

With 5 bedrooms upstairs, one downstairs, an office, a huge living room, a separate dining room, and a basement it'll be perfect. Unfortunately, they're still finishing the last of the fencing and a few repairs before we can move in though Theo did assure me we'll be able to no later than the week before Thanksgiving so won't be too long. Of course, that's another thing I haven't told Jake yet. I'm not trying to hide anything really, but it's difficult to tell him. Of course, it might make things better. I know he's been upset and confused about the money that I've been spending lately. The new house will also help quite a bit with our new in-house security issue.

Everything's already been bought for the house so we'll be able to move in and have the stuff we are keeping brought over there. I even made sure everyone got new wardrobes and they can go through their old ones and decide what to do with them. Granted Theo insisted on a personal shopper so I have no idea what to expect.

As I'm stuck in my thoughts I missed Jake coming in. "Who's this babe?" Jake asks from behind me.

"Oh sorry didn't notice you got home. This is Sierra Travis, Sierra this is my husband Jake." I tell him, but it only seems to increase the concern on his face.

"Nice to meet you," Sierra says as she shakes his hand.

"You too." He mumbled looking confused as hell.

"Hey Jake I need to talk to you can we go to the room for a few?" He eyes Sierra questionably. Jakes has never been the trusting sort. "It'll be fine," I whisper as I pass him to head to the bedroom.

"Of course." He replies as he follows. I close the door after he enters." "What's up Angel? What's going on?"

"Babe please sit down."

"I think I'd prefer to stand. Look if you're going to demand a divorce don't try and make me sit down and coddle me before you ask."

"What the hell Jake? I'm not asking for a divorce. Where the hell did you get that idea?"

"Oh." He says as he sits. "When I came in and saw her, someone you've never before mentioned, I figured that's what you were heading towards. You know you've been strange recently. I figured that must be what's going on."

"Do you want one?"

"What? Of course I don't Angel I just figured that's why you'd been distant."

"Okay, good now that we are sure neither of us wants a divorce I have to tell you a few things. So last month someone came around looking for me, but they used my old name the one I don't use anymore Tyler. So, I didn't tell them anything."

I pause for a moment watching his reaction, then continue. "They had someone watching me because they had to find me, that's why Ian was in the area when that guy attacked the house. So after that, I found out the reason they were looking for me was to give me, my inheritance."

"Okay, that sounds like a good thing why wouldn't you tell me? What is the inheritance and what does that women have to do with it?"

"Well, the inheritance isn't just one thing. Apparently, I now own a security company which Sierra works for. I'm also apparently rich and have many properties. I guess I should also tell you the car across the street is mine and the big yard being put up you noticed is ours. The main reason I've been worried about telling you is there's a catch. The way my inheritance is set up since I'm married, I can't collect it all for five years. Unless you signed an agreement releasing any rights to it. You also have to continue working for that time to prove you aren't in it for the money. It's a ridiculous clause my grandparents put in to protect me. As well I have an attorney."

"Okay, that's not so bad. Does it say I have to keep the same job I have? I was hoping to move closer in when things were in a way I won't screw over Pete?"

"I don't believe so no. I will have to double check with Theo to make sure."

"Okay no big deal. You had nothing to worry about telling me."

"There is another thing. Today someone dropped off a package. Tasia thought it was one of the ones she'd been waiting for and grabbed it and ran in her room. She opened it and inside… inside was a mutilated animal…"

Jake literally leaps off the bed and heads toward the door.

"What?" I grab his arm.

"Jake wait let me finish. On the flap written in blood, it said your next bitch. A security system is being set up tomorrow and from now on we are going to have security personnel here at all times."

"Is Tasia alright? The security idea is good, but where are they gonna stay? We're kind of tight on space."

"Tasia is okay, she freaked out obviously, but we calmed her down. The problem with space won't be a problem by Thanksgiving. The house on the corner is ours, there's plenty of space even for security. We're just waiting on a few repairs to finish and the fence."

"Okay, I'm going to go check on Tasia. No more secrets okay? I get why it took a bit to tell me but you're always yelling at me to communicate, you need to as well."

"Of course," I tell him, through a fake smile. Already breaking that one. I still haven't told him bout the supernatural world of course, I doubt he'd believe me. I haven't told him about the threatening phone call. I sure as hell didn't tell him about the private lessons with Ian.

Halloween night we took the kids trick or treating like every year. Jake of course headed home early also like every year, he's such a poor sport and won't even dress up. Well I got him to twice but those were hard to pull off. He normally knocks off around eight or nine while the kids and I continue until the candy seems to run out. This year we took the car however so I did have to drop Jake off, just a small delay though. So we were parking at the ends of streets walking the street then hopping in the car to move to a new one. With the area being so desolate walking the whole thing simply wasn't an option. Of course with security following us it reminds me more of a procession.

I am kind of curious where our little shadow disappeared to I haven't seen him in a couple hours. Every time I get back in the car their SUV is parked right by it so I'm not terribly concerned but still strange. Tonight, there's a new guy I've never met before named Grant. If Sierra hadn't introduced him, I would have never let him through the door. He hasn't talked as much as the others, and to be honest looks more like a professor than a security Guard. I mean the man wears spectacles and that isn't even a dig, it's what he insists they're called. He's got perfectly parted brown hair and he wears a vest. Of course, just like the rest of the guys I've seen he has a pretty massive stature.

"Mom, look at that house it looks awesome. There's fog coming out of it and everything." Remi exclaims drawing me out of my thoughts.

"Dude look at all the blood and bodies!" of course Fy would notice that.

"Do we have to go to that door?" Tasia asks quietly.

"Of course we do Tasia stop being such a baby!" Fy yells at her.

"Enough guys go ahead. Tasia if you really don't want to go, you can stay with me." I tell them.

"Yeah Tasia stay and hide behind mommy you big baby." Fy teases here.

"Fy…" I begin.

Tasia cuts me off. "No, it's okay I'll go."

I stand at the curb watching them go. I used to go up to the houses with them. They'd prefer to come out alone too old to have mom tag along but this is a decent compromise that they seem to somewhat accept.

"I smell blood." A voice whispers in my ear and I literally jump almost dropping the phone I'm taking pictures with spinning around.

"Jesus fucking Christ Grant. What the Fu…" I start.

He cuts me off " I smell blood."

"Well there's fake blood littering the ground," I say pointing to the gory décor.

"Its not fake. Get the kids back here now." He says heading for the house.

I follow, internally freaking out because the doors open and I barely catch Remi heading inside, Fy must already be in there but Tasia is slowly backing away. I ran up "Tasia what's going on? Why did they go inside? You guys know you're not supposed to." Grant stopped to stand next to me texting someone.

"I don't know mom. The women said to come in there's treats inside and a haunted house. I got a bad feeling and told them we needed to go but they wouldn't listen, they just followed her inside." Tasia is obviously freaked out.

Grant looks at me and before I can respond says. "Angel take Tasia to the street, Ian and Sierra are on their way and should be here soon I'll head inside."

"No offense Grant but Fuck you. Those are my kids and I'm going to get them, you take Tasia to the street and stay with her. Don't leave her fucking side or I swear to everything I will feed you your own balls."

"Angel, there's things you don't…"

"Don't fucking argue with me Grant move your ass now!" The authority that comes out snaps him into action. A reaction I simply don't have the time to think about at the moment. I turn around and head straight into the house. I don't give a fuck who lives here my kids are in there.

It's so dark inside I can barely see. What I can see comes out in fragments due to the strobe light above. The fog is thicker in here and there's such a strong metallic smell, I now know what Grants meant. With how strong it is the wind must have stopped me from smelling it outside. I can barely make out anything. There's three directions to go, upstairs, down a hall to my left or straight through what looks like the kitchen. It's hard to tell with the fog and only having a strobe light going. I pause for a minute. I have to get this right. I don't have time to be wrong. Who knows what these creeps are doing to my kids.

A hear a muffled whimper followed by a soft thump coming from the hall to my left so I go that way.

This house looks like it's been decorated to be a haunted house, but I can't afford to second guess myself. If I'm wrong then I'll just look like a blundering idiot, but if I'm right and stop? I can't risk it.

The end of the hall there's a door with a red light shining under. I pause for just a few seconds and slam my way through the door. The sight beyond the door causes me to stop dead in my tracks. Fy is tied to a chair and gagged. She's bucking like a crazy person and screaming what appears to be very violent threats behind her gag. If I were these guys is be worried her eyes are blazing with anger. Remi is backed into a corner whimpering and shaking. Behind him is what appears to be a vampyr but not like the demon creature that came to my house.

This woman is eternally gorgeous. She's got the reddest hair I've ever seen, up in some old Victorian hairstyle. A hairstyle that matches her blood red Victorian gown. Her eyes are literally glowing red, and a porcelain but oddly beautiful complexion. However beautiful this bitch it's she's holding Remis's neck in her hand, albeit gently and the hell spawn is fucking sniffing him like he's the hottest dog's ass at a dog show. Flanked on either side of her are two more vampyrs but these ones are like the creatures that came to my house. It feels like I've been standing here for hours staring at this terrifying display, even though it's only been a few seconds.

I storm forward and place myself in front of Fy, between these demons and my daughter. "Hey twinkle bitch. Get the fuck away from my son now!" I ground out.

Sparkle tits looks at me. "Oh, little wolf did you finally decide to come out and play?"

"What the hell is with you guys and little wolves? Can we get anymore original? What the fuck do you want hell whore?"

"Why my dear, I want you of course. It's a simple trade you for your children."

"Uh, huh because hell whores keep their word, do they? I come to you, there's nothing to make sure you keep your word." I tell her as I slowly inch forward.

"I always keep my word little wolf? Why would I ever lie? My lord just wants the Alpha, all others are free to go."

"Okay, so where is the Alpha and I'll gladly go get them and give them to you." This demon actually bends over laughing at me. She seriously looks like she's going to burst open. The two on her sides are laughing as well. "What's so damn funny?"

She just keeps laughing and howls "Where's the Alpha." Then continues laughing. While they're distracted, I reach forward and yank Remi to me, shoving him behind me.

"You sneaky little bitch!" She hisses at me.
"Playing dumb to make us laugh at your stupidity. All so you could grab the boy. It won't change anything, you're all going to die tonight."

"We're not dying bitch" I tell her staying in front of the kids. Fy finally gets free and so I slowly back up keeping them behind me. I can feel Fys' tension because she wants to go at these guys.

Thank God she's smart enough to realize distracting me could be a major issue. I'm staring at this insane vampyr who I can barely see move trying to register that the blow to the jaw I just took came from her. Fuck she's fast. I guess it was dumb not too expect it.

"Look lady just let us leave peacefully. I haven't done anything to you. Hell I don't even know who the hell you are. Why don't you take your two companions and go get a motel to work out your aggressions in a fun albeit disgusting fashion. What do you say?"

"I prefer dinner and a movie. It looks like delivery is already here so we should start."

"Look you crazy ass hat I don't wanna playing your fanghead games."

"Listen to all that righteousness smothering the derogatory slang you use. Yet you act better than me? I've been around for thousands of years. I've seen things you can only read about in history books. I've …"

"Ya ya we get it grandma you're older then dirt. You were alive before the dinosaurs. We get it hell you carry your age in your saggy wrinkled cheeks." Granted all lies but an angry opponent is a stupid opponent.

"Why you stupid little…" she stutters out as she lunges.

Shit normally I have more time to react. All I can do is throw my hands up and let her hit me. Hoping that Fy and Remi have backed out of the door I do just that. When I see Fy trying to come around in front to block me. I grab her and twirl her around while yelling no with my opposite hand trying to block the succubus bitch. When the weirdest fucking thing happens, all three vampyrs are thrown into the wall by an invisible force, and I feel what I can only describe as raw power stream through my hands. Queen bloodzilla is on her feet the quickest. I stand up to face her again trying to conceal my shock.

"It's not possible." She mumbles staring at me with her eyes wide and mouth agape. Suddenly she looks over my shoulder then jumps out the window behind her. Her two creepy little puppies chase after her. I spin around and Ian as well as Sierra are staring at me in complete and udder shock.

"What?" I ask innocently. I don't know exactly what they saw. Hell, I'm a little confused about what even happened. I felt power in me, flowing out, but there's no way I did that? Did I? No, Magick doesn't work that way. Did they hear what she said about the alpha? They would be curious about that I'm sure. After all they are involved in that world.

CHAPTER 4

Ian

I was so furious when I showed up and Grant told us what was happening but even more that he'd let Angel go in alone. I know it's not his fault but I can't help how irritated it made me, besides with the smell he should have never let the children go up to this house's door in the first place. Sierra and I rushed in right after his brief explanation and it didn't take us long to find the room. What we didn't expect was that wave of witch magic to flash out of Angels' hands and from the look on Beatrix she certainly hadn't expected it either. The fact that the disgraced noble heir chose to run only speaks volumes to her surprise. The strangest part was Angel's eyes. They were glowing and not the typical golden wolf eyes oh no she had the True Alpha blue eyes. Granted we'd already expected what she was, but her eyes shouldn't glow if she can't shift which obviously, she had never done.

Sierra came out of her stupor before me. "Ian, I'm going to go after Beatrix. I probably won't catch her but we have to try. You, okay? With this?" She asks, directing towards the room.

"Ya I'm good. Go ahead." I turn towards the family we were supposed to protect. "Angel, are the kids okay?"

She looks up a grim smile. "Yes they're okay. Not sure what that vampyr bitch planned with them but she didn't actually hurt them. She just scared them."

"Not me mom. I want to stab her in her glowing red eyes. That's why she tied me up she said I was to much trouble." I can't help but smile at that. This woman's daughter is strong no doubt about that.

"I know you did Fy. I did too but getting you two safely out of here was more important than satisfying my urge to ram her head up her ass."

As Angel looks at me again I notice a bruise I didn't see before and her lips split. Fuck!
"Love, are you okay? Your face?"

"Oh ya. Queen bitch felt my face needed some decorating. Unfortunately for me I wasn't expecting her to flash over and punch me then flash right back out of reach. She didn't look like those other two, she actually looked normal. Beautiful even."

"There's different kinds of Vampyrs. The creature looking ones are more like pets. Guard dogs in a way. The strigoi. She is a royal, a born vampyr descended from royal blood. We better get out of here."

"Right. Should we call the police?"

"Nothing they can do. Let's just get you guys home okay."

Dropping Angel and the kids off didn't take long. She must have messaged her husband on the way because he was on the porch waiting looking extremely stressed. I couldn't blame him driving away tonight was killing me. I still haven't gotten my anger over this to level out. The beast inside me is pissed and it wants blood desperately.
I pick up my phone and dial the last number I really want to.

"**Edward Wulfrik .**" He answers.

"**Hey boss, I couldn't reach Theo. We had a situation tonight. I figure it's important enough to give you an immediate update on.**"

"**Is Angel okay?**"

"**Yes, she's fine. The problem is she and the kids were trick or treating. They came to a house and a Vampyr lured two of her kids inside, the other one said she had a really creepy feeling and refused to enter. Angel went in to get her kids out, I'm not entirely sure about the events. She was extremely vague. However, the vampyr threatened her kids. She managed to get them behind her and when they were lunged at, she threw her hands out and yelled.**" I pause trying to decide the best way to word this. "**She ... Well, she threw the vampyrs across the room with her mind. That's not all though when she looked up her eyes, they were glowing blue.**"

"**Okay so many issues with that, but let's start with are the kids okay? Why the hell wasn't her guard closer? Why the hell was she allowed to go in alone? Most importantly, who the hell was her guard so I know who to fire?**" He rambles out, clearly furious.

"**The kids are completely fine. The boy is a little shaken, the girl wants to train to kill vampyrs and she's bloody pissed. Her guard was keeping a distance to allow the family some freedom and privacy, something that shouldn't have happened. We let our guard down due to no more direct approaches. A mistake we're rectifying. The guard was Grant but before you do anything drastic you need to understand that he didn't let her go. She forced him too.**"

"**Forced him too?**" He asks dubiously.

"**Sir, she used her alpha powers on him. What's worse, I don't** even think she realized or knew. He was powerless to deny her."

I hear Edward take a deep ragged breathe. **"How is that possible? For that matter how the hell did her eyes glow? If she's never shifted, neither should be possible."**

"Sir, I have no bloody idea. There's no way she's ever shifted or if she had, she's forgotten but I doubt that and don't even think it is possible. I'm more worried that this is a precursor to her shifting for the first time. If she shifts with that metal in her we have no idea what it'll do to her. It could paralyze her, maybe even kill her. Then of course there's the Magick. It was pure unadulterated witch Magick. We have no idea how powerful it'll be and an untrained powerful witch? That's as dangerous as it gets."

"Okay you need to talk to the Doc again we're going to have to get the metal taken out. Worse we're going to have to come clean with her about everything. We also need to get Belladonna involved so she can train her in her powers."

"Okay I will get in touch with both immediately. Do you want me to tell her?"

"No, I haven't been able to make it out yet. I was going to send Theo back home next week, I will be coming out with him. If someone's going to break the news to her it should be me. Besides we don't want to damage the trust you two have already built with her. I'll make the arrangements and I will plan to stay throughout the holidays. Have a place set up close by but not underfoot."

"I will see to it."

He hung up and I'm left to sit here in my thoughts. We wanted to ease Angel into her role but this turn of events ruined that plan. It looks like her life is going to implode sooner then anyone planned for. I only hope she's as strong as she acts or this might crush her.

Angelika

It's been a week since Halloween, and I still haven't learned a damned thing about vampyrs. Ian's still been teaching me more about Weres and their culture. We have however been doing more intense defensive training which I suppose is good. I've always been an okay fighter but let's face it, street fighting and knowing a few moves is nowhere close to knowing what you're doing.
On top of the lack of vamp education Ian absolutely refuses to talk about that night. Outside of asking me what I felt, if the kids and I were okay and fussing over my bruised cheek which now doesn't look as bad but is a nasty shade of green/yellow. He dodges the subject every time I try to bring it up.

The only decent thing is apparently today is the last day of our Were lessons. I wanted to immediately jump into my vampyr education but Ian said that after Thanksgiving I will be getting witch lessons. Oh joy, the only race I've had an issue with no one will teach me about. Don't get me wrong I do enjoy learning about these things, but come on priorities anyone?

On top of everything, coyote activity has increased around my house. I'm not horribly concerned about Kyra but I really don't want her to get hurt by one. Oddly enough though the few coyotes we've caught on camera I could swear are wolves a lot bigger than I would think wolves would be but still. Ian assures me that healthy non- emancipated coyotes aren't much different from wolves but personally I think he's hiding something. Yes, I may have never seen a coyote face to face hell, not even a wolf for that matter but I have seen plenty from a far. What's been sulking around my house seems way bigger than either I've ever seen. Every time I ask Ian if he's sure Werewolves aren't stalking me along with the vampyrs, he seems to get uncomfortable, but assures me Werewolves would never work with Vampyrs to hurt me. Sadly, as ignorant as I am to this world, I have no true reason to question him.

In a couple of weeks, I'm finally going to be doing my first family Thanksgiving in years. Truth be told, I can't wait, I'm looking forward to it. I'm not certain who will show and of course can't promise family I would prefer not to show up, don't. However, I am excited to see my dad, brother, and niece again. It's been far too long. Of course, I am nervous because my uncle plans to be here. I don't want my dad to feel like he's not enough, after all, he's been the only dad I've ever known and the best dad I could ask for.

That's in a few weeks though, today is the big day we are moving into the new house. Our move-in date got bumped up because they were able to finish the fixes sooner than planned. It's a good thing too because our house is beginning to feel a little cramped and now Edward will have a place to stay. A company was hired to pack up the house and everything's been moved to an outside storage shed for it to be gone through and moved in gradually. All we're doing is getting the personal belongings we need and electronics. Ian said we have until noon, he planned on giving us more time but apparently my uncle Edward is coming out sooner than planned so they're going to get this old place refurbished and cleaned for him to stay in when he arrives tomorrow. Ian informed me he intends to stay at least through new year's. Once we're finished up here and settled into the new place Ian said we can have our final lesson.

Jake has been surprisingly supportive and understanding about all this. I can tell however he suspects there's secrets and more going on then he's been told. Oddly enough I feel the same way. It feels like I'm only being told half of the story which leaves me feeling like I'm in limbo waiting for the other damn shoe to drop. Truthfully though, I have told Jake most everything I know, however, there is one major detail I've left out, well besides the supernatural bits. Ian, I don't know why but there's a connection to him I can't quite explain. The more time we spend together the stronger it seems to grow. Lately, whenever his skin touches mine I feel jolts of tingling electricity that I can't even begin to understand or explain. What's worse is I can tell he feels the same thing. I keep catching him watching me intently when he doesn't think I'm paying attention, but I can't call him on it because he might call me on the fact that I do it too.

I can't even begin to open that door; I've never cheated on Jake and I will be damned if I start now. Besides I love Jake no matter what's going on with Ian. I know Jake is my soulmate. I won't give that up for some electrically charged infatuation. We've been together since we were eighteen, we have three kids together for crying out loud. I'm sure whatever I'm feeling will subside when Ian and I no longer have to spend so much time with each other. I mean it's most likely some kind of issue with close proximity and working together anyway. That's all it is right?

"Hello love." A deeply seductive voice says from behind me.

Speak of the devil. I turn around. "What's up Ian?"

"Just seeing how much longer you think your all going to be, love. I want to get this last session in so I can get some preparations done before your uncle arrives tomorrow."

"Oh, um I'd say maybe another twenty minutes?"

"Okay I'll head out and grab everyone some lunch then we can meet at the new house to get started."

"Mm-hmm sounds great."

After lunch I head out back with Ian, he's decided we should start with physical training first. I've been gradually improving, however I'm still nowhere strong enough to face off against one of the creatures that have been attacking me. Yet no matter how much I need this training it's the hardest part of my time with him. It's extremely difficult to ignore a physical attraction when your body won't stop responding to even the slightest touch. The fact that he's shirtless and his tanned muscular chest is on full display most definitely doesn't help matters any. The man looks like a damn god with his golden perfectly toned chest.

"Okay, love I'm going to come at you now and I want you to take me down."

"Take you down?" I response with a laugh. "Right that'll happen."

"Just try." He says literally seconds before charging at me.

Fuck! I dodge as quickly as I can but he still clips my shoulder, hard. I stumble a bit but refuse to drop, pure stubbornness is the only thing that prevented me falling on my ass. I turn back around just in time to see him charging again, this time right before he hits I drop to the ground and sweep my leg through his ankles. At least I try he sees my feeble attempt and literally summer saults over it rolling to his feet and spinning around seamlessly. I spin and sit on my ass with my knees bent. This time he charges and I grab his arms plant my feet in his abdomen rolling back and flinging him over my head and across the yard. The look of pure shock as I lift him makes me giddy. I hop to my feet and spin around.

He's still laying sprawled out on the grass staring at me. The look in his eyes while still shocked show a bit of admiration to them.

"Well, that was new." He finally breathes out.

I shrug my shoulders. "Jake taught me it a few years ago, outside of practicing with him I've never used it."

"Well it's definitely a good move. I guarantee I'm not the only one who would be caught off guard by it. Where did Jake go anyway? I thought he was home today?"

"His mom called, apparently she needed him urgently. So no idea when he'll be back. I think Grant was tailing him."

"Happen a lot does it?" He asks as he gets up dusting off his pants.

"It is what it is. What can I do? It's his mom."

"Of course. Well let's go finish your last lesson on Werewolves, shall we?"

I follow him inside and we sit at the table.
"So this is the last lesson but it is the most important. Weres while they can be volatile, act as the policing force of the supernatural world." He starts off.

"Wait so they make the laws?"

"No. The different groups have leaders who create the laws together. I explained the wolf hierarchy; each group has their own governing system. For the most part the leaders govern their own group. Weres however, they act as enforcers when a supernatural or group of supernatural's gets to out of hand, especially if their own leaders can't reign them in. Weres also are the main protectors of humans."

"What so other groups don't help? They don't protect humans?"

"They do, just to a different extent. Of course, they also help the Weres when asked. Each group of Weres as I explained has a High Alpha they serve on the council. Each pack has an Alpha, those Alphas report to a representative for the area, who in turn reports to the council. Then of course there is an Alpha that is in charge of all of the Weres as a whole, the True alpha."

"Okay so like a Super Alpha? How does that Alpha get picked?"

"They aren't chosen. They're born. Every generation True Alpha potentials are born, however not every True Alpha potential ascends. If the current True Alpha dies, retires or becomes incapable of performing their duties a new True Alpha ascends from the potential True Alphas. There was a purge a few decades ago where a group of hostile supernatural's hunted down all the potential True Alphas and killed them. Only one True Alpha survived, the one who was currently leading."

"So how does it work then? Is it a bloodline thing?"

"No, it's not a bloodline thing. Hell it's not even a species thing. True Alphas are just born no body knows why or how they're chosen. It's believed they are chosen and blessed by the Were gods."

"So who's the current True Alpha?"

"The current one is only a place holder. The son of the last True Alpha has been holding the position while the Weres have been searching for the True Alpha. They believe the last True Alpha had an heir that was hidden from the Were community and they've been searching to bring the heir home. Until that happens there will be instability within the supernatural world especially within the Weres." He explained.

For the next hour he continued filling me in on how Were law was written and decided upon. How the punishments get carried out, and what happens when they can't make decisions. It's strange and relieving to find out Were culture while more primal has a heavy democratic presence. I never would have imagined a group of Weres debating, playing politics, voting on decisions, or holding court hearings. Of course, for packs the Alpha has the final say as is true for the True Alpha. Still the groups as a whole act similar to our American government which is shocking and the True Alpha is closer to a president then a king or queen.

Yes, they seem to still have many animalistic attributes like dominance contests and mating but all in all they are a real civilized society at least to a degree. I suppose it's more of an eye for an eye and more violent, but oddly enough it seems way fairer than the human society. The truly guilty get punished while the innocents get protected, it might help that apparently, they're walking lie detectors but still. Not to have to worry if the man you put to death was guilty or if the man you freed was truly innocent must be a huge relief. I almost wish I could live in that type of society.

The next day the kids went to stay the night at Maggie's who picked them up early in the morning. She of course was happy to take them but thought that they should actually stay and meet Edward with me. Jake left early too, so he could go to his mom's and wouldn't be home till late. I was grateful I truly didn't want anyone here when I met my uncle. Now I'm just waiting with built up nervous energy for him and Theo to arrive. It will be nice not to have Theo leaving town constantly to help my Uncle. I've had a lot of questions that only he could answer, but he's never around. I asked Ian when they'd be here before he left last night at the end of his shift, but he said he wasn't certain. Granted if they don't hurry by the time they do arrive I'll be a hyped-up blabbering mess seeing as how I was already on my fourth cup of coffee.

"You okay love? You look like you're about to jump out of your skin?" Ian asks as he walks into the kitchen behind me.

"Yeah I'm fine. Sorry a little too much coffee and way too nervous."

"No reason to be nervous, love. Your uncle will adore you. Let's go practice a bit, it'll take your mind off the wait."

"Okay, that sounds good," I tell him as I follow him to the yard.

Unlike all our other sessions he doesn't even give me a warning mid step he just turns around and swings at me. No idea how I managed it but I spun out of the way, stepped behind him and kicked his knee. He went down instantly.

"Damn love. I was just testing your reflexes." He informs me as he stands. Hands up in mock surrender.

"Well now you know how they are."

"You know the good thing is at least, if someone does attack you, your natural reflexes and instincts are sound. Okay let's do this for real."

We circle each other for a few minutes. He fakes a jab with his left and catches my shoulder with his right. Fuck how did I not see that coming. I swing back with my right and barely clip his chin.

"Close, love." He says as he backs up a bit.

I recognize what he's doing, he's done it before in our sessions he's trying to draw me in to wrap me up. I contemplate what to do for a second. I decide to act as though I'm following but when he reaches out to grab me I spin out and pepper his sides with a few jabs.

A look of pride flutters across his face. This time he drops and tries to sweep my legs out from under me. I leap over them and spin around again. He hops right to his feet and tries to fake with his left again. This time I'm ready when he begins pulling his left back towards him to swing with his right I follow into his left and grab his hand wrapping it up around his back and kick the back of his knees dropping him. Pulling his arm up above his head he finally yields.

Just then I hear clapping and turn to see Theo standing with who I assume is my uncle. He didn't look as old as I thought he would. He has short sandy blond hair, and a well-groomed beard. He was quite tall pushing six feet at least and built like a linebacker. If it weren't for his crisp dark blue business suit, I would think he was one of the guards.

"Well done, well done. You have no idea how long I've waited to see you again sweetheart." He says looking at me with pure adoration and pride shining through his eyes.

CHAPTER 5

I walk up to him shyly. "Hi, I'm Angelika."

"Oh sweetie. I know who you are. I'm sure you don't remember me but I knew you when you were little. You were always my favorite." He replies, as he pulls me into a tight hug. I hesitate for a moment and then I return his embrace.

"Well, why don't we sit down and talk then," I tell him as I lead him towards the patio table. "Would you like anything to drink? I'm going to go get me a soda."

"A coke would be great if you have one." He asks.

I start to head towards the door but Ian stops me. "Go sit down Love I will go get some drinks."

"No, it's okay you don't have to." He gives me a hard stare so I just sigh and say. "Okay thanks." I head back to the patio table and sit down. "So, Ian and Theo have told me there were a few things they couldn't really discuss because you wanted to yourself. I'm not trying to be rude but, I must know what's so important that you, yourself want to tell me?"

Edward stares at me accessing me for a few minutes before he speaks. "Well, what I have to tell you are... well, there's a few things actually. I want to be the one to tell you, but I want you to understand that none of the others had a choice they were not allowed to have this conversation with you. You do understand what I'm saying don't you?"

"Sure, you're their boss and if they don't listen, you'll fire them. I get it, I don't like that they've been here this long and kept things from me. However, I do get it, it's your fault not there's."

He sighs. " You're correct, it is my fault and for that I am sorry. The things we need to discuss, well they're family matters and only a family member should explain them to you. To start I want you to know Tyler was never really your last name."

"I know that much. The Authorities told us my father stole his identity from someone he killed before he married my mom. We just were never able to find out his real name."

"His real name is Ullrich Wulfrik, the family called him Ricky."

" So my real last name is Wulfrik? That's an unusual name." I mummer more to myself then anyone.

"Yes, it means powerful wolf, in German. While we do have other cultures mixed in we are mostly German. How much do you know about our family?"

"Not much really. Just what my dad told my mom and given everything I'm not certain I believe much. He told her that he'd been adopted by your family and that he was beaten as a child before your family took him in. That's really the most I know."

" Okay, well that's not true. I mean there is truth mixed in but it's not really the truth. He's my real brother, he was kidnapped when he was a toddler and we didn't get him back until he was in his late teens. He returned to us broken and dark, but my parents kept hoping their sweet little boy would return. He never did. While he was away, he was abused horribly. We never found out everything that happened but what we did find out was unimaginable. He's the eldest and I was merely a baby when he was taken, our other siblings weren't even born yet, however, he blamed us for our parents not finding him sooner. He was convinced that they catered to us rather than trying to get him back. This was not true of course, due to his absence we didn't have normal childhoods at all they devoted everything to find him. The man who he killed and stole his name from was actually one of the children of the people who took him. He'd been hunting them for a long time, killing them when he found them. I understand the desire and in truth, if those were his worst offenses, we could overlook them but they aren't." He explains the regret and sorrow evident in his voice.

"Damn, that almost makes me feel sorry for him." I say with a touch of sympathy.

"Please don't, he's a deplorable person. Yes, he's had a horrible past but that doesn't excuse his actions." He pauses as Ian sets our drinks down to give him a thank you. "One of the worst things he's done is to his children. He's sired so many of you then would walk away. He'd return and take them from their mothers, when they were a little older then twist them to be like him. For a long time, we feared he'd gotten you."

"No, my mom was so terrified of him she never let me even go anywhere that would be close to somewhere he might show up. Hell, I hadn't been to a fair since I was young because he'd sometimes work them when she was with him. I know he tried to find me once that was when they changed my last name."

"Which is why it took us so long to find you. My parents adored you, and to be honest you were always my favorite out of my nieces and nephews."

"How could that be? You haven't seen me since I was little."

"I don't know. There was always something about you. Something different and fierce but also kind and gentle."

"Thanks, I think."

He Snickers. "So onto the next topic. I understand..." Right as he says that Solas jumps up on the table meowing and rubbing up to me.

Edwards eyes widen with shock and I swear he damn near jumps from the table. "You have a cat?"

"A couple actually, yeah. I love animals though Solas doesn't normally come outside like ever really. He's not allowed and normally follows that rule." Solas is my baby, he's a long haired tri-grey striped cat. He's also super loyal and incredibly smart. Most cats are but he's unusually so.

"But cats don't like us." He mummers. As Solas wiggles in front of him for attention.

Ian comes over. "Solas is a little different. Her other cats are a bit more stand offish with anyone but her and the kids but Solas here loves everyone. He also follows Angel around like he's her shadow never letting her out of his sight. If she leaves he waits by the door for her. If he's locked out of the room he guards her door. Their relationship is quite unique one might say it's blessed." He says with a very odd look in his eyes.

Edwards composes himself and pets Solas who of course starts purring. "This is amazing." He mummers. I sit there utterly confused as to why a cat letting him pet him is such a big deal. I grew up around cats. They've always been big in my family. He finally clears his throat. "Right sorry so as I was going to say I understand Halloween you had an interesting experience?"

"Um, ya I guess that's one word for it. Though I think terrifying is more adequate when it comes to vampyr psychos. Personally." I state sarcastically.

"Yes, I concur. So, it's my understanding that you did something that night. You threw a vampyr with nothing more than your thoughts?"

"Wait, that was real? That was really me? I thought I was going crazy."

He chuckles. "No my dear, that was really you. Your mother's family comes from a long line of witches, did you know that?"

"I heard rumors and stories about my great grandma but I always assumed it was just that. My grandfather swears that she'd cursed him for being mean to my grandma, and once that she tortured him with a voodoo doll. No one ever really paid much attention and merely dismissed it."

"Have you ever felt like you could do Magick before?"

"Sort of. I mean I've had dreams that come true. I've wished for things that shouldn't have happened but did anyway. I do practice a little witchcraft and have had results. Never on the same scale as that night though."

"Well what I want to do is call in a friend of ours. Her name is Belladonna and she is a witch. I think she can help you if that's alright with you?"

"Of course I think that would be great."

"Fantastic. So while she helps you with Magick, Ian will continue your physical training and I'm going to have him move onto teaching you about vampyrs since Belladonna can better teach you about witches."

I start to get excited. I've been dying to learn about those bloodsucking idiots. "That would be awesome," I exclaim.

"Yes well there is one more topic we need to discuss. I'm not certain how you will feel about this one but…"

He got cut off by a woman standing beside him. She's quite average looking in my opinion. with brown hair and matching eyes. She's around my height of course she does have huge boobs.

Solas is instantly on alert and hisses at her which is weird as hell because he never hisses at anyone.

Edward turns to look at her. "Yes, Tala." He replies in blatant irritation.

As soon as she opens her mouth to speak I hear a mans voice in my backyard. "How dare you expect us to follow this outsider bitch!" Pointing at me. Solas is tripping out now, Ian thankfully grabs him and takes him inside. The new girl I hear say "fuck" and the anger radiating off my uncle is like nothing I've ever felt.

The man is in nothing but shorts breathing hard. He has a long scar down the side of his face. While he's fairly muscular he's also pretty short, maybe around five foot five if that. He's not an imposing or impressive man, but you can feel a power to him. He has a shaved head and dark eyes that promise danger.

My uncle's voice is grating and angry. "What in the hell are you doing in my niece's backyard Connor?"

The man looks even more irate. "I'm here making sure you don't destroy us over your fucking family. It's bad enough your parents did it for your brother, I am not going to let you do it for his spawn!" he screams with an accent I can't quite place.

"Now listen here…" Edwards begins saying but he doesn't finish because right before my eyes this crazy ass man in my yard turns into a fucking wolf.

Yes I knew they existed Ian told me so, but to see one? What's worse is that this man is talking like everyone here is a wolf like they are his people. He turns towards me and growls. He's not a very impressive wolf which doesn't surprise me since he's not a very impressive man. His scar on his cheek shows through his dull grey fur, and his dark eyes shine with hatred and the promise of death. I realize this wolf has every intention of ending my life. He sees me as a threat that must be destroyed. I hear the others screaming for the wolf to stand down, I can see his confusion and him fighting what appears to be the commands coming from my uncle. It looks like he's fighting a struggle of nature versus want.

At that moment it clicks, my uncle is an alpha and this man is fighting to deny an alphas command in order to end my life. Slowly I stand putting my hands carefully in front of me to show that I pose no threat to him. "Listen, Connor, was it? I truly don't understand what the hell is going on here, but if you have a problem with me, we can talk about it. I would like to understand what your problem is, I would like to help if I can? Please let me?" I say.

I can See the conflict in his eyes, he's torn. He doesn't really want to murder me but he feels like he has to. By this point I've moved towards the stairs of the deck, my uncle puts his hand on my shoulder. I look up, keeping an eye on the wolf out of the corner of my eye and see the fear in him. "It's okay uncle. I'm not afraid." I lie I'm terrified but I won't let them know it. I can see in my uncle's eyes he knows I'm not fully being honest but I also see pride as well as fear, but he lets me go. I hear a banging from the house but I can't afford to turn completely around and see. I see Sierra and a few others sneaking up behind the wolf and I shake my head for them to stop surprised when they do. I see the conflict in their eyes as well. They want to do their job but they want to listen to me as well. I put my whole focus back to the wolf and continue my slow approach. He hasn't attacked yet which I think is a good sign and his growls are softer, the conflict is still present in his eyes though.

"Look I can tell you don't want to hurt me, and I'm not going to lie I really would prefer you didn't. I understand your animal is apart of you, but it's not all of you. You are still a man after all and we can talk about this. I heard what you said and while I don't fully understand all of it, I can promise you I'm nothing like my father."

He continues looking at me. I can see his bunched muscles beginning to loosen a bit. His growls become even more soft. Everyone else around us is in complete silence and the tension is stifling.

I'm close enough now to where I reach out and place my hand on his fur, he tenses but then relaxes and stops growling completely, his eyes appear almost blissful now.

Out of now where I hear a crash the wolf begins growling and tensing again a new wolf this one massive and midnight black slams into his side. He's snarling and snapping I stumble back as they roll further into the yard.

I stand and look towards the wolves and the black one raises his gaze to mine and I see his piercing eerie blue eyes. "Ian?" I say questioning. While he stares at me the grey wolf leaps on him. I'm reeling from this to be honest I had already guessed he was a wolf but to see it verified? Not to mention his unreasonable and vicious attack.

I hear my uncle mutter, "God damn it!" while everyone else begins whispering to each other. While the whispering is soft and low I hear it as though they're screaming right in my face. I glance at my uncle and he's holding his lips tightly together and looks like he wants to intervene with the wolves, but doesn't know if he should.

Suddenly I hear a loud yelp followed by a pain filled whine and the smell of blood floods the air. Even though I'm still filled with shock and have stood here for what feels like ever frozen, in that moment I snap back into reality. Without thinking I flung myself towards the wolves. I hear my uncle yelling at me to stop and what I guarantee are his footsteps behind me but it doesn't even make me pause. The wolves are now squared off ready to fling themselves at each other again and I literally jump in between them stopping them in their tracks.

Both wolves growl at me though it's not menacing, it's more like a warning to move. Ian is limping, his front paw hanging awkwardly In front of him. Connor is unsteady on his feet and I notice a gash on his rear flank and blood pooling under him. "Stop!" I yell as they begin to try and move around me. They both literally freeze; in fact, the entire yard has frozen even my uncle. "If you want to kill each other you'll have to kill me first," I state in a voice far more calmly than I'm feeling. "Now change back!" The voice carries the kind of authority that leaves no room for argument.

They both instantly change back, completely naked.

Connor is staring at me, his mouth hanging open, standing carefully, his injury even more apparent. "How?" He quietly asks, his voice filled with shock and wonder.

Ian steps forward. "Love, what were you thinking? You should never get between two wolves. You could have been hurt." His anger and disappointment is evident but I don't care.

"What was I thinking? I was thinking some dick-lint decided to take it upon himself to attack a wolf I was trying to speak to who at that moment wasn't trying to harm me. How about what the hell were you thinking!" He flinches as I scream at him. I know he was trying to protect me but I'm furious right now.

"Angelika, he came here to attack you! Bloody hell, what is wrong with you women?" That is literally the first time he's ever used my name. Oh ya he's pissed.

But so fucking what? So am I. "He may have come here with the intention to hurt me, but we were working it out just fine without your interference. I'm sorry if I'm not stupid enough to think a man full of fear resorting to violence, when he doesn't want to, deserves to be met with violence. Wait actually I'm not fucking sorry, not one fucking bit! People react out of fear, I don't know what he fears but we could figure it out and figure out a solution."

"There is no solution he fears YOU! He thinks you're just like your father and he thinks that once you become Alpha, you will destroy us just as he would!" He snaps his mouth shut, and flinches as though saying that hurt him, as I feel my eyes fill with shock. "FUCK!" He loudly mutters.

"Alpha?" I say quietly. "What the hell are you talking about?" I glance around and no one will meet my eyes. I look to my uncle. "What the fuck is he talking about?" I ask.

"That was the part I was about to get to Angelika. You're a wolf and you're the rightful Alpha. The rightful True Alpha to be exact." My uncle replies softly.

My head is spinning. They're wrong they have to be I'm not a fucking wolf! How could I be a wolf? Sure a witch I can see but a wolf? I turn and start heading to the door. I'm in desperate need of a few minutes to myself and some fucking caffeine.

When I reach the stairs, I look up and see Theo. He instantly turns away. Fucking coward. As I get to the backdoor, I notice the door isn't fully on its hinges almost like something busted through it. That must have been what I heard Ian was inside; he must've busted through the door. I glance over and Tala is standing pressed against the wall, for a moment I could swear hatred flickers across her features. As I head inside I hear talking coming from the yard now. Of course Solas is waiting for me and instantly greats me rubbing around my legs.

I head to the kitchen grab my coffee and then go into the office and close the door. Solas follows and I just sit down letting him climb into my lap petting him as he calms me.

As I'm sitting there with my thoughts I hear the door open and look up and see Theo. " Angel sweetie are you okay?"

"Nope I'm pretty damn pissed actually. I don't like being lied to or misled and while you guys didn't really lie you most definitely didn't tell me everything. I understand some of it, sure but the big stuff? What the fuck Theo?"

"I'm so sorry Angel. We were ordered not to say anything, we can't disobey or argue with an Alphas order. How Ian managed to break that order I don't understand but your uncle wanted to be the one to tell you. It was important to him."

"Look Theo, you guys have to be mistaken. I'm not a wolf I would know something like that. How's Connor?"

"Not necessarily you were raised away from this world, hidden from it sheltered. There's no reason you would have known. I don't know why it was hidden so deeply but for whatever reason it was. What I can tell you though is that you are definitely a wolf and definitely an Alpha. I felt it even your uncle felt it. He wasn't even able to resist your commands and he's strong. Angel there's no mistake. As for Connor he's fine the doc is meeting him next door and he's requested to officially come see you Edward told him he'd call him. Ian is also fine. His shoulder is tender and he's a little upset but otherwise fine."

"I didn't ask. Is my uncle still here?"

"Of course he's still on the patio."

I get up and head out Solas follows of course. He stops when we reach the back door where two guys are already fixing them, and lays down. I head outside and over to where my uncle is passing Ian who still looks furious and hurt all at once. I look into the yard and see other guards just casually standing around but Sierra is giving me a death glare. All well fuck her; she's never liked me anyway.

I return to my seat and look at my uncle. "Alright look your my uncle I don't have much family left well who want anything to do with me anyway. So I can't afford to just drop new ones so how about we cut the bull shit…" I hear a gasp from Sierra, but continue anyway. "and you tell me what the hell is going on? No more secrets, no more lies, no more half truths. Just fucking tell me?"

He stares at me for a few amusement dances in his eyes. To me, it seems like an odd emotion to see but whatever. "Okay, Angelika, no more bullshit. Yes, you're a werewolf, my mother, your grandmother was the last True Alpha. I understand you've finished with your werewolf learning so as you know all True Alphas and Potentials outside of my mother were killed prior to her death. All but one, of course, that one is you. We knew it from when you were a baby. Your father knew it, we suspect, that's why he cast you out even as awful as he was, he'd never kill his own offspring." I started to open my mouth to argue but he put his hand up to stop me. "I know he's threatened it but the truth is he would never do it. He couldn't even ever really bring himself to kill one of the mothers, which is why he would kidnap his children. We knew he tried to find you but as far as we can tell it was never truly to take you or even harm you but to watch you. He didn't want you to take what he deemed his rightful place but he also never wanted you hurt." He pauses and takes a drink. "In his own twisted way, he loves his children. However, it didn't matter he was never a True Alpha and wouldn't hold the place forever. As soon as another came, he would be out, that's why he's suspected of killing them all. To try and claim what he felt was his by birth. "

"Okay, but I've never shifted. You're right Ian did teach me, and while I do know a wolf can never shift technically. That's never been a thing for True Alphas."

"True it's never happened. The proof though is in your Alpha command. Only a True Alpha can command another Alpha and you commanded me. Not to mention your eyes."

"My eyes? There just blue nothing special."

'No. Wolves eyes can glow during extreme emotions. However while a normal wolf glows gold or yellow depending on pack position, a True Alphas glow blue. Angelika, yours glow blue. Also there may be a reason you can't shift."

I sit there letting what he just said absorb. My eyes glow blue to be honest I've been told that before but people have always contributed it to a trick of the light. Hell even I did. Then something he says jumps out at me.

"What do you mean there might be a reason I can't shift?" I ask him.

"Well, we've been discussing that. Actually, that's why I couldn't meet sooner and why Theo's been with me. There are a few factors we believe are at play here. The first is your ignorance of our world. While yes, a wolf will still usually shift regardless of knowledge of our world it can still play a factor. Of course, then we have the fact that your family obviously shielded you from our world. It is possible they put a spell on you to prevent your shift and hide you from detection. Your great grandmother was in fact a powerful witch and your other had a shaman for a father. It's entirely possible they did it to protect you "

"Why? Why would they do that? That doesn't seem wise at all. They didn't even tell me about this world, they left me defenseless. Why would they do that?" I ask in outrage. Furious that anyone felt they had a right to make that choice for me.

"Well the spell wouldn't just prevent your shift. You're undetectable to us, we can't even tell you're one of us. That's in part why we didn't tell you sooner." I don't respond and just stay silent so he continues. "The last possibility and one we have to fix even if it has no effect if you want to shift is the metal in your back. It's possible the wolf refuses to shift because doing so will hurt you.'

"I don't understand." I ask in confusion.

"When we shift our body shape reforms. We can't, however , reform foreign substances. So, if you were to shift you could hurt or even kill yourself because of the metal. We can't figure out what went wrong, the doctor who did your surgery is one of ours and he tested you, nothing came up suggesting you were a shifter of any kind. Hell, a supernatural of any kind. Your new tests however we can tell the wolf gene is there he would have run more tests before surgery if it popped up sooner."

"Okay so I won't shift ever. Ian said beyond a certain age it won't matter most likely anyway."

"True usually but not always. Definitely not in True Alphas. It's a miracle you haven't shifted yet. If you do shift when your emotions get too strong you could hurt yourself. We can't take that risk." My uncle explains.

"Its my risk to take. Besides, I know how to control my emotions." I say firmly.

"That may be the case normally, but things can happen to change that. A forced shift like you gave Ian and Connor, though near impossible to do to a True Alpha, can be done with Magick. An intense threat that is so strong you can't control your emotional reaction. Grief." He pauses looking from Ian to me then says, "imprinting or a new mate bond, even a threat to your mate." I notice Ian stiffen.

I scoff. " I've already faced intense threats, nothing. If I have Magick I will just learn to block others. Grief I've had an abundance of and have never shifted. As for mates I have a husband mate or not I'm happy with him and won't be changing that."

"Even so, my dear…" He continues trying to plead I cut him off.

"No. If I get the metal taken out I may never walk. I can't afford that and I won't do that to my kids. I'll do whatever else is needed but I won't do that. I won't risk hurting my kids even that much. So what do you need from me?"

"Well I'm going to have to introduce you to the packs of course. The councils will want to meet you. It's set up to where I will still be in charge for the next two years to help prepare you so you can adjust to your new role before fully taking over. You'll continue your training with Ian in addition to myself and Belladonna who I'll have here the day after Thanksgiving. The beginning of January is when I would like to start introducing you so we have until then to prepare."

"Okay fine. Can you be here Sunday night for dinner? I would like to introduce you to my family."

The most genuine smile appears on his face. "Of course my dear I would love that."

We continue chatting for some time as he tells me stories about the family I don't know. I know I've just officially met him but it really does feel like I've known him forever. As we are getting ready to call it a day Solas leaps on the table In front of me and starts hissing. I look in the direction he hisses and I see Tala heading this way. His reaction is weird as hell; he never acts like this towards anyone.

"Uncle just curious earlier when you said Solas was strange. What did you mean?"

"My dear, cats don't like werewolves. The fact that he doesn't care about us is very strange. Of course he obviously doesn't like us all." He says with a chuckle.

CHAPTER 6

Sunday evening Edward shows up just as I'm finishing dinner. He's apparently extremely punctual unlike me. As I open the door I realize he's not alone, I honestly didn't expect him to bring anyone with him but standing next to him is Tala. It's fine of course, I didn't tell him he couldn't bring anyone I just didn't think he would, and for it to be her? I don't know she gives me a strange feeling that I can't describe. I guess it could simply be Solas' reaction to her, but I've always trusted when I have these feelings they've never steered me wrong before. Screw it, I don't want to cause problems so I merely smack a smile on my face.

"Hello, Uncle I'm glad you could make it."

"Of course, I wouldn't have missed it. You two haven't been officially introduced yet, this is Tala. She's my personal assistant and we lost track of time working earlier. Normally I would have ordered food for us but I didn't want to miss tonight."

By the look on Tala I'm not so sure their losing track of time was accidental on her part. "No problem at all there's plenty of food. Good evening Tala, nice to meet you."

"You too." She replies meekly. For some reason it seems like an act but I try to ignore the thought.

"Well let's head to the dining room shall we? Jake and the

kids are already there. You'll have to excuse the kids if their manners aren't too great. We don't usually eat at the table, we're barbarians that way."

This comment earned a chuckle from my uncle. "No need for that dear we are family."

We head into the dining room and I'm suddenly very grateful for the decorator having the foresight to set it up even though I said it wasn't necessary. The room actually looks amazing to be honest, not quite as grand as the one I designed for my dream home but amazing just the same. The nice oak table that seats ten people, the beautiful china cabinet that displays my more decorative china dishes beautifully and even the bar they added off to the corner. We still usually don't eat in it, but it's nice to have it available for occasions like this. The kids and Jake stand up as we walk in.

"Guys, this is my Uncle Edward and his assistant Tala." They all murmur a hello. "This is my husband Jake, and our children Tasia, Fy, and Remi."

"I'm so pleased to be meeting you all. Of course the best part is I brought gifts!" Edward exclaims as Tala hands him a bag I hadn't noticed.

"Oh, that wasn't necessary," I tell him.

"Nonsense dear girl." He replies and starts passing around a gift to everyone, he even got Jake one it appears. Then he hands one to me as well as two fancy bottles of wine. "I wasn't sure what was for dinner my dear so I brought both red and white."

"Oh, it's nothing special. I made scampi, with garlic bread and salad. I think white would work well. Let me just grab my wine opener and a couple glasses."

Of course I didn't have them out already. We were used to just grabbing a soda. So I end up grabbing a couple glasses for the kids and some juice as well then head back in. Everyone had already torn into their presents by the time I'd returned. Remi and Jake have watches which actually look really nice. Fy, and Tasia have a couple of beautifully created necklaces. All the pieces have a wolf howling at the moon on them and they look like they were costume made. Even Fy seems pleased with her gift which surprises me since she's not exactly a girly girl and doesn't do much jewelry. I pour the drinks for everyone and then take my seat.

"Well my dear why don't you open up your gift and then we can get to this incredible food I smell."

I can't help but blush a little at that I've never taken compliments well they embarrass the hell out of me which just seems extremely stupid. Slowly I open the box and I find a necklace like the girls but quite different. In it there's a girl with her hair blowing in the wind wildly and a wolf at her side. The wolf is a gorgeous white wolf with glowing blue eyes. They are in a forest under the stars and a full moon shining down onto a small stream. It is stunning and the extreme detail that was put into such a small piece is not lost on me.

"It's beautiful. Thank you." I say quietly.

"Of course my dear I'm so happy you all like your gifts. What do you say we eat and get to know each other?" He suggests.

So we do. After we finished the meal I got out desert . I bought some tiramisu, my absolute favorite which I learned is also my uncle's favorite. We talk and get to know each other even Jake who normally doesn't talk to anyone much is fully engaged in the conversation.

What strikes me as odd however is Tala isn't saying anything. The whole time she just sat there watching and listening. I guess she could be just letting us get to know each other but it seems more somehow. I'm not sure why, I can't really put my finger on what bothers me about it. I keep trying to tell myself I'm just working myself up over nothing but still Solas reaction to her bothers me. I had to put him in the room because he wouldn't stop hissing at her once he woke from his nap and what's weirder is when we let Kyra in she growled at her too. Both animals have always been so sweet to everyone and have never behaved that way. Granted Kyra I have no doubt would be protective if we were threatened. The problem is no one is threatening us.

I did try multiple times to bring Tala into the conversation but she never gave more then a clipped response. Another thing that keeps bothering me is that I keep catching her staring at Jake as though she'd prefer him for desert. I'm not above admitting I tend to get a little jealous and a tad possessive. Hell, that's probably my issue. After a few hours they leave and we head to bed.

My phone dings letting me know I have a text so I grab it.

Restricted: We didn't forget you bitch! You will die painfully and begging.

Me: Not bloody likely go fuck yourself.

Restricted: I think I will wait to fuck until I have you.

I cringe and decide not to reply. At least they haven't sent me any more presents that's something.

Thanksgiving finally comes. Sadly, I haven't been able to get out of my thoughts, and I was hoping today would improve that but it hasn't yet. Even so I was extremely happy to see my niece though as always she likes to tease me not letting me hold her unless I bribe her. Of course, that might just be because she knows I will bribe her, the little manipulator.

What I'm not excited about is my aunt's and cousins decided to show up. Of course I invited them, but it was more out of a necessary politeness I never actually thought they would come. So now I'm hiding in the kitchen finding last minute things to prepare just so I can try and avoid the awkwardness and blatant dislike I see every time I look in their eyes. It's been like this since my grandma passed away Jake can't figure out why I tolerate it which of course I do it for the kids. I understand where he's coming from, since I can't understand why he tolerates his mom.

Speaking of which to my utter shock his mom actually showed up with his grandma. Though I think that was more to nit pick and make snide comments about the house and our new situation. She knows I've heard her talking about how I couldn't wait to show her son up, and how she doesn't get why I couldn't be content with the cozy house we had. Boy is she going to go nuts when our real home is done, something I don't think Jake has informed Rachele about yet. She definitely doesn't like the security she keeps going on about Jake deserving privacy.

"Hiding away are you, Love?" Ian says from behind me. Speaking of smoking hot security.

"Nope, not at all. Just gotta finish dinner is all."

"Come now. Don't lie to me. What's going on?"

"Nothing important. Just not thrilled to see a bunch of people who hate me, but I'll be fine."

"If they despise you, why invite them?" He inquires.

"For my kids. The kids love them, what I feel about it or them is irrelevant. It's that simple."

He stares at me for a moment. "You're a good mom. Here let me help I will take some of this into the dining room for you." For the second time today I'm grateful the dining room is a good size. We were able to set up a few extra tables in there so we aren't all squished together. Given the awkwardness it's a very good thing I don't think I could handle it otherwise.

"You don't have to it's not your job."

"I know but I want to. So stop it and let me help."

I do as he asks. I finally get the last bit of stuff done and get everything set up in the dining room. I had Tasia gather everyone up and bring them in. Dinner was going okay for the most part everyone was in their own little groups talking to each other. Edward thankfully didn't bring Tala with him today, I didn't really look forward to explaining that on top of Edward and the security. Oddly Jake's mom took Edwards being here quite well and of course his grandma Joy instantly was welcoming to my long lost family member. My dad and brother were even very supportive and thankfully my dad didn't seem too put out by this new relationship.

Of course not everybody was copasetic with the situation, as my aunt Racheal was eager to point out. "So Edward, I'm curious how it is that her mom can struggle raising her and no one cares. Now however you show up and give her everything? Hell, how can she even get anything at all when her dad was a low life?"

"That's not needed Racheal." My dad points out.

"I disagree, I think it's a very valid point." She replies.

"Moms right, we should get an explanation." My cousin Saddie says. Her sister Haddie however remains quiet which is usually the case to be honest. I don't think she agrees with most of what those two say and do but she rarely if ever speaks up unless it's to defend them.

"Well, it's simple really. My parents couldn't find her or her mother. They would have loved to have a relationship with both of them, it just wasn't possible." Edward says this very calmly which amazes me seeing as how I'm not the least bit calm over their questions.

"Maybe we should talk about this at another time? It's

thanksgiving, a time for peace and family, not drama." I say as evenly as I can.

"I don't see what's so dramatic about asking reasonable questions, Angel. We do have a right to have these answers." My cousin Pam adds in.

"They have a point Angel. We had to take on the burden of helping raise you and we didn't get a single thank you for it. Now this big shot comes in and hands you the world and we're just pushed aside." Of course aunt Jessie just couldn't stay out of it.

"Excuse me, but I believe I'm the one who helped raise her. In case you've forgotten I've been taking care of her even before her mom married me barely six months after they left her real dad and I can promise you it was in no way a burden. It was a pleasure and I couldn't be prouder than I am now." My dad states as he walks by and squeezes my hand. "I'm going to go watch some football sweetheart. Too many knives and too many stupid people in the same room together for my comfort." My dad whispers in my ear and I can't help but giggle.

"He acts like we did nothing that whole time," Jessie says with irritation.

"Seriously, some people have no appreciation." Racheal mumbles.

I'm trying not to snap but I kind of want to start using those knives on people. I refuse to ruin everyone's holiday so I just keep eating and ignore the bullshit.

Edward looks at me and I think he sees it and grabs my hand. "I think I will go check out the game with your dad sweetheart." He says and kisses my cheek as he gets up and heads out.

"Jeeze." Saddie mumbles.

"Oh my god will you guys shut the hell up and stop ruining my sister's thanksgiving already?" DJ, my amazing brother, has finally had enough and says what I can't. "She was nice enough to let you into her home after all the bullshit you put her through after grandma died and all you can do is bitch and whine? Seriously the world doesn't revolve around you self centered assholes. Sorry sis." He gets up and heads to the living room with little Ro and Darlene.

"Wow people are quite sensitive today I see," Racheal says. Haddie is still sitting there quietly, Saddie at least looks a little chagrined. Jessie and Pam just look miffed.

Jake gets up and calmly states. "This is why I don't like certain people around and why I don't socialize. Some people just don't know how to act." He leaves too.

Even Rachele adds. "It's sad that she and I have issues and not even I would act like that. Good grief." As she follows Jake out.

"So anyway, Angel, I was hoping to ask you. Rich and I aren't doing too well lately and I'm going to be leaving him. Is there any way you can loan me some money to help me get out on my own? I would be so greatful." Racheal actually has the fucking gall to ask me that? Seriously? After everything even before today she thinks that's okay? What the fuck?

"Seriously?" I all but yelled. I merely stand up and start to walk outside.

"God it was just a question she could have simply said no. I just figured she might be willing to help me after everything..." I don't hear the rest as I close the back door behind me.

I go over and sit by the fountain in the backyard. It's pretty gorgeous actually, a unique design that looks almost like a waterfall with a stream. Theo had insisted Ian have fish put in it when he was told about the fountain.

My aunt's and cousin's words bother me quite a bit and sadly, I can't really talk to Jake about it. He tries to be understanding but he thought I should have cut them out a long time ago. His family is not near as close as mine is or at least as mine use to be. In my family we were taught to never turn our backs on each other, to always be there and that family is the most important thing. Apparently I was the only one who paid attention, but still it's ingrained in me . That all changed as soon as my grandmother died, at least for the rest of the family it did. I'm still stuck in the past and keep forgiving them no matter their sins no matter the pain they cause me. As long as they're good to the kids, that's all I care about, I can deal with whatever they say or do.

"Hey Love, are you okay?" Ian asks from behind me.

"Yeah I'm fine."

"You don't look fine. You shouldn't let them get to you."

"What the hell do you know about it?" I snap.

"I heard how they were talking, it's uncalled for. Remember I've been watching you for a while now, you're too good a person. Too kind. Too forgiving. For that treatment to be justified. Just remember that okay?" He says and then walks away before I can reply.

Thankfully not long after Tasia comes to let me know my aunt's and cousins are leaving, so I say a polite goodbye. I spent the rest of evening with the family I'd planned on showing up.

CHAPTER 7

I spent the next week training with Sierra, Ian still was making himself scarce and I rarely saw him if ever. It sucked of course and Sierra was no doubt good and knew what she was doing but she wasn't near as good or patient as Ian. We hadn't actually talked much at all nor had I seen him much since the incident with Connor, so I'm sure he's still pissed at me no matter the excuses my uncle gave him for avoiding me. I know he was still guarding us but he seemed to do his shifts when we were all asleep and never when we were awake. Of course with the exception of Thanksgiving my uncle made everyone be on guard duty that day. He's worried those demonic assholes would take advantage of my guests if we didn't have everyone. Ian actually seemed like his old self that day, but the next day he went right back to avoiding me. Personally, there are a few of my guests whose disappearance wouldn't have been such a terrible thing.

Granted saying that is one thing, but if it happened I would probably be racked with guilt something my uncle seems to acknowledge. It's kind of strange that a man who barely knows me understands me better than those who practically helped raise me.

This morning while I was training with Sierra my uncle's assistant Tala came by to let us know that we were summoned by the Were council. Apparently, he had been trying to hide my being found for a while to give me time to adjust but, someone had shared the news with the council and now they are demanding to meet me today. He attempted to push it off until after the holidays but they denied that. The good news however is that they have decided to come and meet us out here.

This is why I'm currently getting "*dressed to impress*" as Tala said, so I can head over to my old home where my uncle is staying to meet these Weres. Ian surprisingly decided to set his anger aside to give me some advice and he told me not to allow them to intimidate me. He said to hold my head high and not show any fear. He also assured me he would be right there. To be honest I was shocked he even bothered while I wasn't certain what angered him so deeply. The simple fact is I expected him to not even bother with me, nor did I expect him to try and help support me now.

I'd gotten dressed in a pair of nice dress slacks that my uncle sent for me but I refuse to wear the stupid shirt and tie. Instead, I opted for my pint striped spaghetti strap blouse, it's low cut sure, and maybe more librarian fantasy than business but so what?

I'm not going to lose who I am for these people. I also set aside the suit jacket I placed aside for a cute black half jacket. Of course, I'm wearing the pendant I always wear but I also put on the wolf moon pendant my uncle got me along with a moon earring set my dad got me for my last birthday. I change out my nose ring for an opal, and my eyebrow ring for a glowing ball. For my make up, I settled for some lip gloss and a bit of highlighting. Finishing it off with eyeshadow I did to look like the night sky with sparkling stars and a moon off to each side at the end of my winged liner. I chose to put my hair up in a ponytail at the top of my head with ringlets flowing down. I'm pretty happy with the outcome and barely recognize myself if I'm being truthful I look like a moon goddess dressed for court. Kind of fitting.

I hear a knock at my door followed by Sierras voice. "Angel are you ready were going to be late."

"Yup just finished coming out now." I quickly put my beauty supplies away and head out my bedroom door where she's waiting.

She looks at me for a long minute and I can tell she's appraising me. "Decided not to wear the outfit your uncle sent over huh?" she asks.

"I'm wearing the pants, it's enough. Sorry but I'm not a fucking Barbie people can dress up however they like. If I'm going to dress like a trained monkey I'm going to do it in a way I'm comfortable doing and if people don't like it to fucking bad." I reply a little more angrily than I intended.

She holds her hands up in mock surrender. "Hey, kid, I think you look good. This is ten times better than what they gave you and while I may think things about you a trained monkey would never be one of those things. You're your own person and I truly do admire that. Anyway we better get over there. It may only be next door but we're already close to being late."

We decided to just walk since it's literally right there. The rest of the security team didn't like it they said it was easier to protect us in a car, which might be true but too damn bad. Granted I do wish I didn't wear my heeled boots I forgot how hard walking in heels have been since I had my surgery. Too late now though I will just have to push thru I'll be damned if I show that weakness. I can tell Sierra isn't use to the desert scenery when she becomes practically mesmerized by the dust devil we see off in the distance. It's kinda funny to me how uncomfortable the environment makes most of the security.

We get to the door and the guard rings the bell. Of course Tala answers and I can't help but feel angry to see her answering the door to my old home. I truly wish I could figure out why I can't seem to get past this disdain for the girl, it's not like she's done anything to me. Aside from Solas obvious hatred for her I have no other reason to have an issue. She steps aside without so much of a word and lets us pass which just adds to my irritation.

She leads us to one of the bedrooms which has been converted into a conference room for today. There's five others sitting in there with my uncle. Tala stays by the door with Ian while I take my seat and oddly Sierra follows and stands behind me.

"Good morning Angelika, how are you my dear?" My uncle asks.

"I'm fine."

"So, as you were told, the Were council wished to meet you today. I believe Ian taught you the basics of Were hierarchy. I'm not sure how much he went into detail so I will simply explain. There are different types of Weres, and each of the main types has a leader. We have Caine the leader of the Canine, Katya the leader of the Feline, Bryan the leader of the Bruins, Koto the leader of the Avian, and Draco represents the miscellaneous faction which is made up of all the groups with smaller numbers." He informs me pointing to each member as he names them. Oddly I wouldn't have even needed him to, you could almost see their animal sides, except for Draco, not quite sure what he is.

"Nice to meet you all," I replied.

"So Edward informs us, you know nothing of our ways?" Koto says with a sneer. "Yet we are expected to just accept you as one of us though you were raised human." You can literally see the hate in his eyes. I'm not sure why, if it's merely my ignorance or something more.

"True, up until recently I'd been ignorant to the supernatural world. I'm not going to lie. However I have begun being educated in it, and I am learning. I know my uncle isn't planning on immediately putting me in charge, and I would never ask him to and even after he does I plan to keep him as a trusted confidant to help guide me. I am not naïve or arrogant enough to believe that I will know everything by the time I take my role." I say with my head held high.

"Yes Edward has explained this to us. We are surprised you are willing to agree to such an arrangement, most young alphas are eager to take over as soon as they are allowed." Bryan points out.

"Yes well as it was pointed out I was raised human and ignorant to our ways. I was raised by a great man who taught me that sometimes a person needs guidance and that a person should not take a role they are not ready for. In truth what is being seen as a weakness on my part is actually a strength that allows me to be patient and wait until I'm ready to do what is needed."

"There is no strength to be had from human ways. Humans are weak and frail; they don't know how to do what needs to be done." Caine says harshly. Out of the corner of my eye I see Ian's eyes flash. He seems as upset as I am.

"Well, let me put it this way. I'm not here to play games. I didn't choose this role. I didn't ask for it. I'm merely accepting what was given to me by fate. If you'd like me to walk away, you've simply picked the wrong girl. I will learn what is needed and fulfill the roles that've been pushed on me."

"You truly are insolent aren't you girl?" Caine growls. "You're not only ignorant of our ways but you're disrespectful of them as well. Why fate would pick someone like you for this role is beyond me. I believe we should keep things as they are. We don't need an ignorant little child sending our people to distraction. Hell you can't even dress appropriately for this function."

"Now, Caine..." My uncle begins. I hold my hand up signaling him to halt which thankfully he does.

"You want to lecture me on disrespect? Seriously? Yes I choose to dress the way I choose, not to be disrespectful but simply because I'm not yours or anyone else's puppet to be dressed up and paraded around. I will not be intimidated by you, nor will I be cowed by your misconceptions of who I am. Yes you're right I was raised by humans but what you see as weak I recognize for what it truly is, strength. A supernatural putting themselves in harm's way takes way less bravery then a human doing it. Yet humans do it every single day for a multitude of reasons. I've placed myself in danger to protect others well before I knew anything about this life. I will do as I am needed to do, period and nobody will stand in my way, not you or anybody else. Simple fact is sir, you do not now, nor will you ever scare me away from my responsibilities. This is a fact that will be easier on all of us if you merely accept it, because I'm simply not going anywhere and I will not ever live under your thumb." The anger rolling off the man amplified by a thousand. He looks as though he wants to kill me. My uncle however looks proud as does Ian. I can't see Sierra but I do know she's stepped closer to me and Tala looks like she might just piss her pants.

"Oh, I like her. Yes, I like her very much." Katya says warmly.

The rest of the meeting goes on, people stop with their insults and snide remarks and while Katya and Bryan actually seem okay with me Caine and Kota do not. Draco however is very difficult to read. For the most part the meeting seems to be about introducing me to the supernatural world as well as the attacks that have been made against my family. The council feels we need to speak with the vampyrs. Something they all seem to feel I should be present for, all except my uncle and Katya who both feel that my doing so would be a horrible idea since at least some vampyrs are targeting me. They also discuss my inability to shift which is another reason those two don't want me going. Of course Caine argues if I want to be an alpha I need to solve problems myself, and while Bryan seems to fully agree, Kota only feels I'd have better luck getting information and Draco simply voices no opinion on the matter.

At this point I'm not really participating in the conversation anymore, I'm merely listening. However I completely blank out all together when I notice Tala is hanging on Ian, flirting and giggling loudly like a complete and total idiot. I can't even stop the intense wave of jealousy that washes over me and takes over everything else. I don't know precisely how long I'm sitting there simmering in anger but my uncle finally touches my arm which jolts me back to the present.

"So, I think it's time to call it a night. I will schedule the meeting with the Vampyrs and I suppose we will go from there. Does that appease everyone?" Everyone present agrees. "We will however wait to introduce Angelika further than this group and the Vampyrs until after the holidays, that's not negotiable. She needs the time to adjust and deserves to have time with her kids for the holidays."

"That sounds fair," Katya says. The others simply nod their heads. I excuse myself and head out with Sierra trailing me. Ian tries to stop me to talk but I ignore him and my uncle calls him back. Once I reach the street Katya catches up to me.

"Angelika, I have a question for you, if that's okay?" She asks.

"Angel, please and of course it's completely okay."

"Do you plan to take a mate soon? I can introduce you to a few eligible suitors who I think you will like, unless you have one in mind already?" She asks this while eying Ian who I didn't realize was standing outside the door. I just stand there looking like a fool for quite a while and can feel the blush creeping into my cheeks which is ridiculous since it's not like I'm a school girl or anything. "Oh dear girl I didn't mean to embarrass you, I was only offering to help. You're not limited to the wolves you know and even if you want a wolf there's more than what's here." She continued obviously misunderstanding the issue.

"It's not that, I'm um… I'm married already. I'm faithful to my husband. I have no interest in finding a mate." I explain.

"Oh dear girl. In our world we can have our cake and eat it too. If you want more than one you can have it, hell take all of them you can get."

I chuckle at that. "Ya I don't know about that. Men suck one is hard enough to deal with. I'm not sure I would ever want more to try and cope with their moody bullshit."

"Well that's your choice. Some of the men especially on the council will eventually try to push you, but whatever you choose I will support your decision. Good luck dear girl and don't let these fools walk over you because they fail to see your strength." With that she gives me a quick hug and walks away. Leaving me to return to the house and deal with the idea of having to meet a bunch of blood suckers.

It's just over a couple weeks before Christmas, the council apparently took over scheduling my meeting with the Vampyrs. My Uncle was attempting to push it off until after Christmas, however, I will be going tomorrow the thirteenth instead. I've been assured I will be back no later than the twenty-third, though it's supposed to only take one night, so it won't interfere with my holidays. Granted I don't trust this much given how my luck is, I will probably end up returning after Christmas. I planned on going shopping with Maggie tomorrow. It's really sad the one year I didn't have to shop at the last minute due to lack of money. I still end up doing so due to how busy I am.

Thank the Lord that after Thanksgiving we all agreed not to do a huge thing for Christmas if I had to plan for a huge dinner on top of everything else I don't think I could do it.

Today however I'm shopping with Ian and Sierra. I don't think either of them want to be here since they keep trying to convince me I can just have someone shop for me, I can't get them to understand Christmas presents are personal and can't be passed off to anyone else. Since money isn't the issue it normally is, this year I'm not limited to big lots, the dollar store and Walmart. Yes I did go to Walmart first but that was mainly to grab some stockings and stuffers.

Thankfully Jake had already done the tree since I completely forgot and I pulled out the ornaments and decorations for the kids before I left. One less thing to worry about. While I'm at Walmart though I grab a few things I need some melatonin for Jake, some hair dye, pet food the usual. I decided to get bath and shaving kits for everyone to put under the tree. I also found a few brush sets with holders, and I checked out the clothes and toys and found a few things as well.

Sierra comes up to me as we're loading everything in my car. She's been riding with me today while Ian follows. We thought this would be easier to give extra space. "You know some of those things you bought like the hair dye and melatonin have better options for you right?" she asked me.

I just kind of stare at her. "Um… What?"

"There are herbs, potions and even spells that help with those things and work a lot better. I know there's a hair dye potion that will actually last for a year or until you change it. There's a tea that works better than melatonin."

This actually catches my interest. "Where is this Belladonna again? Now I really want to see her."

Sierra laughs at the. "She's apologized for the delay but she's leading the winter solstice celebrations for her coven and can't get away until after the season, unless she can find a replacement which she hasn't been able to yet."

"I can see that. I need to remember to ask her about those things."

"So, curious you were looking at that laser tag game in there did you want it?"

"I thought about it for the kids but there's only two guns and I might be too busy to referee."

She nods. "So where to next?"

"Sephora, for Tasia."

We hop in the car and head out. We went to Kohl's, Sephora, and Game stop but I still wasn't able to find a few items so we decided to head into Chandler and go to the mall. We didn't finish until ten at night but I finally got everything I needed.

Thankfully we aren't leaving first thing in the morning so I can sleep in a bit since I have to get these wrapped so the kids don't peak. Then tomorrow off to see the Vampyrs oh joy!!!!

CHAPTER 8

Ian and Sierra have been the only ones allowed to accompany me to meet with the vampyrs. According to my Uncle they are the most experienced in handling them outside of himself and the council won't allow him to come with me. They say it's too much of a risk and that he is too important to lose right now, of course they claim I am too, but I somehow think some of them would be content to see the blood suckers kill me. The Vampyr council has been adamant with my uncle that they in no way condone or have given permission for any of their "Brood",none of their "Seeths", ha yes that's what they call themselves, to be tormenting me. As such they are sending me to speak with the local Seeth at their mistresses home with nothing but a damn letter from their grand elders to their mistress.

Admittedly I still haven't learned much about Vampyrs so most of these damn terms that keep getting thrown at me as if I might understand are utterly confusing. I think everyone forgets my extent of knowledge is from television and reading.

My Uncle says it's easy to forget because of how easily I've accepted everything and due to the fact that I seem more knowledgeable than I really am, so apparently my love of mythology and reading makes me appear smarter than I actually am, go me!

Ian hasn't talked to me much lately. I think he's still pissed that I told him off but now he won't shut up. Granted he's trying to give me a crash course before we get there which is apparently a cozy ass four hour fucking drive. I had to tell Jake I was going out of town for business which I suppose is slightly true. He seemed totally okay about it until he noticed Ian would be coming and then he threw a tizzy fit.

I kind of get it but it's not like I have a choice in the matter. It didn't help that after I said goodbye and walked away Ian put his arm around me. I shook it off but Jake still looked like he wanted to choke Ian to death. Such is life I guess.

So now here we are with Ian explaining that compulsion is real and that I must be careful about eye contact. He seems to believe this will be a major problem for me. He said they have other powers of course including enhanced senses, speed and strength, but compulsion is by far the worst. He's also told me to under no circumstances give my blood or let them bite me or feed me theirs, like no shit dude!

Additionally my attitude needs to be curbed apparently while Weres respect independence, and strength to at least some degree vampyrs do not. Vampyrs prefer blind obedience and hive mentality. Ian explained there are two main seeths in Arizona, while the closest is in phoenix they are currently out of the country so we will be meeting with the Seeth in Parker. The Vampyr from Halloween and their mistress has a history so Ian assures me this is the better option anyway.

Unfortunately I've effectively zoned Ian out by now so I've missed a lot of what he's said. Hopefully I didn't miss anything important, but to be honest I can't stop thinking about how I'm about to walk into a cluster of blood drinking lunatics. Even worse that I'm so far from the kids.

"So should we stop and eat or check into a hotel first?" I hear Sierra ask Ian this gets my attention because I'm starving even though I've refused to say anything.

"Let's check in then I'll go out and grab some food." He replies. I now notice we've entered Parker and both Ian and Sierra seem extremely alert.

We pull into nothing I would ever name a hotel, this is more like a church camp I use to attend but on the water. I see a sign for Benton's resort, it's directly off the river, with an old fashioned lodge type feel to it. Truthfully it's gorgeous, and a place that under any other circumstances I'd probably love to be.

I'm too busy looking at the peaceful river to even notice that Ian has left and come back with keys, and directs Sierra over to a cabin marked twelve.

"So I got us a Cabin we will all stay in. Hopefully we will only be here for one night, but just in case I booked us for two we'll go from there. Charles is the closest alpha in Havasu Falls; it's only an hour away. Edward has notified him and he will be standing by if needed. We're going to go in. I'll go and get some food and come back Sierra. You'll stay here with Angel."

I don't pay attention to her response, I merely get out, grab my bag and follow Ian inside.

"There's two rooms you can each take one I'll sleep on the couch." He states and immediately heads out.

I head straight into the left bedroom and set my stuff on the bed, immediately pulling out my clothes. Taking them I head into the adjoining bathroom, yep the real reason I took this room I'm not big on sharing my bathroom. The bathroom is not at all what I expected, yes I didn't pay much attention to anything else in here but by God this bathroom is even better then the one I had them put in our house. There's a his and hers sink with black marbled porcelain, set into a deep dark wood countertop, with plenty of drawers and cabinets underneath. The tile while still white has deep black lines marbled throughout and the toilet matches the sink.

There is a shower in the far corner with a bench inside and so many sprayers including a rainfall one on top and a waterfall one along the rocked wall, it's big enough for a whole football team. Okay an exaggeration but it's huge.

The most attractive feature though is the tub. In the center of the room there's a huge circular tub sporting the same marbling, it's a deep Jacuzzi tub full with six seats. A rocked canopy held up with four rocked poles. Plenty of room on the edges for anything you'd want and a small set of stairs with the same rocked design. Next to it is a fireplace with again the same rock features and a window behind the tub.

This is literally my dream bathroom with very very few missing pieces. I took a few pictures since nobody understood the design when I described it. I might as well take it home and show them. I set my stuff on the counter and walk past the tub staring longingly at it and take a shower. Sadly I don't have near the time I'd need to enjoy that beauty right now.

I had to take my shower too quickly to actually be able to enjoy it as much as I should have as well but what can you do? After I step out I dress quickly, my uncle told me to dress respectfully yet intimidatingly, not sure what he meant but I took this to mean a pair of black flared jeans, with a deep red low V-neck long sleeved skirt, and my combat boots. I do my make up with a simple smokey eye look but I add a sweep of red glitter. Deep blood red lipstick and pulling my hair up in a tight pony at the top of my head braiding it half way down. I throw my leather jacket on to complete the look.

On my way back into the living room I notice the bedroom has a huge canopy bed, along with a balcony that has a small waterfall rock wall to one side. The coloring matches the bathroom including the wood floor. I notice Ian's back and that he's putting what looks like a plant everywhere.

"Whatcha doing?" I ask him.

"I'm putting Juniper limbs around the cabin. It can be effectively used to keep vampyrs out." He replies offhandedly.

"I thought they couldn't enter without invitation?" I ask confused.

"That's true with very very few exceptions for private homes. However for public places? No, they can go anywhere public and temporary places to stay like this are considered public."

"Good to know. I thought we didn't need to worry about them. Aren't they are supposed to be our friends?" I ask using air quotes when I say friends.

"According to their grand Elders yes. For the most part we don't often have issues with the seeths however there are rogues. Either way since we aren't sure what's been going on I think it's best we be prepared for anything. There's food on the counter, go eat."

I noticed Ian didn't even glance at me the entire time we were speaking. I don't know why it bothers me but it does. I shake it off and head over to the counter to grab some pizza.

As I'm finishing it Sierra walks in the front door. I had figured she was in her room, but I guess not. She walks over to me and drops a bag in front of me.

"You're uncle special ordered these for you. Since we're close to where he ordered them from he asked us to grab them, I figured getting them before we go is better than after." She tells me.

I open the bag inside and I find three dark wooden stakes with silver tips inside a leg holster. A set of five throwing knives in another thigh holster, a large serrated blade about half the size of a machete with a hip holster and a smaller one with an ankle holster. I also found a small jewelry box opening it. I find a beautifully adorned silver cross with deep red set stones on each limb of the cross. I notice it's also got an intricate design that matches all the blades and stake. I'm pretty sure it's Celtic designs though I could be wrong. While on one hand I love them I'm a little apprehensive by the fact that she felt I should have this first.

"These are great, but I thought this was a political meeting and that our safety was guaranteed?"

"In our world there's no such thing as safety. The elders in my opinion think too highly of their abilities to control their brood, they also strongly lack discipline for failure to follow rules. Actually more like their ideas of what requires discipline lacks. You'll want to wear those, they will probably take the stakes and the cross, though they think so little of us I'm sure they'll leave the knives and try to conceal the ankle one just in case. You should still wear the cross instead of the necklace you're wearing." She explains to me.

I've been wearing my herbed necklace everyday lately. It seems silly and knowing this world exists I'm sure the protective intent the necklace was put together for is useless since I probably did it wrong anyway but I'm not taking it off it makes me feel better. It's a simple urn necklace with a mixture of what's named as protective herbs and oils, a little dragon's blood, some rosemary , some verbena and a few other things inside.

"I'll put the cross on but I'm not taking off the necklace." I say sternly.

"Suit yourself. I see you've already dismissed the dress

code advice. You're really going to wear pants?" Sierra asks incredulously.

Ian looked at me then after finishing what he was doing he simply sat on the couch not even looking my way. Oddly he simply smirks.

"Yes, why wouldn't I you are?" I replied as I began strapping on the weapons.

"I'm an enforcer nobody cares what I wear."

"Well nobody should care what I wear either." I snap, "Are we ready to go, don't we need to be there by eight? It's already seven-thirty."

Sierra looks like she's about to say something more but Ian cuts her off. "Sierras is right you probably should wear a skirt however I think you'll end up intriguing the mistress, not to mention this will prove you're new to this world. Let's go."

The drive to the property itself is short, but after being buzzed through a gate we head up a windy dirt road that seems to go forever. There's thick crops of trees off to each side and I keep seeing what looks like eyes staring at us. Granted where we are, that's probably exactly what I'm seeing. I try to ignore the chill creeping up my spine and not show the bit of fear I'm feeling. We come to the opening and a four story mansion that looks like it's been here since the town was built looms before us. No it's not run down in any way you can just tell that's it from a different time all together.

At the bottom of the stairs that lead up to the massive gothic style front door stands a lone figure. We park and Ian opens the back door because I'm a stubborn jerk. I decide to open the one on the driver's side for myself and get out. Ian slams the door and Sierra just scowls and shakes her head. I guess I should stop antagonizing people here to protect me but what can I say?

As I round the corner of the car the figure comes into full view. He looks the same as he always had with his thick shoulder length black hair, lanky but muscular figure and tall stature. I bet he'll have the same sinfully enticing blue-green eyes as well. "Nicky?" I squeak. He looks at me then and my heart stops.

Ian immediately whips his head to me, and before Nick can say a word he snarls. "You know him? So you lied about not knowing anything about this world?"

Seriously? " Oh fuck off you douche canoe! Yes I know Nicky but I knew absolutely nothing about this. So why don't you get bent, you bastard."

Nick of course looks torn between anger at my presence and amusement at my telling Ian off. "Nicolai, Angie." He snaps at me then turns to my companions. "It's Nicolai Kearne."

"Kearne? Aren't the Kearne's in Ireland? Let alone born Vampyrs?" Ian asks then turns to me. "How the hell could you have not known? When he's a born Vampyr?"

Nick speaks before I can. "I never told anyone what I was so no she didn't know. At least about me, as far as I know the only thing she ever knew of our world were myths and legends. Then again it's her so who the hell knows."

"Fuck you Nicky boy I'll still beat your ass!" I snipe at him. Of course the asshole stills believes I'm a liar, fuck him, fuck all of them. "If you don't fucking mind I'm not here for you and I'm starting to lose my fucking temper so can we move this the fuck along before I get stabby." I notice other figures begin to emerge from the shadows until Nick holds up his hand and they slink back in.

"I see not much has changed, you're still snarky as ever. You'll have to leave your stakes and cross in the vehicle, you can keep your knives no one in this home is afraid of those. I advise you to be a little more polite with the Mistress of the seeth and to probably find a new favorite word at least temporarily."

"Fuck you, I can be diplomatic!" I argue and notice everyone Snickers and Nick mumbles how he'll believe it when he sees it. I walk over and throw my contraband into the SUV and slam the door. "Lead the way asshat!"

We follow Nick into the house, while outside it could almost be mistaken for a historical dream home, inside is quite another story. The entire décor is gothic which in and of itself isn't bad but the only colors to be spotted are black, red and bits of gold. It makes it look ghastly. The stench of blood is overwhelmingly disgusting. Seriously, who thinks black floors and red walls are in any way good design? Well maybe other then Fy but Ive accepted she demented as hell. The windows have heavy Black curtains with gold designs and the furniture is a mix of black and red.

Do these guys even realize there's a whole lot of other colors in the color wheel? I figured we'd be meeting in the living room or even in what looks like a meeting room but instead we follow Nick upstairs to the second floor where I imagine the bedrooms are. Not freaky at all. The phrase *let me suck your blood* keeps cycling over and over in my head and try as I might, I can't make it stop. Like what the fuck are they playing at.

Both Ian and Sierra seem completely fine with this situation and don't even seem to find it odd at all which irritates the hell out of me. We walk down the long hall at the top of the stairs straight ahead. The dark motive along the hall is the same as downstairs, black and red, black and red everywhere you look. With fake torch lights lining the long hallway.

We come up to a room at the end of the hall, Nick knocks softly on the door. "Entre." A soft musical voice from inside calls out.

He enters and we follow, this room is quite different from the others we passed on the way here. There's what appears to be a full bar in the corner, with a long table In front of it. A coffee table to the other side of the room surrounded by plush lounge chairs. What strikes me as the strangest is everything in this room is a rose pink, and passion fruit purple color mixed with white and silver trim. It seriously looks like a pampered princess room display from a home design magazine. Behind the bar is a small kitchen and there are three closed doors lining the back walls. It's quite strange and not at all what I expected. I glance up to find Nick smirking as if he knows my thoughts, but Ian and Sierra are not in the same state of shock I am.

I am so stunned I don't even notice the stunning brunette bomb shell that glides up next to Nick and caresses his chest seductively. "Bonjour mon amour." She says to him in the same musical voice which only variation is the husky undertone it takes. She's extremely tall with a thin but curvy figure and huge breasts. She has long flowing deep brown hair but eerie blood red eyes. Her skin is flawless but pale and she appears to only be a teenager. "Oh I see you've retrieved our guest Mon Amour. Come, come introduce us please Ma colombe." Nick seems uncomfortable but he has a smile on his handsome face. If I didn't know him so well I'd believe he was enjoying her attention but since I do I know he's not. This must be a secretary or something.

"Mistress, this is Angelika of the pack, and her two enforcers Ian and Sierra." He says to her, then turns to us. "and this is the Mistress of this Seeth Corentine Bellerose." Nope not a secretary and not at all what I'd expected. Come on, the girl is wearing a frilly pink mini skirt and a blink 182 Shirt. Not what one expects from the mistress of a Vampyr Seeth.

"It's a pleasure to meet you, Mistress Bellerose," I say as sweetly as possible.

"Yes, yes do you have the letter from the elders Cheri?" She asks.

Ian steps forward and hands her the envelope then steps back. She reads it quickly then sighs. "It would appear the elders have demanded we help in any way we can. Tell me Cheri how did one such as you, with no respect for our customs endear them to you?" She asks, though her voice takes on a tone I can only describe as jealousy.

"I won't lie to you, I was told of your customs and while I intend no disrespect I hate dresses in any situation that might end in my fleeing for my life."

She stares at me, then starts smiling. "So Cheri, you don't trust the grand elders' word of your safety? Nor that of your own council?" She asks with a strange tone that I can't figure out.

Ian and Sierra seem nervous now, but what strikes me is so does Nick he appears to be fighting an urge to grab me and run. "It's not that I don't trust their intent that I will be safe, but no matter what at the end of the day you can't control every single thing another does. The elders and council may wish for my safety but that does not mean they can ensure it especially if they themselves are not here to do so. While you've shown me no ill will yet I can not see your heart, nor can I read your mind for all I know you may wish me dead. I would be stupid to trust anyone's word that I am safe especially if that safety is meant to be enforce by a mere letter. Besides, rogues themselves show that not everyone follows orders given."

She literally busts up laughing, when it dies down a bit she glances at Nick. "Oh my, I think I like this girl too bad I can't keep her, of course you know about that do you not mon amour?" Nick gives a disgruntled look, and Ian well he looks pissed. She turns to him and Sierra. "I'm pleasantly surprised to see a smart wolf, one that does not blindly trust and obey. If all of you were like her I dare say your species would thrive more so then it does." She finally turns to me. "Cheri, I wish you no harm, of that

I promise you. Though I trust you wise enough not to grant me blind devotion, hopefully I will earn your trust. You no doubt would be a strong ally to have in the future." Nick visibly relaxes, Ian and Sierra however do not. "I am curious Cheri, who is it you do trust?"

"I trust my friends and family those closest to me, but I am not stupid. If it were to come between me and someone they care deeply for I would not hold in against them to turn on me. So at the end of the day I can and will only ever trust myself with full certainty because my mind and hearts are the only ones I can ever know."

"Very wise mon Cheri, very wise. Do you speak from experience? Would you betray to protect those you hold dear?" She inquires curiously.

"At the end of the day the only person I would ever sacrifice is myself. I would never choose between two people to save, I would save them both at the expense of myself."

"What is this? An honorable wolf? Why I would never thought to have seen the day." She says, astonished. It's clear there's a species divide. Both the wolves and vampyrs seem to believe themselves above the other in all respects. Ignorance has always been fascinating and their beliefs can clearly be contributed to ignorance. "Well, Nicky mon amour, I have gleaned all I wished from this meeting. You shall take them to the meeting room downstairs. I will be down shortly. I must change before I meet our people. Keep them safe until I join you." She turns to me and takes my hands, hers are cold and while my nails are bland hers are beautifully manicured with deep red polish and three diamonds on the tips of each. "Mon Cheri you will be safe with Nicky here of that, I promise you. You have nothing to fear from me, though you are wise. Everyone believes that vampyrs are of a hive mind this is not exactly true my dear. While yes we must obey direct orders of our sires, masters, and mistresses and even the elders, direct orders are a tricky thing. Say I order my people to do you no harm; they may decide that harming your companions and imprisoning you does not harm you. Then of course we do have the rogues who follow no edicts at all. Thus your lack of faith in the protections of a letter is a wise one, do not let your guard down here mon Cheri, and remember in the face of the public we must all play our roles." She brushes the lightest kiss on my forehead and turns her back to me.

Nick looks completely stunned and Ian and Sierra well I don't think they even know what to say. I truthfully didn't know what to expect from the mistress but that definitely wasn't what was imagined. Not by a long shot but their reactions to it seem a bit extreme, I will definitely need to ask them about that later.

Nick leads us back downstairs and then down another set behind the staircase that leads to the basement. I hate basements I always have and have no idea why. Basement and attics though just have always given me the heebie jeebies and I have to fight the urge to run. It gets worse when we reach the bottom of the stairs and I realize the walls are all cobblestone and resemble a dungeon. My apprehension intensifies and we pass through a hall with a room on each side one side is a room full of coffins, like seriously coffins I thought that was a fucking myth! Just rows and rows of coffins. While the other side looks like another hallway that's got bars for a door and looks like jail cells on each side of the hallway.

I turn my head straight and try to ignore everything else we pass including what appears to be a blood storage room and a torture chamber.

Nick keeps glancing back at me as we walk. I'm curious if he remembers how afraid of basements I am. All the time we used to spend in Tyler's basement as teenagers. While I was always okay when everyone was down there with me, one night I completely lost it. We had all fallen asleep down there after a few drinks, playing never have I ever. I woke up and everyone had left, I was in the middle of a panic attack when Nick came down for another beer, he saw me and helped me calm down. It was the first time we kissed, and the first time I ever truly saw him as anything more than my fun, sensitive stoner friend.

This room has the same dungeon feel as the others and no windows. There's a huge chandelier with candle lights that add to the gothic feel of the house. With torches, real torches lined along the walls. There was no seating with only the exception of what could only be described as a throne towards the other end of the room up on a stage area with about five steps leading to it. It's massive and I can't imagine the mistress' tinier mass sitting upon it. It too is extremely gothic looking with what gives the appearance of two horns sticking out on either side at the top of it. The floor is basic stone, nothing special except what looks like blood stains in various places. The strong smell of blood leaves me to further believe this.

Glancing around the room I see a lot of people, most of which appear perfectly normal. While yes a few have red eyes or fangs showing and most are pale as hell those are the main differences. However I do see about six of those creepy ass demon looking vampyr guard dogs, but these ones are on chains being held by others. They are the ones who first react to our presence hissing and straining against the chains being held by their masters.

Nick notices them immediately. "Why the hell did you guys bring your pets to this meeting?" He snarls at the ones holding the chains.

The six holding the chains who were huddled turn towards him. The man in the front speaks first, he's not what I would expect from a vampyr. He looks older, not ethereal as the Mistress or even Nick does. He has long black hair pulled back in a band by his neck. His eyes are glowing red and he's extremely tall. What catches my attention is the scar he has that goes down the center of his eye. He's wearing what I can only describe as an old suit from colonial times. It's classic black with a white blouse but still very out of place for today's times.

Hanging on his arm is a girl who looks as though she's sixteen. In contrast she has long blonde hair which is braided, with half of it wrapping around a bun on top of her head and the rest flowing down her back. She's shorter than him though still taller than me by quite a few inches, and she has bright blue eyes. She's wearing a dress that seems to appear to be from the same era as his suit though it's in a deep blue shade. While he glowers, she's smiling as she looks at Nick.

"I will bring my guards or my pets where I choose to. I do not answer to you boy! None of us do!" He sneers at Nick with blatant irritation.

None of us heard the doors open, but we realize it when we hear Corentines voice behind us. "No but you do answer to me Cornelius, and anyone whom I deem necessary to act on my behalf. Or have you forgotten?" She demands with an authority to her voice that she did not use while conversing with us earlier.

Her comment about playing our roles makes much more sense now, this is her role. She was not kidding when she said she was changing she's now wearing a slinky deep red thin strapped dress. It flows all the way to the floor dragging at the back, there's a slit that literally goes up to her hip. She's barefoot as well and is wearing a crown of thorns with black roses. It's hard to recognize the girl before me from the one I met.

"Of course I do not question you mistress only this dog who barks at your command." He replies.

"This dog as you call him has a higher rank than you ever will.

Further if he does bark at my command it is still my command is it not?" She snaps.

"Of course mistress my apologies."

Another male clears his throat. "Mistress, would you like us to remove our guards?"

" That won't be necessary for now Luis. I merely advise those of you who have brought them to keep them in line or they will be disposed of." She replies with dismissal then continues up the steps of the platform turning to face us in front of the steps. Everyone else bows except for me, she merely raises her eyebrow and then smirks at me before sitting. As soon as she sits everyone rises.

"We gather today to grant an audience to the wolves before us as has been demanded by our elders to do so. We have been told to grant both information and aid to them in regards to one of us who has been rogue for some time. It seems as though the true Alpha Heir has returned to the wolves which should be a time for celebration for them. Instead turmoil has befallen them as the Heir has been being threatened by Beatrix Stone and her brood. "She announces.

"That is why you've gathered us? For this? To subjugate ourselves and to betray one of our own to a bunch of dogs?" Cornelius all but yells and everyone else gasps. I'm unsure if it's his manner or if it's her announcement that caused the gasps. "She doesn't even show the respect our costumes demand. She did not bow, she dresses as a peasant, and she hasn't even bothered to speak for herself!" Corentine appears completely calm and is merely tapping the tips of her nails on the arm of her chair. Still the room is filled with fear and anger in equal measure. A few men I never notice behind the throne begin stepping forward she merely holds up her hand and they step back into their original places.

" Who is asking subjugation to the wolves? I don't believe I said that, did I mon Amour?" She asks Nick.

"You did not, Mistress." He replies simply.

"Good, good I was worried I misspoke. We are being demanded by our own council as we should since Beatrix is one of ours. I believe you were her suitor once, were you not Cornelius?"

"You know I was, but I am not responsible for what she does neither is the seeth. She left us and went rogue. She is no longer our concern or problem!"

"Yes she has gone rogue, but honor dictates we control ours who go mad. Does it not?"

"It is not our way!" He continues to argue.

"You are wrong. Our way is to follow hierarchy and rules put forth by our elders, masters and sires in that order. Our laws say we dispatch those who are beyond control and our elders say we help. So help we shall, your displeasure will be noted but it changes nothing. Understood?" She asks.

"I understand, you've made friends with the new wolf. Don't think we didn't notice your private meeting. You've gone too so ...."

He doesn't get to finish because faster than anyone's eyes can track she's launched herself at him. He is now dangling in the air gasping for breath. Her nails are digging into his neck with blood dripping down. He drops the chains around his guard but Nick who followed her has already snatched it up.

"Weak am I? You call meeting a stranger in private before bringing her into a room filled with my people to make sure she won't pose a threat weak? You call being a leader first weak? You couldn't even control your lover which is why she's here in the first place! You have the highest number of rogue sired who manage to survive and escape the laws then any of us and you question me?" She snarls inches from his face.

"Apologies Mistress." He whispers.

She drops him to a heap and returns to her throne after he's standing Nick hands him the chain then heads back towards me.

"Angelika, please explain to the fools among us who do not understand why you did not bow? Why you did not dress appropriately for this meeting?" She asks me her voice returning to her musically soft tone.

"Simple mistress. I wore what I am because I do not know who wishes me harm other than they're vampyrs. A dress would hinder my ability to fight back or too run if I need to do so. As for the Bowing its truly simple: *a queen does not bow before a queen.* If I am the heir to the True Alpha that would be as a queen I could not bow to you any more than I could demand you bow to me or bare your neck to submit." I replied.

She nods her head. "Does this satisfy your lack of propriety Cornelius?" She asks. He merely nods his head and glares, still rubbing his throat. "Very well let's move on from this ridiculousness. The Vampyr who has been troubling you Cheri is Beatrix. She was an unholy demon even as a babe." I hear Cornelius grumble but nothing more. "She was never fully in control but she went fully rogue about ten years ago. We have sent many to dispatch her but they all failed and many never returned. We believe she killed them but can not be certain. She is pure evil. I understand you're relatively new to this world so you may not know much about our kind, but we are not evil. Yes we prefer the darker side of life but we do still value life. Our kind have rules, one of our highest being not to kill or turn humans without permission Beatrix disagreed with this among many other laws. I have had a folder of information put together for you to take back to your people . It contains all the information we have. Additionally I will be sending some of our most trusted to return with you to aid you in dealing with her."

"That's preposterous!" Cornelius exclaims. He also dropped the chains on his stupid guard who immediately launches itself at me throwing both Ian and Sierra out of the way and slamming into Nick throwing him across the room. It's on me so quickly I don't have time to really react. It knocked me flat on my back and sliced down my shoulder in the process. Without thinking I withdraw my knife and stab it through the throat. It flings itself off me, clawing at its throat while making a gurgled screaming sound. I stand shakily Ian, Sierra and Nick are now standing before me and the guard. The mistress is directly in front of me.

"Are you okay mon Cheri?" She asks.

I nod not trusting myself to speak.

She turns and walks up to the guard before I can even think of what she's doing. She rips it's head off. Taking my knife she hands it to Nick then walks calmly over to Cornelius and shoves the head in his arms. "I warned you." She hisses. To the room she says. "This meeting is over, get out Now!" walking back to me. "I will have Nick escort you out. I must ask you to remain at your hotel until tomorrow at sundown. The people I will be sending with you will meet you then before you leave with everything you will need. Go now and get yourself taken care of. I am sorry that this has happened Cheri, but now you understand why I said you were wise." She softly brushes her fingers along my cheek and leaves the room.

Nick takes us back out to the car. When I'm about to get in, he grabs my arm. "Angel, I'm really sorry that happened back there. Cornelius normally doesn't contend with Corentine so openly. I really didn't think there would be any issue or I would have warned you. How badly were you hurt?"

"It's fine Nick. I'm not your responsibility. It's just a scrape no big deal it's not even bleeding anymore." I immediately turn and get into the car closing the door.

We returned to the hotel without incident, both my guards are sullen and haven't spoken a word. I should probably care but I truly can't bring myself to, fuck them. It's not like they got hurt in any way.

Once inside Ian immediately tells me to sit on a kitchen chair and runs back outside. I of course ignore this and head straight for my bathroom. I just finished peeling off my shirt and bra when Ian barges into my bathroom.

" I thought I told you…." He begins irritatedly.

"Ian what the fuck!" I yelp glaring at him. I don't even bother trying to cover my breasts, I've never been one who is afraid of nudity. Still though him barging into where I should have privacy annoys the hell out me. He's still standing there with his mouth open like a fucking guppy out of water, starring at my tits. "Hey big boy eyes up here," I say.

He recovers. "Um, ya sorry. I need to see where you were cut. Claws from their guards can cause infection easily and with not being able to shift you're at a higher risk."

"Fine whatever but I'm taking a bath first I'll come out when I'm done."

After he leaves, I take a nice long relaxing bath. Afterwards I went out with a towel wrapped around my chest and let him patch me up. Sierra and him were quite upset when I informed him I didn't want to talk about it then and that I was going to bed but I simply ignored their objections and went to bed anyway.

CHAPTER 9

The following day we didn't have anything really to do so I made them take me into town to go shopping. They immediately tried taking me to the outlet mall which I of course objected to. Instead we hit up a few of the second hand stores, antique stores, and even an apothecary. At the last minute I saw a rock shop I just had to go into and among other things I bought four large quartz rocks which had solar lights behind a piece of Plexiglas in the center. Of course Ian and Sierra thought I was nuts. By the time we finished it was already five Ian decided we needed to grab some food and head back to the hotel to wait for our vampyr group who would be sent with us.

We all had talked this morning before we left for shopping and I found out why they were so shocked by the mistress's behavior towards me. Apparently she is a born Vampyr and had lost all of her family to wolves a long time ago, and while she has always sworn she holds no grudge whatsoever she is usually more reserved when it comes to wolf kind.

Instead she showed me a rare fondness that is normally reserved for her children which most definitely was not expected. Normally those who enter her personal quarters are intimidated. Ian explained that she came here from France not long after losing her family as a slave to the former master. She ended up overcoming his tyranny and killed him which is how she became the mistress. The wolves who had killed her family were strays working for her former master, she has certain gifts though Ian is unsure what they are that the master had sought to use for his own gain.

Neither of them know Nick personally or a whole lot about him. What they do know is that his original Seeth is in Ireland but his father fled here when he was young. They don't know why exactly but do know he and Nick's sister belong to the Phoenix Seeth by choice. Nick on the other hand refuses to belong to either Seeth and is under the mistress by choice and loyalty alone. She allows him to remain in the central area only calling him back for important reasons when needed otherwise he's left alone with merely the need to check in by phone or email to assure her of his safety.

They are unsure of her relationship with Nick though there are rumors of a romantic relationship and that she has some kind of a friendship with his mother who still lives in Ireland something I actually did know. I still can't wrap my head around dating him for half a year let alone being friends with him for as many years as I was and not knowing what he was. What's even weirder is how cold he was to me, yes we did have a bad falling out but I thought we'd gotten through that. We've talked and seen each other a few times since then of course about two years ago he deleted me from all social media and stopped talking to me together. I'd just figured his girlfriend got jealous and made him, though now I'm wondering if it wasn't something more. Granted I'm not curious enough to go through hell trying to drag it out of him fuck that shit he was always hard to get anything out of. Besides, it's not like I will ever see him again anyway.

We're just finishing loading our things into the car when Ian and Sierra both tense, I feel it too but I've been expecting them to show and apparently lack the natural apprehension they both have. Not necessarily this promptly since the sun literally just went down minutes ago but it was still expected nonetheless.

"Right on time," I say without turning around.

I had not expected his voice to answer. "The Mistress was extremely persistent that we were on time and not a second late. So here we are."

I take a deep breath. "Nicky poo, I didn't realize you'd be coming to see us off." I respond by turning to face him. I see the irritation in his face. He's always hated that name. It's the main reason I've always used it when I'm annoyed with the bastard.

"Oh, my dear angel I'm not seeing you off, I will be accompanying you." The wicked smirk forming on his face tells me he noticed how uncomfortable that idea made me. "The Mistress has assigned me to be in charge of the vampyr guard she's sending with you. You should be honored she is sending seven of her most trusted guards to help aid you and keep you safe. I've never seen her do so much for someone not her child and I doubt I ever will again."

"Oh, great she's sending a stoner to lead my guard?" His eyes flash in anger. "Maybe I don't want you to be here, have you ever thought of that? Besides as I understand it you have no obligation to follow the mistresses' orders, so why do so to protect me? We both know you could care less about if I die or not." Ian again is looking upset. I swear this is a new operating mode for him and it's starting to piss me off. Sierra however looks completely amused by our interaction.

"I follow her orders out of mutual respect and appreciation. She keeps me from having to subjugate myself to either seeth and allows me the freedom to live where and how I wish. So no matter who she were to request I guard I will do so even if it were my own father." I gasp at that, I know how much he hates his father and rightfully so he's a right bastard and always has been. Anyone who can convince him to guard that man must mean a lot to him. Maybe Corentine is the new girlfriend I had heard about, the one I assumed forced him to drop communication with me. Then again if that were the reason he stopped talking to me why would she push him on me now?

"Look, Nick I don't know how Jake is going to react to you being around. He knows our past, and he's already having enough jealousy issues with Ian without adding you to the mix. Besides where will you all stay? I don't know about opening up my home to vampyrs, endangering my children by letting vampyrs around them just to possibly be safe from other vampyrs. Besides, you can't be around all the time. What about the sun?" I explain hoping he'll back down and stay here.

He looks to my companions. "You guys haven't told her? How much does she know? Has she really been walking around thinking the sun will save her?" He demands the anger in his voice is blatant.

Ian just growls but Sierra replies. "We haven't had the time to teach her much about your kind. We had to teach her about us first so she could be introduced to our world. Then she showed some unusual talents so we had to reach out to a witch but that training has been delayed as well. It's only been a few months she grew up completely ignorant of our world."

"Angel doesn't know many things but she's never been ignorant. She knows more than even she realizes, and she's a fast learner she'll catch on quickly. I was unaware of anything witch related, but that does explain her necklace." Ian and Sierra look at my necklace with confusion. "It's a good thing that wasn't mentioned in the Seeth and you must be cautious to who you mention it to. No one here will say anything and neither would the mistress but there are some who… let's just say it won't be good. I need to know more about this and about who knows." He turns to me. "I am the only vampyr who will be given access to your home for now. While these guards can be trusted, they can be compelled by Beatrix whereas I can not. My access is non negotiable as for Jake he'll cope. We've gotten along before it won't be a problem."

"That was before…" Before what? Before he hurt me? It shouldn't have hurt when he stopped talking to me but it did. Jake had been furious about it. It was strange that he was so mad about another man not speaking to me, but he always knew how much Nick meant to me. I can't get into this now, I won't not in front of everyone. Maybe not ever, so I change the subject knowing Nick's stubbornness I realize nothing's going to stop him from coming. "What about my necklace?" I ask instead.

"I will explain later, for now, let's just say Alec was always right about you." He responds. Alec a blast from the past if ever there was one. How I miss that carrot-topped jerk. I haven't spoken to him since the fallout with Jonah. Nick waves over the others with him.

"This is Emilio, Celene, Thyone, Eva, Tara, Doyle, and Draven." He says pointing to each vampyr as he says their names. "You do not have to worry about the sun, we can each walk in it. Guard this is Angelika, and her enforcers Ian and Sierra. We will be guarding Angelika and her family while also tracking down Beatrix. The mistress has made it clear how important this is and the consequences of failure do not forget."

They all express their agreement. While a thought strikes me one last ditch effort before giving up on getting out of having Nick around. "It doesn't look like there is enough room for all of you, Nick I guess one will have to stay behind. You should take one for the team and let it be you." I state with a smile.

To my astonishment he smiles back. "Nice try angel, I will be riding with you."

"Excuse me," Ian shouts. "I don't remember inviting a bloodsucker for the ride?"

"You didn't and it doesn't matter. Load up, you all will follow us."

Nick orders the vamp guards before hopping in our car in the back.

I exhale slowly then hop in the other side looking at Ian. "Let's just get this over with. I miss my kids and am quite honestly done with this shit."

The drive back was fairly quiet for the most part, that is until we hit the 1-10 about twenty miles outside of Chandler. We were quite literally in the middle of nowhere, normally it wouldn't be that bad, it was only around midnight. Usually, the 10 is still pretty busy around this time, tonight though the highway was pretty dead. We haven't seen another vehicle since we passed the casino. I don't know why it bothered me but I found it quite concerning and couldn't shake the feeling we were being watched. That's probably why I was so freaked out now that we were on the side of the road changing two tires. Thankfully both SUVs had a spare otherwise we'd have to wait for someone or try to pile into one vehicle which would be a nightmare. Still, it's odd that both the passenger side tires on our SUV went out at the same time. Ian made me stay in the car as he and the Vampyr guard all were outside working on changing the tires and watching the perimeter. I don't think they'd realize that my sense has been improving recently. If they had, I don't think they'd have been talking so openly since it was clear they were trying to keep it quiet that this was sabotage.

I know Sierra could hear every word they were saying, I could tell by watching her facial expressions. Apparently something, either magically or in some other way intentionally, took out the tires. Nick and Ian seem to believe it was done to our car on purpose and that both tires were hit hoping the other SUV wouldn't notice us not following or otherwise, though unlikely, not recognizing they were with us. We switched positions with them once we hit the 10. Nick thought it would be a good deterrent given how desolate it was if someone were following us. Unfortunately, it looks like whoever did this knew exactly which car I was in. Thankfully the Vamps saw and stopped since this is the dead zone for cell reception.

Sierra looked at me in the mirror and smiled. "You heard everything they said, didn't you?" she asked. Ian and Nick instantly stopped speaking and turned to me. I merely nodded my head. She rolled down both our windows.

"I thought you said she didn't have abilities?" Nick asked Ian.

"She's never displayed any." He replied.

They were both staring at me expectedly. I shrugged. "My senses started improving a few weeks ago, it's been gradual," I informed them.

"Ian, you're an idiot! I noticed this and I'm not around her near as often." Sierra exclaimed. Not quite true recently at least not since Thanksgiving. However, it started before then so she's not exactly wrong.

Ian went back to the tire and continued his work quietly. After they finished the last tire he and Nick moved towards the other SUV to confer with the vampyrs. I heard Sierra mutter something about idiot males and lack of information being dangerous. She didn't even get a chance to react when a Vamp flashed next to her, not one of ours, and knocked her out with a fierce strike to the temple. In my head, I began cursing myself for packing my stakes and cross why the fuck did I even do that? Here I was traveling with a vampyr right next to me for fucks sake! As these foolish thoughts went rushing through my brain I was yanked from the car by the Vamp thankfully I wasn't buckled he might have decapitated me with the force he'd used.

I kicked him in the knee hard and he faltered enough to release me and I used the advantage to back away quite a few paces. I took the opportunity to glance to the other SUV quickly and saw the vamps, Nick and Ian fighting at least a dozen of those stupid guard dog vamps. The one that dragged me out recovered and was approaching me again.

"You will come with me. You will come without fighting. You will come silently. You will co…." he began, with his eyes glowing red.

"Like fucking hell I'm going with you! The only thing I will be doing with you is killing you!" I snarled, cutting him off.

"YOU WILL COME!" He demanded.

"Fuck you, blood breath. I take demands from no one." I yelled back.

I was still taking small steps back knowing it won't do much if he comes at me using his speed but it gives me a little comfort.

"How are you defying me? This isn't possible you stupid bitch. You're a mutt! You can't defy me!" He screams in self righteous anger.

At this point I think he's just ranting to nobody in general but I can't help but respond. "Wow you really think a lot about yourself don't you? What's the matter Dracula, your power impotent at the moment? Your impotency hurts your ego and you can't take it?" I can't help but laugh at the furious roar he lets out in response.

"When the master is done with you, I will kill you!"

I shrug my shoulders. "Why wait? Why not do it now if you think you're strong enough?"

He flies at me, I'm able to pull my knife out but barely in enough time. I slash out at him just as he crashed into me. I fly back and hear a pop in my left shoulder as I land and roll. I feel the brushes scrape against my skin and I know my arms are covered in road rash before looking. Odd fact if you hit dirt hard enough you can get road rash just as well as you can on asphalt. I feel a little better looking up and seeing the front of him covered in blood, his shirt torn in half, but only a little his eyes tell me he's pissed. I force myself to stand ignoring the pain, blocking it out the best I can letting adrenaline take over.

"You're right bitch I'm not waiting I'm going to kill you now. Nobody makes me bleed."

"I just did twinkle bitch!" I yell

He's charging me already I fling my left arm back and thankfully this time going for accuracy instead of speed he's not using it. Once he's close enough I fling my limp arm at him with all my might ignoring the intense pain. I've only ever done this once fighting a guy in high school so I already know the hit if nothing else will confuse him just enough to stall him for a few seconds. I mean come on? Who hits someone with a dislocated arm? Nobody sees that coming. So I use it repeating what I did with the vampyr guard at the seeth and slamming my knife through the soft flesh of his throat with my good arm.

"Check bitch!" I wheeze as I shove him away. He's too busy clawing at his throat to fight me.
Sierra, who must have just regained consciousness rushes over as fast as she can bleeding from a gash on her head, assesses and grabs me. "Lets go!" she says, dragging my good arm behind her. "I'll say one thing: you're smart and thank the Goddess for that."

Once we're back at the SUV I look over to the others who have just finished dispatching the last of the guard dog vamps and are walking away from the piles of dust. That's at least a good thing and where the legends come from. While most vampyr bodies don't disintegrate the lower ones like these do. Which means less mess.

"Where the fuck did Amon go?" Nick growls.

I glance over and realize the vampyr is gone and only my knife remains.

"My knife," I whisper.

Nick looks to one of the other Vamps who rushes over to grab it. "Angel are you okay?" He asks me softly.

"I'm fine. I need to get cleaned up and take care of these before I go home though I don't want to worry the kids."

"We'll take you to your uncle's. I will call him and have the Dr meet us there," Ian says. "I need to let him know we might be bringing guests anyway or he'll shoot first ask later."

I'm pretty sure I passed out on the way there. Everything hurts something awful. I had thought it was just the scrapes and my shoulders but no, my back, hip, and head all hurt too. I know I should open my eyes but I just don't want to quite yet, instead I just sit here in pain and listen to them talk. Ian and Sierra are freaking out I can tell, I'm pretty sure they're scared my uncle will blame them but fuck that this is hardly their fault. I have every intention of making that clear to them once I can open my eyes.

I think this hurts worse than when I fell out of the back of the truck which surprises me. I thought that was the worst pain I would ever feel, God was I wrong. Though it might still be the dumbest. Like seriously who the fuck gets in a fight with their husband then sits in the bed of the truck not alerting him you're there when he peels out? That was a trip and a half. Poor Jake would've been arrested if I was unconscious because everyone actually thought he'd run me over. Like seriously? Jake run me over? Ha! Damn though does road rash and a 4th degree concussion take forever to heal. Actually the stupid strep throat a week later causing a weird staph infection stalled the healing but still. The Dr was so confused over that he said it was extremely abnormal. For me? It was par for the course my body always does weird shit. Ya though half my body was covered in road rash it was so bad I couldn't even wear a shirt and lived in sports bras for quite a while. This though? This hurts worse. I wonder if they'll give me pain pills this time? I mean I'm not drunk so they should right?

"Did she seriously hit that Vamp with an arm attached to a dislocated shoulder?" I hear Sierra ask.

"Yeah, she did. I have no idea how with the bloody amount of pain she must have been in, but she did." Ian replies to her.

"She's done that before. It's really not the first time, she can be a crazy ass bitch when she needs to be." Oh yeah I forgot Nick was there for that fight. It's weird he's seemed so angry with me yet he sounds worried.

"So you mean she's always been this crazy? When I met her she was clueless and outside trying to fight a guard Vamp with a machete! It's the craziest shit I've ever seen!" Ian says.

Nick chuckles. "Ya that sounds like her. In high school this guy was fucking with one of our friends. Our friend didn't want to fight him but he wouldn't back down. He threw in a cheap shot and wouldn't stop swinging, none of us could get there fast enough. Angel, though she flung herself in there, shoves the guy and starts screaming about how he had a tiny dick and was over compensating. When he shoved her she hit the wall hard we all heard the pop she didn't cry nothing just started pounding on him with that same arm. The crowd who was stopping us from getting there finally let us through and were now yelling at the guy for pushing a girl. We had to pull her off him she was still screaming about his small dick as we pulled her away."

"That asshole deserved it and he probably does have a small dick," I mumble. Nick jumps and looks down at me. Both Sierra and Ian glance back. "Hey, got any caffeine? I'd kill for an energy drink right now."

They all shake their heads at me. Nick reaches into the back in the cooler and pulls out a Dr pepper handing it to me. "Didn't know about energy drinks but I remember this used to be your favorite."

"Technically still is but the hubby drinks it like water so I don't drink it as often anymore. Now I live on energy drinks since I'm always so tired, and I drink 7-up a lot though I might have to change that since hubby started drinking that too. Like seriously is nothing sacred?" I respond and see Nick smirk. I take a few drinks then ask. "So where are we?"

"Almost to casa grande. The Dr is meeting us at your uncle's. Did you want to call Jake? Or head home after seeing the Dr?" Sierra asks me.

"Naw I'll just stay at my uncle's tonight. Jake goes to work tomorrow so I'll head over after he goes in that way. I have all day to figure out what to say to him about everything. Sadly with injuries I have got to tell him something just not certain he'll like anything I say."

"Won't you heal by tomorrow? Wait you haven't told him?" Nick asks confused.

"No I've never shifted so I don't have their woohoo healing. As for Jake of course I haven't told him. He doesn't believe in any of this shit. He'd never believe me and he'd think I'm a lunatic!"

"Wait if you've never shifted, how do you even know you're a were? As for Jake, why doesn't someone just shift in front of him?"

"They did blood tests, my father is a shifter, and well my eyes they um… glow sometimes. As for shifting Jake would just shoot them and convince himself the weed was really good."

"Wait your eyes? They really glow?" I nod. "I wasn't hallucinating," Nick mutters to himself.

"What?" I look at him.

"Well, um… a few times when…" He looks upfront, "well when you'd get really… excited? I could have sworn that your eyes glowed."

I hear a growl upfront. "You mean when we had sex?" I ask him, and he nods his head.

"Had sex! You two have had sex? You had sex with a Vampyr?" Ian screams with a growl. He's looking back at us and he swerved.

Sierra smacks him hard. "Watch the road asshole and don't scream I have a concussion!"

"Ya what she said. Besides it's none of your business who or what I fuck or who or what I have fucked. So fuck off asshole!"

"I hadn't matured yet, so I wasn't a Vampyr back then. To be more accurate she took my virginity so we didn't just have sex. Also we were close friends for a long time and in a relationship for almost a year. Not that it's any of your business or anything. I mean there's no bonds there right? Or are you hiding one you didn't tell Angel about?"

"No there are not any bonds, and it's not his fucking business," I say sternly.

Nick just smirks. "Really though, are you okay?" He asked me.

"Of course, perfect, no worries."

I feel the car speed up quite a bit it scares the shit out of me and I latch on to Nick fuck! I didn't mean to do that just like I didn't mean to back then. Strangely he just rubs my back and whispers that it's okay. The car slams to a stop and Ian immediately gets out and slams his door, by this point I'm in Nick's lap. Nick opens his door. I watch Sierra walk over to talk to Ian, they argue a bit and she shoves him then heads back to us.

"He's going to go take a walk, before I kill him. I can take her from you?" She offers Nick.

"Yall know I can walk right?"

"It's okay I've got her. My guys will wait out here but I'm not leaving her until I know she's okay and with someone not losing their mind." Nick says, ignoring my objection altogether.

Sierra nods. "That's fine this is a temporary home anyway so you won't need an invitation to come in. Follow me."

She turns around and Nick follows holding me. She opens the door and walks in.

"What are you doing? Edward won't like this? Why would you bring a Vampyr into Edwards house?" I look and of course it's Tala. God I really don't fucking like her.

"Good thing it's my house huh TALA? Listen I'm not in the fucking mood for your shit tonight little girl so don't fucking start. Besides he's my friend so fuck off!" I informed her.

"Your uncle won't like you having Vampyr friends." Tala says in disgust.

"Ya well I don't like him having hanger on bitches like you, but I cope don't I?" I hear Sierra snicker. "Besides I've known him longer than any of you so guess who I trust more? Now back off and get the fuck out of the way!" I fire back at the stuck up broad.

"Your uncle…"

"Her uncle can speak for himself, and I knew he was coming. You're excused TALA." My uncle says coming up behind her. She looks from him to me pouting and looking devastated. He turns towards us. "Though I didn't know he'd be carrying my injured niece. Where's Ian? Will someone explain what's happening? All he said was vampyrs were coming with and a Dr was needed. He didn't say it was for Angel. Sweetie, are you okay?"

"I'm fine, he just won't let me walk. Ian's outside somewhere throwing a temper tantrum. We were attacked on the road on the way back obviously I got hurt but I hurt him too so I'm happy! Where is the doc, does he have some Vicodin cause I kinda hurt a little?" I inform him and he just stands there staring at me like I've grown another head. "What?" I ask.

He just shakes his head at me. Nick laughs. "Angel, not everyone is used to your nonchalant attitude about injuring yourself."

"You seem pretty used to it though. I'm Edward Wulfrik, her uncle."

"Nicolai Kearne, I went to high school with Angel."

The front door slams. "Ya he shagged her too!" I hear Ian's voice.

I jump out of Nick's hold before he can stop me. I wince hard when my feet land jarring my hip more than it is, but ignore it and get into Ian's face.
"You listen here you self righteous prick! Yes I dated Nick, yes we fucked quite a lot actually and it was fantastic if you must know so much about my personal life, but it's none of your fucking business. Get the fuck over whatever is going on with your fucking head and grow the hell up. None of this is about you nor is it your business!" I scream at him.

He growls back at me. "Ian that's enough you need to go to the guards house now! Send grant back over here. You need to calm down and let this go or I will move you out of here altogether." My uncle says and looks over at Sierra who moves immediately.

She grabs his arm and pulls him out the door. " This is ridiculous, she's hurt, and she doesn't need this." I hear her berate him on the way out.

"I'm sorry dear, he's struggling right now. Please come sit. You too Nicolai." My uncle says. I'm too tired to argue so I just do it. "The doc will be here shortly. So, you two know each other?"

"Please, call me Nick." I snort because of his reaction to me calling him Nick when I first saw him. The only reason he hasn't corrected me again is because he knows better, and that it'll only encourage me. " Yes, we were good friends in high school, and dated for a while. Before you ask she didn't know what I was and I had no idea about her. I hadn't matured yet. We had a falling out, but reconnected a few years after. However, we lost touch again a while ago." I snort again because the last thing I'd call it is lost touch.

"Dear, are you more hurt than you let on? Would you like a drink maybe? To help with the pain for now." My uncle asks.

Before I can respond Nick cuts in. " She will never tell anyone how much pain she's in. If she's crying or if she's telling you she hurts really bad she's probably dying. So yes she's in pain and a lot of it. She also prefers whiskey." I stick my tongue out at him. Jerk.

My uncle gets up and comes back with a bottle of whiskey and a glass sets in on the table then goes and grabs a coke and brings it back. I grab it before he can mix it yuck, and pour a glass then open the coke. I take a chug and chase it. My uncle chuckles. "So I see you know her well?"

"I hope so she was my best friend and more for a time." Nick replies solemnly.

"Alright, so I can tell you have a few things you aren't saying." My uncle says to Nick as he eyes me. "I won't say I'm completely okay with it, because I'm not. I don't like secrets especially when they can affect my family but since you know her and you kept her from a moody werewolf already I will let it be for now. I will ask this however, will you put her and her family's safety first? That's all I care about."

As the door opens Nick replies. " That is one thing I swear on my life."

His response stuns me! Like what? Really?

Dr Smith walks in. "Awe, so you're my patient! What on earth did you do, poor girl?"

"Fought with a Vampyr."

"Well let me have a look at you."

CHAPTER 10

Ian

Sierra pulls me out the door and over to the house we purchased to be the guard house. It's directly across the street from the house Edward is staying in. It's more of an old trailer home than a house, and while the inside is spacious and well kept the outside is quite run down. With peeling blue paint and a yard full of cacti. Seriously, this yard could be a cactus store. It's got so many different types of cacti. There was so much we actually had to take some out to be able to have a clear view of the house. Of course now that she moved into the house on the opposite side we can only watch Edward from here. Which is why he purchased the one on the next street over directly across from her new place though he's not moved us yet.

The inside of the guard house has a decent sized living room and kitchen. Though the real appeal was the five bedrooms and three baths. Even with that we still have to double up with the rooms, the two girls of course were given the master bedroom on Edwards orders. Always being a gentleman he wouldn't have it any other way.

"Grant, Edward wants you to head over to his place," Sierra informs him.

"What? I just got off duty?" Grant whines.

"Sorry dude, this moron couldn't behave himself so he's been relieved the rest of the night." Does she really think I'm a moron?

"There's guards at her house already."

"Sure, but she's at Edwards for the night. There was an incident on the way back and she was injured so she's going home tomorrow. Just a heads up there's an SUV with some Friendly vamps and one in the house. Don't shoot any of them Edward won't be happy."

Grant gets up grumbling and shoulder checks me as he passes. "Watch it!" I growl at him.

"You watch it asshole, if you'd behave yourself I might have some damn down time." He snarls as he slams the door.

"What the fuck is your issue Ian? That was completely out of line and out of character for you! The last thing an injured wolf, let alone a woman needs is someone challenging them!" Sierra all but yells at me.

"I don't like fucking vampyrs damn! I thought we agreed on that?" I yell back.

"That was more then just not liking vampyrs Ian I'm not fucking stupid so stop acting like I am. You're right I don't care for vampyrs but he was sent to help and seems to want to that's all that should matter."

"They slept together of course he wants to watch her!" I yell, not believing she doesn't get it.

"Yes they have a history but he didn't seem too inclined to rekindle it at the moment, so I don't think that has shit to do with it."

"He wants her I can tell!"

"Even if he does Ian it's their business not yours. You're letting your jealousy get the best of you and it's getting out of hand."

"I'm not jealous. It's just unnatural that's all." I say defeated because we'll what else can I say? She's right I am jealous!

"Bullshit Ian, I've known you, your entire life. I know you imprinted Ian and at first I was pissed at her for seeming to just dismiss you, but she doesn't know does she?" Have hit the nail on the head with that one.

"Of course she doesn't. How am I supposed to tell her."

"Why did you do it? Why would you do that to yourself? Hell to her?"

"I didn't do it on purpose, it just happened. I didn't even realize what had happened until I'd lost it with Connor."

"Ian you know how it works on some level you had to have wanted it. Has she accepted it? Even without knowing."

"No she hasn't. She probably never will whether she knows or not. Besides, why do you care when you hate her?"

"I've never hated her. I thought she was screwing with your head, and wasn't sure she had what we needed. After seeing her in the Seeth and with that Vamp tonight I might be changing my mind. You need to fucking tell her Ian either she can accept or reject the imprinting. Whichever she chooses this lunatic behavior can stop. The longer you wait the worse it'll be." With that she walked out to leave me to stew in my thoughts.

Seriously I can't believe Edward kicked me out over that damned blood sucker! I thought for sure he'd be as furious as I am. Yes I get Angel didn't know what she was, but he knew what he was. Granted maybe I'm not being fair to either of them but I don't really care right now. I probably wouldn't be as pissed if she was anyone else. Hell Sierra was right I'm being crazy, and

I probably should tell Angel what I did. I didn't mean to do it, I didn't even know it happened at first. Hell I don't even know how it happened if I'm being honest. It just snapped into place when I looked at her that first night. Even though I hadn't realized it until much later.

Then when she mentioned her husband it almost killed me but I deluded myself thinking she'd just leave him the second she found out what she was. So far that doesn't seem like it's going to happen. The man is hardly ever home and doesn't seem to help much with the kids. Outside of paying bills I don't really understand what he even does for his family. His relationship with his mother is extremely unhealthy and creepy. Sounds more like he's her husband not her son, hell just last week he didn't come home until two in the morning when I asked Angel about it she said he went to his mom's because she had a bad couple of days and needed to talk to him. I don't hear him talk to Angel much and I've never heard him discuss plans with her it's always were going here, so and so is coming here, I'm doing this meanwhile she talks to him about all her plans and tries desperately to tell him about her and the kids days but he doesn't bother listening or calls her boring. She deserves way better than he treats her, but she keeps saying he's her kids father, and she loves him.

It's so heartbreaking to watch and now I'm going to have to watch this damn blood sucker drool over her for who knows how long. I look up and see the Vamp ahead of me damn I must have really been lost in thought because I didn't even notice I left the house. I think it's official I'm going mental. I watch as he hands some keys to his guys then heads off in the opposite direction and I decide to follow him. Maybe I will get lucky and he's up to something. Actually I wonder if anyone would notice if he just disappeared. It would definitely solve my problems. Instead of doing something stupid and getting myself in more shit with Edward I decide to have a little chat with him.

Nicolai

After the Dr had finished seeing Angel and I knew she'd be okay, I took my leave. I let her uncle know I'd be getting a location for my group in the morning but he'd simply handed me keys and told me he'd already secured the house across the street from Angels. He explained it was originally for the added guards he had coming, but that he had at least a week to worry about that problem. I'd gratefully accepted because I needed some time to decompress myself and that's more difficult to do while standing outside or in a cramped SUV. I told him I'd be back in the morning since I still had to talk to Angel.

I gave the keys to the guard and then opted to walk there instead, giving myself a chance to get familiar with the area. I've never been out this way before so it's entirely new for me, it seems very spread out which at least makes it easier to secure being able to see people coming from a mile away. Unfortunately there's a lot of new houses being built so in no time that's going to change quite a bit making it more difficult to keep an eye out for enemies. I definitely need to talk to Angel about that or maybe her uncle.

Angel… damn it's been a long time. I know I should hate her after what Christian told us, I normally wouldn't believe the asshole if it weren't for what happened with Jonah. Truth be told though I've missed her a lot more than I ever had any right too. I'm curious if she even knows why I ghosted her? Her hostility would suggest it's possible of course I guess I was hostile with her first which as always she called me on. Does she know I know about it though? Ugh, I've got to forget about that shit for now, I have a job to do. The mistress trusted me with this and I can't let her down no matter how I feel about Angel or my personal bullshit issues. Hopefully, though I can keep an emotional distance while doing my job, I've always had a weak spot for this woman. Hell when she passed out in the car I thought I'd lose my mind with worry.

"Hey Vamp!" I hear a man call behind me and turn around. Great it's that Ian asshole he definitely doesn't like me. Of course why would he? He sees me as competition.

"What do you want, wolf?" I respond as he approaches.

"You shouldn't be out here walking around until you've been introduced to the guards. I'd hate for Angel's "friend" to turn to dust over an honest mistake." He says friend with a disgusted sneer.

"I'm sure I'll be fine doing a simple walk around the block to check things out." I say as I begin walking again. I know he's just trying to get a reaction due to his saying I'd turned to dust. He's experienced enough to know how incorrect that is.

"Well we are watching for your kind and mistakes can happen easily enough. It be a shame to have issues caused with your Seeth over your own stupidity. The stress that would cause Angel is hardly fair." He replies now walking beside me.

"Yes, you totally seemed concerned about causing her stress earlier with your toddler like temper tantrum."

"You can hardly blame me for being upset. Vampyrs and Werewolves do not belong together it's not natural."

"That's always what bigots say. They never admit their own insecurities do they? That's an outdated concept that doesn't apply in this century. Besides which as I made perfectly clear she didn't know what I was and I didn't know what she was."

"Sure, that could be understandable. You still have feelings for her though and that's NOT understandable. That's what makes it disgusting and wrong! I saw it on your face when you saw her but I didn't realize then it was something that had already happened."

"Yes, and we broke up. No matter any feelings I might or might not have, they no longer matter. You have no reason to be threatened by me. Her husband though well…"

"Threatened by you? I have no reason to be threatened by you. There's nothing between her and me."

"I'm sure there isn't, at least on her part. You however want there to be." I point out bluntly.

"I just don't want a vampyr screwing with her mind!" He says fervently denying the accusation.

I come to the house Edward sent me too and turn to Ian as I reach the door. "Look, I can see the bond, it's one of my abilities. I know you imprinted on her and I can tell she doesn't know. Instead of getting your panties in a twist over me, you might want to start worrying about what she's going to do when she finds out. She's going to be pissed I can promise you that and the longer she doesn't know the more likely she'll cut off your balls. So how about you worry more about yourself and less about me pup?" I tell him then walk inside and close the door in his still shocked face.

The nerve of that asshole being worried about my screwing with her mind when it's obviously he imprinted without her knowledge or approval. If that's not screwing with someone's mind I don't know what is. What's worse is she probably doesn't even understand why he's acting like a possessive asshole, let alone her own conflicting feelings she must have. I'm slightly curious if he acts that way towards Jake too or if it's just me? Eh, as much as I probably should tell her I need to let it be, I can't get emotionally involved. I just can't.

Angelika

I lay there with my eyes closed working my way up to opening them and you know moving. I haven't been this sore in quite a long time. For a second I woke up confused as all hell, it took a moment to remember what happened last night and why I was in so much pain let alone not in my own bed. For just a few minutes I imagined everything had been a dream and that I was the same old me with only basic normal responsibilities like the kids, pets and making sure the husband doesn't forget to pay the bills. I'd almost be willing to give up all the money just to go back to how things were. The money is nice. It means Jake doesn't have to work as hard, less stress and fighting over bills and a better future for the kids, but really is it worth it? Then again even without the money I do still have Vampyrs after me, I still might change into a wolf, hell my kids might. I wonder if time travel is real? Maybe I can go back to before I found out about the money and everything else and move to a different state? Country even? Let's be honest though as much as I wish I were that coward who could just run away from everything I'm not.

Ugh, Jake, I wonder if he's going to pull the usual disappearing act he does whenever he's left out of what he thinks might have been fun. Yes, he's been better since he quit drinking but still, he can be a serious whiner sometimes. I swear it's like I have four children not three. Last I checked I signed up to be a wife not a mother, hell it's been ages since we've had sex. Granted that's not for lack of trying on his part but it's hard to get in the mood when he seems to have a more romantic relationship with his mother. I try, I really do, not to get pissed about their relationship but it's hard, it's not normal at all. I mean what son goes to his mom's boobies cancer appointment to help her pick out the new implants she'll be getting? No way in hell would I ever have Remi go with me to one of those appointments. His mommy however begged and pleaded and whined about how she didn't want to inconvenience her friends or her mom who all actually wanted to go. Even the nurses and Dr seemed to think it wasn't quite right. They reacted with confusion and disgust when they realized he was her son. Before they'd realized that, they seemed dazed thinking she was just a cougar, which to be fair you probably find a few of those getting implants. Probably doesn't help I'm irritated he took every single appointment, surgery, and chemo treatment off work to take her which while killing our ability to pay bills and almost costing him his job aside, he didn't bother coming to anything for my back appointments. Even when I scheduled them for his days off, he did come for the surgery which I appreciated but really nothing else? I don't know, I think I'm just a petty bitch. I need to just stop whimpering about it and let it go. Even if she does hate me and is petty, spiteful and mean every chance she gets.

Then there's Nick. It had to be him, really? It couldn't have been Christian or Jaxon even? I'm sure Nick thinks I just used him to get close to Jonah but that's so not true. Yes I'd always thought Jonah was hot and we got along well, but I never thought of him romantically until after what happened with Christian and Sheri, and by then I'd already been half in love with Nick. Hell if Nick and Linda didn't lie to me I probably never would have broke up with him. Then I never would have dated Jonah and I definitely never would have thought about what Nick and Jonah would be like to have at the same time. Plenty of batteries were wasted on those thoughts, hell the amount doubled once I found out Jonah was Bi and started wondering what it might be like to watch them. Fuck, no sex makes for one horny as hell brain! Point is though my feelings for Nick never fully went away. I've only seen him a couple of times since Jonah, but every time I walked away confused and still half in love with him. I'm worried the strain with Jake currently might make that worse. It is what it is though.

Then there's Ian. I have no idea what's going on with him. He was basically the one I was closest to and to be honest I started feeling an intense attraction to him, but now? I just wanna beat him over the head until he grows brain cells. He's been an ass since the whole Conner thing and it's only getting worse. I might need to just ask someone else to train and teach me and keep my distance from him. If he keeps up this attitude and wolf or not I might have to knock him the hell out.

Damn it now I have *"momma said knock you out song stuck in my head*!" Fuck me running!

"Sir, you're seriously letting her get away with too much! She brought a Vampyr to where we sleep!" I hear Talas squeaky and annoying ass voice.

"I let her get away with nothing Tala. I do not nor am I meant to control her. Yes I allowed a Vampyr where I'm staying but he could have come in even had I not. I've already told you, you can stay at the guard house if you like, or I can put you up in a hotel." My uncle replies then pauses. "I can send you home if you would like?"

I hear a soft gasp. "Sir, that's not at all what I'm saying. I must be here with you. What would you do without me?" Okay gag seriously! "I'm merely pointing out you're putting yourself in danger for that girl."

"That girl is my niece, my family. If you don't put yourself in danger for your family , who do you put yourself in danger for? I'm sure I will be just fine if you wish to, go home my dear."

"No, sir. I'm just worried she's bad for you, she's bad for all of us…."

She continues prattling on in her annoying voice. I try to drown her out and focus on getting up. I doubt they intended for me to overhear that conversation well at least I doubt she intended it. It's not like my uncle had said anything bad. Like Ian and Nick in the car though I don't think they've noticed my improving senses yet. I finally manage to get myself to sit up, thank the gods. After that standing is a bit easier, I wait a few seconds to make sure I'm not going to fall over before heading out the bedroom door. Of course right outside Sierra is standing guard and nods at me.

"Oh my good God, TALA stuff a sock in your hole to muffle that grating noise you call a voice won't you?" I say casually, earning a snort from Sierra.

"Why are you eavesdropping on private conversations?" She sneers at me.

"Um, did I mishear myself? I don't remember saying I understood anything you were saying though I'm not claiming I didn't either just don't put words in my mouth. What I said was that your voice is like that squeaky wheel that just drives people to madness. Besides you can't really call it a private conversation when you're having it in the living room of the house I'm sleeping in and own you dumb Twat waffle." This time Sierra actually starts laughing while even my uncle had his hand over his mouth to hide his laughter. Tala though she's turning red, like beet red. I think I pissed her off which oddly makes me immensely happy. As amusing as this truly is, I really don't feel up to sparring with a whiny bitch today, so I turn to my uncle. "Is there any coffee? Energy drink? Something with enough caffeine to wake the dead is greatly preferred."

He points to the coffee maker, so I go over and pour a cup, and mix in my ridiculous amount of cream and sugar to make it taste less like tar.

"So my dear, are you feeling any better?" my uncle asks with genuine concern.

"Right as rain! Just gonna wake up a little bit then head over to my place. I'm really hoping Fy and Remi made it to school and that neither Fy nor Tasia killed Remi while I was gone so I gotta check on them. They've not answered my texts since yesterday morning so I'm a bit concerned"

"No need to worry my dear they're just fine. I'm unsure why no one's answering but I know they're safe. Their Grandmother has been coming over daily."

"Of course, she has been," I mumble. "Curious question, was the vaca home up north able to be purchased yet? Is it ready if it has been?"

"Of course, it has been and is. What's on your mind, my dear?"

"I was actually thinking about going up north for Christmas, maybe having just you and my dad and brother come. If you wanted to of course. We wouldn't be able to leave until Christmas Eve night or Christmas morning but I think it would be nice to get away."

"I will have to get that sorted out and to send someone up to make sure it's stocked and everything is ready, but I think that's a fantastic idea and I'd love to come if you'd like me to be there." He tells me sounding genuinely happy I'd invited him

"Of course, I would love for you to come. You don't have to get it ready, we ca…"

Tala comes up and intentionally interrupts our conversation. "I know Edward, I can stay at Angel's house! I'd feel safe from the Vampyr there. "

I can't help it, I spit out my coffee with it coming straight out my nose causing me to start hacking up a lung. "Say…what… now?" I grate out through my coughing.

"Your uncle earlier was trying to find a solution to make me feel comfortable with the Vamps you invited here. You know because he actually cares about others feelings." She says in a manner that has me wanting to bury her in the backyard and not invite her to be my guest. I roll my eyes but wait to see if she's leaving it there or continuing her ridiculous thought. "So I can come stay at your house."

"Um how would that make you safer?"

"Your place isn't temporary living." She states like it explains everything going through her stupid little head.

I glance at my uncle to see he's just watching waiting for my reply. I fold my arms across my chest more so I don't punch her than anything else. "No I get that part, what I don't get is why you would be safer when I'm inviting at least one vampyr inside. I'm also confused why you think you can just volunteer my home as a solution to your paranoia?"

"You can't invite a vampyr in! What's wrong with you? Are you crazy? Oh my God, why are you even being guarded? Edward you can't….." She whines. I swear to God she sounds like she's a two-year-old!

"Enough Tala. The Vampyr she's inviting in I have a suspicion not inviting him wouldn't even matter anyway. However she's an adult, it's her choice to make. A guard is always in the house and one vampyr won't be a problem. Just stop this morning please." My uncle finally speaks up and from the looks of it Tala didn't like what he said.

She storms into her room slamming the door behind her. It's then I notice the room I slept in must have been hers, cause she just retreated to it. Maybe she had somewhat of a reason to be pissy with me after all because I know she wasn't in that room with me last night.

"Well, I better go. Sorry for the drama." I tell my uncle sincerely.

"No, no my dear none of that. Tala was out of line. I wouldn't think you fit for alpha if you didn't slap her back into place. I will talk to you more later tonight about the north trip, okay my Dear?"

"Of course," I reply and head out the front door not even remotely paying attention and slam right into a hard, sexy as hell chest. No not shirtless, but with the skin-tight tank, he might as well be. I glance up into those sexy as sin blue-green eyes. "Morning Nick." I breathe out.

"Are you okay? I heard yelling while I was on my run and came to see what was happening." Nick asks with worry.

"You run since when?" I ask. The man was never athletic in anyway, so I'm kind of stunned.

The look he gives me is pure exasperation "Yes I run, why is that so hard to believe? Are you okay?"

"Oh, ya sorry I'm fine just a disagreement with Tala no big deal. We weren't really yelling I wouldn't say, she just drives me insane." I explain.

"I've noticed. You seem just as easily annoyed as ever."

"Oh shut the hell up dickwad." I say slapping his chest.

He chuckles at that. "Case in point. Anyway, I was going to head over to your place after my run, I could just save time and walk with you now."

"Sure if that's what you want works for me."
With that we head in the direction of my house. Nick keeps glancing in my direction like he wants to say something, he's always had that sweet innocent look to him that gets even cuter when he's curious.

"What do you want to say Nick ? Just spit it out before you explode and I have to clean the gore you leave behind out of my hair." I hear Sierra snort behind me. I figured she would follow what she usually does but I haven't heard her. Damn she's sneaky.

"Well that's not an easy question, there's a lot I would like to say. Let's go with how much do you know about my kind?"

"You mean aside from what I've seen on TV? Not much, I was

told y'all have a hive mind I didn't get that impression. I was told you didn't value independence and strength that didn't seem correct either. I'm guessing stakes and crosses work since my uncle got me some and Ian did explain you don't all explode in dust when dead. That's about it."

"Okay well while I'm here I would like to teach you more about us. If there are vampyrs after you, your lack of knowledge will only serve to grant your death."

"I've been saying that for a while now but I was told it was more important to learn about the weres. You're offering to give me what I want so I'm not going to turn it down."

"Good, we want to keep you alive."

"You do?" I ask incredulously.

"Of course. Your death would displease the mistress." He says emotionlessly.

"Of course it would." We get to my house and once on the porch I turn to him. "Look, I'm inviting you in only because I don't believe you will do anything. However don't forget that if you do I will kill you slowly and painfully. You can do anything you want to me but don't hurt my family. Got it?"

"Angel, you know, no matter what, I would never hurt children."

"That's the only reason I'm doing this. Heads up my daughter is boy crazy." I say as I unlock and open the door. "You can come in Nick."

"Wwwho is it?" I hear Tasia ask from upstairs. Of course she's scared that child is going to give herself a heart attack.

"It's me, Tasia. Come down here please." I hollered up the stairs. I then looked at Sierra. "Do you know if Fy and Rem made it to their bus this morning?"

"The morning guards have said everyone made it where they

should be." She replies.

Before I can say anymore I hear clomping coming down the stairs and turn to see Tasia glaring at me. "Finally you get home mom, where were you? Grandma said you were probably out sleeping around!" Tasia demands.

"Of course she did because she apparently thinks every woman sleeps with every man they see like her. Sorry to disappoint but like I told all of you when I left I had to go do some business. I'm really not in the mood this morning I hurt and I've had a bad couple of days." I tell her as I take off my jacket to hang in the closet.

Tasia gasps, "Mom what the hell happened dads going to flip out!"

"No big deal Tas I fell nothing big. I would have been home last night but I had to see a Dr and make sure I was okay."

"You fell?" She asks not believing me. She glances over my shoulder towards Nick and Sierra. "Mom, whose that?" She asks me.

"Tas, this is an old friend and associate Nicolai Kearne. Nick, this is my oldest daughter Anastasia but we call her Tasia."

"Hello, Tasia. You look just like your mother at that age. Please call me Nick." There we have it Tasia's blushing, she's already smitten with the charming asshole!

"Hi." She mutters shyly.

"Have you started your classes yet today?" I ask Tasia.

"Mom, it's too early! I'm tired. I made sure Remi got on the bus and went back to sleep." Tasia whines.

"Have you done school while I was gone?" I demand.

"Um, well I took a few days off, it's no big deal mom!" She

explains like I'm overreacting.

"Did you take Kyra out? Actually where is she?"

"Oh um, I forgot she's still in your room." She tells me finally looking guilty.

I sigh, "Damn it Tas, go take Kyra out then get started on your school work. I mean it don't argue or I'll take your phone!"

"Mom you can't, I need the music to concentrate. Do you want to be the reason I fail class?" She whines at me dramatically.

"Tas stop with the dramatics and move your ass now." I turn to Nick. "If you don't already have kids my advice is don't have them fuck!" He just chuckles. "Sierra, can you take Nick to the office? I'll be there in a second. I'm gonna grab a couple drinks."

After she leads him away I head into the kitchen to get the drinks. I decided to message Jake while I'm at it.

Me: Hey babe I'm home.

Jake: Okay good. Going to moms after work.

Me: Can it wait we need to talk?

Jake: No she needs me, she had a hard day. I wasn't gonna go since you were gone but your home so I need to.

Me: Of course you do.

Jake WTF you know what IDC talk later.

I put my phone back in my pocket and stood there for a bit to decompress before heading to the office. I'd grabbed a few of everything so I can bring them a drink as well since I'm not sure what they'll want.

CHAPTER 11

It had taken me a while to head to the office. Longer than I had realized apparently. When I walked in Nick and Sierra didn't even notice me. They were too busy chatting away and I'm hit with a pang of jealousy at how comfortably they are talking to each other. It's stupid and I know that, but at one point in time Nick was my best friend and I would have called him to vent about my irritation and Jake. Unfortunately, that's no longer an option for us. I should have taken the opportunity to call Maggie. Well, maybe not Maggie as much as I love her. She sucks to vent to plus I think Brian is home right now and I might reach through the phone and choke him to death if he gives his opinion. For such a smart woman she somehow found the biggest idiot to marry. Sara would have been a better option or even Vivi. Lisa maybe but we get too sidetracked and I don't have time for that right now. I'll have to make this quick so I can give one of them a call before I explode and murder someone who doesn't deserve it.

"So..." I start to get their attention once they are both looking at me. "What do we need to talk about right now?" I ask.

Sierra answers first. "I decided to give Ian a few days off to figure out what the hell he's doing. He needs to get himself under control. Your uncle is thinking about sending him off to meet with the local security office. Hopefully it'll give you a break. I'm sorry about how he acted the other night. It was unacceptable. I will be moving into the spare bedroom temporarily as well. No offense to Nick but your uncle would prefer someone in the house with all the vampyrs around and it was myself or Ian. We should have already had someone in there to be honest. It was the whole point of this move to begin with but instead we've just had someone on the door at all times."

"Thank you. You're not responsible for Ian's behavior though, so I'm not holding it against you. If he doesn't knock it off I'm going to rip his balls off and feed them to him." Nick chuckles at that.

"If he doesn't knock it off I will help you. Unfortunately, if your uncle pulls off the Christmas thing you asked for, which I'm betting Ian will have to come with us, there'll be no choice." Sierra states simply.

"Well if he's still being an asshole I will bring a dog house he can sleep in." I reply

"What Christmas thing?" Nick asks.

"I talked to my uncle about going up north for Christmas. He's working out the details for me."

"You know I will have to go with you right?" Nick asks me.

"What why? Won't you be with your family?"

"I haven't celebrated holidays with my family for quite a few years. Some of the guards would need to go for it but most of the ones who came with me have no place to be." He explains. Hmm I wonder what happened with him going to Ireland on holidays.

"Okay well that's fine I guess, but there will be humans there. I'm also not sure of housing accommodations." I say, by this point I know I really don't have much choice.

"Your uncle will make sure there's a place for the guards don't worry about that," Sierra informs me. I just nod. I'm not certain how I feel about Nick coming away with us for Christmas. The point was to get away from everyone and everything all the stress.

"I don't…" I hear scratching and faint meow, so I get up and open the office door for Solas to saunter in. After a brief hello he struts over to the desk and plops down In front of Nick begging to be pet. Nick looks utterly dumb founded, meanwhile Sierra being used to the attention whore just reached over and rubs his cute little chin.

"You have a cat?" Nick asks.

"I've always had cats, Nick , you know that. I currently have four but Solas here is the only one who likes other people." I tell him at this point exasperated over the shock of my boy.

"Cats don't like Vampyrs. Or weres for that matter. Hell, most supernaturals." He tells me in shock.

"Solas doesn't care what you are. To him, everyone is his bitch who gives him love and attention. He's my baby boy. Just don't pick him up; he doesn't like it. I'm going to have to give him a bath soon. He's setting off my allergies."

"You're allergic but you have a cat? A cat you bathe? What kind of parallel dimension did I step into?" Nick muses.

"Oh grow up. Bathing keeps the dander down and I'm fine as long as they don't get in my face too much. It's a small sacrifice to take care of such a sweet boy. It's not his fault I'm allergic. Cats really don't mind baths if you do it right and teach them early on. I bathe all my cats, always have."

"Alrighty then, I really don't know what to say to any of that." Nick still looks terribly confused; it's actually kind of adorable. Solas however is just rolling around In front of the freaked out Vampyr.

"If you don't give him rubs he will do that all day," Sierra tells him. He tentatively reaches out and scratches the little guy behind the ear. Solas instantly begins purring.

"Okay, um so I was thinking I could get started explaining more about Vampyrs today. I'll have to run back, take a shower, change and eat then I'll come back and we can get started. If that works for you?"

"That'd be fine but we'll be doing it in this office. I had Theo add soundproofing to this room for a multitude of reasons, one being neither my husband nor kids know about any of this. I'm going to have to tell them at some point probably but I don't want to until I know more about myself."

"Okay we can meet in here though honestly you really should tell your family. Ignorance isn't always bliss." He tells me disapprovingly.

"I know and to be perfectly honest I even agree. I just know my husband won't believe it, my oldest will probably go try and find an *Edward Cullen* to marry and the other two I'm not even sure."

"Your uncle is trying to get Belladonna out here in the next couple of days. Maybe she can help with a protective spell at the cabin? It would help protect the humans." Sierra informs me.

"That sounds great. Alright well, I need to make a phone call so I guess we can meet back here okay Nick?"

"Sure I'll be back in a bit." He replies then gets up and heads out after giving Solas one more scratch.

After Nick left I glanced in on Tasia who was at her desk in her room on her computer. She was so engaged she didn't even notice me looking in, satisfied she was doing what she was supposed to be. I headed out onto the back patio to call Vivika. I haven't talked to her in some time. We keep missing each other so hopefully, she'll be able to answer. It's funny Maggie didn't seem to want us to get to know each other at all and I really can't help but wonder if that's not because we are more like each other than we are like her. I love Maggie and always will. She's my oldest friend and like my sister but she can be super weird about things and sharing friends is one of those things. Vivi and I got close after Maggie and Brian got together. Vivi was extremely hurt and felt betrayed by that entire situation of course Maggie being Maggie simply avoided the whole confrontation and stopped talking to Vivi and her kids even though she's the kids' godmother. I get it to a degree she's never liked confrontation and she's never understood what's okay or not when it comes to friends or boys. However, she was still wrong with that whole thing. So while I didn't stop being friends with Maggie I did tell her what happened was wrong of her and I stepped in to help Vivi however I could. It wasn't much and I wish I could have done more. Maybe she wouldn't have moved if I had but I did what I could. Now though Vivi is one of my best and dearest friends and like a sister to me. Who needs blood anyway? Chosen family at least you know who you're letting into your heart. I've been trying to keep a relationship with my real family but they make it so hard outside of my dad and brother they are all so damn judgmental, controlling, and psychotic. Ugh, I don't even want to think about that right now.

Vivika though is an amazing friend and I'm glad we started talking. I know Maggie and Brian aren't thrilled with my being friends with her and they're even less thrilled I don't buy into the bullshit they tell everyone else blaming the whole situation on Vivi but I don't care. I made it clear I won't choose between them and that in the situation Maggie and Brian were the ones in the wrong. I mean dating your friend's ex-fiancé is bad enough but sleeping with him in your friend's bed only days after they split up? Who does that? Add to it lying for a week about liking him? Then lying about moving him in after your friend throws him out and having her find out when she comes to get you for plans you forgot to cancel on her birthday? Friend or not your wrong girl, sorry. Vivi is loyal as hell too; she still loves Maggie and would be there for her in a second. Sorry, but I would never give up her friendship for any guy but especially not a whiny lying little bitch like Brian.

"Girl, you will not believe the bullshit going on here! Let me tell you I am about to lose it on mother fuckers!" Vivika answers with clear annoyance.

I chuckle. I love her. She always makes me smile. **"What's going on hun?"** I ask her.

"The stupid child support my state has made me file still hasn't come through. They are saying they can't find Ronnie like what? I told you where he lives, where he works, how in the hell can't you find him?" She fumes.

"That's bullshit. I've heard it's hard to file when you're out of state. Our state sucks at that shit. It's fucked up though cause they made you file and shit." I tell her as I play with a blade of grass.

"Right! I didn't even plan to file those bastards, now they're telling me they can't find him? On top of that, he hasn't called his daughter in a few weeks. I can't keep protecting him. She's getting upset and to the point where she doesn't even care."

"You shouldn't have to protect him. It's not that hard for him to call his kid or send a birthday present."

We kept talking for a while about the shit going on with Ronnie. She still loves him, Maggie had told me about the new girl he was living with. It broke my heart to do so but I told Vivi about it because she deserved to know, especially since she was still holding out hope for the two of them. She says he's her lobster, her one true love. I don't know if she'll ever move on but for her, I hope she does. She's such an amazing person with so much love to give. We joke about how if Jake and I ever split we will become platonic monogamous life partners. Actually, I'm not so sure it's a joke. I'm fairly serious and I'm pretty sure she is too. Who the hell needs men? Sure they're great to look at and during the honeymoon phase, they can be very good at taking care of you. After a while, though, they seem to become complacent and they seem to stop caring. Then it's a lifetime of disappointment and mutual misery. Jake always points out that with my sex drive I couldn't live without a man, I say he's wrong after all I use my vibrator more than his dick anyway. To be honest, it can be more fulfilling, men more often than not only focus on getting themselves off and not the girl. Of course, that's part of why Nick was so great, yet again I did take his virginity so sex was completely new to him at the time so who knows how he would be now. Oh my fucking god horny brain again!

"So what's up with you hun?" Vivika asks.

"A lot I can't really talk about it all right now, but I might need you to post bail soon?" I tell her in frustration

"Ooohhh who do I need to come to help you bury? Please Tell me it's Brian I'm game for that!"

I chuckle at that. **"Nope, today it's my husband, not Maggie's."**

"Oh god, what did Jake do now?" She inquires with curiousity.

"It's totally sad that you have to say now with that."

"True but he does so much."

"Well I had to leave town for a couple of days and I came back this morning. I wanted to talk to him after work about what to do for Christmas, and that stuff but guess what?"

"Um, he left his phone in the bathroom of a gay bar again?"

I literally burst out laughing. A few years ago he left to run to the store and after a few hours, I started calling his phone to have a bartender at a gay bar answer and tell me the phone was found in the bathroom. When Jake finally got him he said he got in a fight with a couple of guys who took his phone and left it in the bathroom at a gay bar on purpose to get him in trouble. He later changed it saying he stopped to use the bathroom and didn't even notice it was a gay bar. Who knows really but Fuck him either way on it.

"Nope, apparently mommy had a bad day and he needs to go to her house. Am I a bitch for being annoyed over it?"

"Hell no girl. Their relationship is weird as fuck, she acts more like he's her husband more than her son." She agrees, still as unbelieving of their weird relationship as I am.

"See that's my thing! Shit dude, he's always putting her before the kids and me. I get she's his mom and all but shit."

"Exactly. I'm sorry hun."

"It's not your fault, it's just ridiculous. He complains and bitches we don't have sex enough well sorry it's hard to get in the mood when it feels like I'm in a love triangle with your mom." I hear the door close behind me and turn to see Nick. **"Shit hey, hun let me call you back tomorrow okay? I love you."**

"Okay, babe love you too."

We hung up. "How much did you hear?" I ask Nick.

"It's none of my business." He replies.

"That's not an answer." I point out.

"I know but it's what you're going to get."

Of course, he's going to be a stubborn pain in my ass. "Whatever, let's just go to the office and get this over with. I wanna take a hot bath and be done with everything and everyone." We head on into the office of course Solas follows us back in before I can close the door. "So…" I prompt.

"Okay well I know you don't really know shit so this will take more than one day to go over. I'll start with what I think are the most important weaknesses."

"That doesn't bother you? Telling me your weaknesses knowing my temper?"

"Not really." He says confidently.

"Arrogant." I muse back.

"Let's just start okay? Yes, crosses do work, actually, all religious emblems and symbols work but only if the wielder actually has faith. As such our Seeths don't allow any of them in our homes. Also as you figured out, stakes do work. However only ash, willow, Aspen, juniper, and Hawthorne work. Some of the stronger vampyrs will not be taken down with just wood which is why many stakes are dipped in silver."

"I'm assuming my stakes are one of those woods?"

"Hawthorne, yes. Garlic is completely useless other than to give you bad breath. Vervain, also known as Verbena, is extremely useful." He says and I reach for my necklace, he nods.

"What's up with you two?" Sierra asks.

"Her necklace has vervain in it. Along with Magick, it's actually why Amon wasn't able to compel her when he tried."

"You knew when you let me in the seeth you knew?"

"I did, and so did the mistress. We both felt the protection might be necessary. As it has been, it won't fully protect you but it will increase your safety and prevent compulsion."

"Thanks," I say I mean, what else can I say really.

He just nods. "Also fire, cutting off our heads, and witches. Finally, sunlight however it does not work on all of us of course."

I point to him. "Obviously."

"The last thing only works on the pets, wolf venom. Now keep in mind biting them will be next to impossible as they are ridiculously fast and vicious. Also, it will take time to kill them, they aren't like the rest of us pain, illness, etc don't slow them down the same way. The rest of us except the oldest and most powerful a bite will weaken us long enough to give you a chance but it won't kill us."

"You mean her bite, I've never shifted."

"Well true. Especially since you would have to have your wolf teeth." I simply nod and he continues. "So we have the ferals humans have called them strigoi which we use as pets or guard dogs. They are the strongest, fastest and most dangerous. They are the easiest to kill however they are also completely mindless and rabid. The day walkers, as known by humans, are the Born and Royals are basically the same; they both have gifts though they vary. Most believe the royals are stronger in everything though really the difference is family. They can walk in the sun. There's the turned, which is pretty self-explanatory, a newly turned will be faster and stronger and might even be confused for a while. That's why their sire cares for them, most turned are extremely loyal to their sires. They can not come in the sun though it won't immediately kill them, it will do so slowly. Then of course there are the elders. There are many reasons a vampyr may physically age. These vampyrs can be the wisest, however, their bodies are weak, and their mental abilities are unparalleled. Of course the rogues, they've turned against our laws and ways to become outcasts and hunted. Like Beatrix. Of course, there are others but these are the main ones you'd ever come in contact with. "

"I'd actually beg you to tell me about the rest of I weren't so worn out right now," I informed him.

"It's okay, why don't we call it a day and we can cover more tomorrow?"

"Works for me." I sit there for a while after he leaves before heading upstairs to take a bath.

I really wasn't kidding about needing a nice long soak. I'm exhausted both physically and mentally. Solas of course follow me and stands guard inside my bathroom door. I seriously think there's something wrong with that damned cat. Still longing for the tub in the hotel I settle for the garden tub In front of me. Make sure the temperature is right and add my oils, bubble bath, and bath salts. Yes, these things are important to a good bath people, the only thing that would make it better is wine but I'm out. I strip down and get in with my next Briggs book ready to escape into the fantasy world she created.

CHAPTER 12

J ake didn't come home until after two in the morning last night. I was awake but I pretended to be asleep because, to be honest, I didn't want to deal with his bullshit. Dealing with his mom's crap is so completely draining it hurts my head. I swear my brain is going to implode one day because of that woman and I truly hope she has to clean up all the gooey brain matter. I do love that man more than anything but if he doesn't cut the apron strings I'm going to cut something! Needless to say, we never got to talk and now he's back at work so it will have to wait until tonight.

Today however I'm supposed to be meeting Belladonna. I don't know much about her except that she's a witch and apparently extremely powerful. Maggie had asked if Tasia could come to babysit tonight while normally I would have said no since it's a school night, but not knowing what to expect I would prefer her not be here. Of course, she was all too happy to go. Not sure if I should be concerned about that.

"Angelika, Belladonna is here. Your uncle had to head to the phoenix office so he won't be here today." Sierra comes back to let me know.

"Okay, thanks," I say and follow her inside. "You've met her before right? I mean you know it's really her?"

"I've never officially met her, but yes I know it's her."

"Okay, just making sure." She nods at me.

We walk into the living room and there is this woman with raven black hair down past her hips, with dark golden skin crouched down petting Solas. Who of course is lapping up the attention, the little shit. She looks up at us as we approach she has full lips that most women dream of painted in soft pink, high cheekbones, and to my approval glitter like everywhere. Her eyelashes are ridiculously long and thick. She's wearing a pure white peasant-style dress. What strikes me the most is her eyes, which are the strangest shade of green I've ever seen. They are like the color of sea glass and I swear they are sparkling.

"You must be Angelika, you are the new witch I'm here to teach, no?" Belladonna asks me.

"Yep, I'm Angelika. You can call me Angel." I replied.

"Forgive me, but I was told I was to train a budding witch. You are a wolf no?"

"Unshifted, yes. I have witch Ancestors, and have unintentionally performed Magick."

"Ah, I see. What did you do?"

"She threw a vampyr against a wall with her mind," Sierra responds before I can.

"Is that all?" Belladonna asks.

"Well, I don't know that I would call it Magick but I sometimes get feelings I would normally call instinct. I've had some dreams that do come true. I have done spells that seem to have worked however it could be a coincidence. Of course, I made this." I say showing her my necklace. "Its effectively prevented vampyrs from compelling me, but I've also always had good luck wearing it."

"Yes the power in the necklace is strong, I just assumed it was given to you."

"No mam I made it."

"Please dear, call me Bella none of this ma'am nonsense. Besides, I am not much older than you my dear."

"Of course."

"Okay so first let's see what power you got. Come on, show me…" Bella says expectedly.

"Um, I've only ever done anything by accident while trying to keep a vampyr from my children."

"Oh, I see. Okay well, I don't have what I need to test your Magick levels any other way so why don't we try a few spells and see if we can get you to do any manipulation? A few other things just to see where you're at. Sounds good, yes?"

"Great actually."

" I notice you dye your hair but it looks like you need a touch-up, how about we try a spell to change your hair color?"

"That sounds awesome!"

I take her out back so we can do this with less distractions from the animals. Normally I do anything like this in my room but I don't feel comfortable bringing a practical stranger in there. Once we are out back she instructs me to sit on the grass, which I do. She then hands me a mirror and three red candles and then instructs me to place the candles in a triangle. She tells me to meditate and relax and again I listen. After I'm relaxed I begin casting my circle of protection without her prompting.

"What are you doing?" She asks.

"Casting a circle of protection?" I say more as a question than a response.

"So you have the basic concept of Magick, yes?"

"Somewhat, I've studied it for a few years hence the necklace. I even have a book of shadows and grimoire I began, but it's still in the garage unpacked." Contrary to popular belief a grimoire and BOS are not on different spectrums of the magickal spectrum they are neither good nor evil on their own. The owner and intent are what makes them bad or good, nothing more. A grimoire is actually more of a reference book that contains information on herbs, stones, gods, etc whereas the BOS is for spells, rituals, recipes, etc.

"I would like to see them if that's okay. Your knowledge will make this easier for sure. Please continue. I apologize for the interruption but I was not told."

"That's my fault I haven't really told them much," I say to which she nods, seeming to understand.

She then tells me to light the candles and hold my hair while focusing on the flame for fifteen minutes while envisioning my hair becoming the color I wish. Unfortunately, this part has always been the most difficult for me because you have to keep your mind clear and we'll that's not an easy task for my dumb ass.

It takes me hours to fall asleep as a result. Currently, I'm musing over how badly I want to beat the hell of Jake. To be honest I'm probably being unfair but damn it. He acts like he's the only one who keeps what's bothering him locked behind a wall, what a foolish man. If I ever unleashed everything going on in my head I would send a shrink to a psych ward. Even Vivi and Sara don't get everything and lately Lisa gets even less. Mainly because we don't talk as often.

She tells me to recite the spell and to continue picturing the color. She made me memorize the spell so thankfully I won't have to fumble reading through it. I've never understood that issue. I can say something I've memorized no issue but reading? I always mix up the word.

Fire warm and fire red
Charm the hair upon my head
Fire dance and fire shine
From this fading red to a vibrant wine red this wish is mine.
As I will, it so mote it be
By fire, water, wind, and tree

I sit there still visualizing or trying to for about ten minutes before we decide it's a bust. I was expecting her to just give up but she surprised me by telling me we would keep trying until I get it.
Three tries later I succeeded, sort of. I changed the color alright but I changed it to a glacial blue. Of course, Ian's God damn eyes had to pop into my mind. Bella asked me if I wanted to leave or try and change it and of course, I chose to change it. For one Ian doesn't need a bigger head, he might stop fitting through doors if he gets any bigger. For another Jake would probably get pissed and give me shit for it neither of which I need if I plan to talk to him tonight. Finally the next try I get it right.

"Good job Angel," Bella says.

"Not really. It took forever." I replied.

"Actually you did it quicker than most of those new to the craft. I'm quite impressed. What do you say we try a few more things, yes?"

I told her of course for which she seemed ecstatic. The first thing she had me do was tarot cards. As in my reading her cards. She said the reading was accurate and identical to what she got prior to coming. She also had me do a protection potion, charm, as well as ritual. She said my potions and charms were strong but where I seemed to struggle most is spells as rituals which she feels is due to concentration. I could have told her that. The last things we did I failed horribly at. Mental and physical manipulation. I couldn't even get power flowing. To be honest those are the only major differences from the Magick I studied. As I studied it, there was no real physical manifestation; it was merely asking for what was needed with intent and waiting. Bella did explain that this type of Magick not everyone has access to, most people have the potential for witchcraft but real power? Most don't have that, and she's unsure I do. Sierra argued that however because she witnessed it, Bella assured her we'd keep trying regardless.

"I believe this has been a good day. Yes, a very good day. I will get what we need to test you but I do not know how long it will take. I will return when I have it unless it comes after Christmas. Your uncle informed me you would all like my presence to ward the cabins, yes?"

"Yes, I have humans coming ones I do not want in any danger."

"Of course, I understand I will keep to the shadows, yes?"

"No need for that, just no Magick In front of the humans."

"As you will it."

"Um, do you need somewhere to stay?" I ask out of nothing else but manners.

"Oh no, dear. Your uncle is having me stay at the house with him. The shrilly troll girl there is unhappy about this, but I do not think I care. She is rather abrasive, yes?"

"Oh, she's something alright."

"Your uncle told her to sleep in the office or go somewhere else. She began mumbling poorly about you. I do not think I like her."

"I don't like her either."

"Well, I must be off. See you soon my dear. Blessed be."

"Blessed be."

She heads out the door as soon as it's closed Sierra asks. "Why didn't you tell anyone you studied Magick?"

"Well, I did tell Theo sort of. Not the extent really but I told him I know a bit about Magick just not being able to freeze things or move things with the mind or anything like that. Maybe because of that he just didn't take me seriously."

"Awe." She says understandingly.

I look at the clock and realize Remi will be home soon. Shit! I rush to go get the laundry and dishes done before he gets home. It was Tasia's turn but she's not here and Remi dirties dishes like nobody's business. If he doesn't get these done then Fy will lose it when he dirties a ton more. I swear they fight more than my brother and I ever did. My grandma did warn me that having a third would change dynamics and oh boy was she right. The two were actually easy as hell having Remi was like dropping a raging bull in a china shop! Don't get me wrong I wouldn't change having him for anything in the world but damn! Talk about chaos.

Hours later after Fy and Remi get home and we deal with homework and all the fun stuff that comes with being a stay-at-home parent, Jake finally gets home an hour late no less. Dinner is already done, which of course he wants to wait for because he needs to "decompress" something he claims I wouldn't understand. As always he starts to load the stupid video game that does nothing more than piss him off even when he's in a good mood and then he goes to grab his headset.

"Jake, wait!" I exclaim.

"Fuck, what Angel? I've worked all fucking day, something you don't understand can't I have a little bit of time to just fucking relax?" He replies angrily.

"Don't even start preaching your mother's bullshit right now Jake! I needed to talk to you yesterday, you spent damn near the entire time I was gone with your mommy and you couldn't say no for just one fucking day!" Though I'm not quite yelling my voice is slightly raised and he can tell I'm fucking pissed. "Yeah, Jake I know your mommy was over here helping you while I was gone."

"What do you expect, Angel? I work all damn day!" He points out to me in anger.

"Are you kidding? It was only a couple of days and they are your fucking kids Jake. Yours! I did not fuck and reproduce with your mother. Shit the days I was gone she worked too and she didn't even get out here until you did. It would have made sense if she was here while you were at work but being here when you were? That's ridiculous!" I can't help or even curb the anger I'm felling at the moment. This is utterly ridiculous.

"Oh, right I forgot you have spies all over my house!"

"Don't even start that Jake. This is my house remember? They're security, and they shouldn't bother you if you aren't doing something you shouldn't be."

"According to you, I shouldn't be speaking to my mom." Jake accuses.

"Oh don't twist my words. Your relationship with your mom isn't normal. You are the only MAN I know who needs mommy for everything. Who talks to mommy about things you should talk to your wife about? Besides, don't forget I'm the only reason you even talk to your God damn mother, a mistake, that if I could, I'd go back in time and erase!"

"I'm done with this shit Angel. What the fuck did you want to talk about?"

"Well for starters dick lint…" He gets a puzzled look on his face at my use of Vivi's name. "did you not notice I looked like I went ten rounds with the asphalt and lost?"

"Of course I did. I saw it when I came to bed last night."

"Oh, and you didn't even think to ask if I was okay? Seriously?" I say now even more hurt then pissed which is very bad for him I lash out when I'm hurt.

"Well, I figured if you weren't you or one of your goons would have told me. It's not like you've been open lately." He states acting like that justifies anything.

"Nice. Real nice dickhole."

"Fine, are you okay?" He asks only to shut me up.

"Just fucking forget it, Jake. God damn!" I try to take ten deep breaths, something I do when I feel my mood elevating to a point I might kill someone. The joys of bipolar really are not flipping your switch, something that takes years of practice to recognize the signs. Once I'm calmer, of course only if I ignore the asshole staring at me with his headset in his hand like he wants me to just give up and go. "You know what fuck it. If you don't see my being injured as important enough to bring up I'm done with that."

"Whatever. Can I play now?" No longer even pretending to care, just eager to play his game. I'm tempted to smash his system and stupid TV.

"No asshole, hold your Goddamn dick a minute before jumping in, will you? What I actually wanted to talk about is I want to go up north for Christmas."

"No!" he says firmly.

"What the fuck do you mean, no?" I ask him putting my hands on my hips. Who the hell does he think he is.

"I mean no. You know Christmas Eve is my grandma's birthday. I'm not missing that because you randomly decide you want to do something."

"Oh of course because you've never interfered with my family because you randomly decided you wanted something?"

"Oh yeah? What family?" He says rudely.

I can't help it but I have to fight the urge to cry at that. He's never understood my attachment to family. His family wasn't close-knit, almost no one talked to anyone else except on Christmas Eve and when they had to.

"Wow, amazing you fucking fairy dust fuck!." A few more deep breaths. " For your information not that it should matter as I AM YOUR WIFE and if I need something that should come before your backwater eat your young bitch of a family! I was planning on still going for Christmas eve you dumb fuck. Mainly because I like your grandma but also because I support family traditions. I was going to get your opinion on whether we should leave on Christmas eve or Christmas morning?"

"Neither, we're not going, period."

"Oh, no, the kids and I are going. You can decide if you're coming and I will decide if we're going to deal with your fucked up family Christmas eve or leave the morning of." I tell him bluntly.

"You can't do that. The kids have to be there."

"I can and I will. The kids are all legally old enough to decide which parent they want to go with and guess what? Since your mom is a bitch to them too causing them to not like her more than the money she spends on them they would rather go with me. So you better fucking decide because I'm not playing this game with you. This could have been a simple and polite conversation but of course, you being the husband of the year thinks a video game is more important!" I finalize completely over this argument.

"The kids aren't going and neither are you!"

"Okay, *Tybalt*! Whatever you say!" I say and get immense satisfaction from the look of confusion, frustration, and anger on his face as I storm out of the bedroom.

He hates book references because he never understands them. *Tybalt* is a character in a book I read about a changeling detective, no not *Shakespeare's Tybalt*. It's an amazing series. *Tybalt* is an extremely frustrating character who is more stubborn and sometimes even stupid than anyone I've ever met. Overall though he's probably everyone's soul mate. I think that's why I say it Jake's my soul mate I know that, but fuck I want to kill him sometimes. Almost how Toby always felt.

I head out through the house reassuring the kids I'm okay and not to worry as they ask. I hate that they do that when they see me almost cry. Don't get me wrong I'm happy my kids love me, but I don't like them worrying and I hate when they hear us fight. Jake used to be so frustrated with the fact that I would stop or hold off a fight until the kids were gone to protect them from it. I did that until we moved in with grandma about five years ago and she told me that was the worst thing you can do. Apparently, she did it, and when her and grandpa divorced her kids blamed themselves for ridiculous reasons not understanding that they had problems long before. She said she hid their fights so well that the kids thought she had a perfect marriage.

Not wanting that of course I eased up a bit. They still don't see the bad fights, but mild arguments, they do. It's actually hilarious we never fought when his mom wasn't in the picture. When we first got together he'd stopped talking to her. I pressured him into talking to her again and the fights started. She's selected to vacate our lives on multiple occasions once for three years actually! Every single time we didn't fight at all yet when she came back, poof fighting. I know how awful that sounds, but I really don't like her. Unfortunately, it's not quite that simple. She whispers in his ear all kinds of bullshit and he takes it out on me or he'll hold it in and just blow up at me. It's ridiculous really and he's lucky I'm not other women, most wouldn't tolerate this bullshit. However I know the real him, he's a caring and truly sweet man to those he loves and I do know he loves me. He just unfortunately is dying for that mother-son relationship so he acts like the conniving bitch who hung the moon. I try to let it go but sometimes like now I simply can't.

I didn't even realize that I'd wandered to the front porch and was crying at this point until I heard a voice behind me. "Angel, are you okay?" The owner of those blue-green eyes, the one I use to confess my deepest darkest secrets to asks in concern.

I turn to face Nick. "I'm fine."

"Angel, you can't lie to me." He pauses. " I know you too well, but regardless I heard everything. I'm sorry I wasn't trying to eavesdrop but I wanted to wait and make sure you're okay."

"I'll be fine Nick. It is what it is. It's not even him talking anyway it's his mom. How can I hold him accountable for being a good son?"

"Angel there's being a good son and there's being a bad husband. All of that was being a bad husband." He tells me.

"It'll get better. He's just stressed and there's stuff you don't know. Things she holds over his head."

"It doesn't matter, Angel. How he treated you wasn't okay. He didn't acknowledge you were hurt. He didn't even listen to what you said and jumped to conclusions. He tried to tell you what to do, not discuss what to do. He didn't even want to talk to you, he only wanted to play a stupid game something he started doing as soon as you left. I was just a kid back then but do you remember what I did when you left when I was playing a game and wouldn't listen to you?" He asks me.

"You followed me and gave me my valentine's gifts early to make up for being a jerk as you put it." I remember that day very vividly in fact.

"Exactly."

"We're married, Nick. We have kids. We've been together for seventeen years. It's different."

"Is it? Or do you just want it to be?" He asks earnestly.

"Thank you, Nick. I do feel a little better. Really though I'll be fine. We'll be fine."

"Okay. I won't push I'm not stupid and know you. Just know if you ever need me, I'm here okay."

I get up and head to the door pausing. "Thank you, Nick, good night." I walk in, close the door, and welcome the chaos of the kids.

CHAPTER 13

Christmas Eve morning finally came, things were tense because Jake being Jake wouldn't admit he was wrong let alone admit he was out of options. It's a serious character flaw he needs to work on. He'd taken to be abrupt in his demeanor while I merely pretended as if nothing happened. It sounds childish I know but after trying everything I can think of over the seventeen years we've been together it's literally the only thing I've ever found that has any real effect.

So on Christmas Eve morning I got up and gave the kids their Christmas eve gifts which are always their outfits for the day and pajamas for that night. After they'd finished I made some cinnamon rolls and hot chocolate for breakfast. I didn't even bother to wake up Jake since I normally do, not doing so will point out I'm still irritated. After breakfast, I went and loaded the bags and Christmas presents into the back of the traverse, because I'm not going back on what I said. If Jake still refuses to go then I'm taking the kids. My dad and brother's family will be heading up to the cabins this afternoon after they finish at Katie's family's house which my brother surprisingly convinced my dad to go to. Jeff and DeeDee, Brian's parents, ended up coming over yesterday to bring gifts to the kids and us. They are truly amazing people. I can't get over how they raised such a petulant child as Brian is, it's truly astounding. Jake of course hid out in the room like an anti-social teenager throwing a tantrum.

I just told them he wasn't feeling well which they accepted gracefully.

After I'd finished packing the car I headed into my bathroom to start getting ready to leave, Jake hasn't said when we were supposed to head out for his grandma's he usually doesn't until the last minute. The way I figure it, if he hasn't said anything by the time I'm finished getting ready we're heading for the cabin and he can deal with his succubus of a mother. As I walk by I notice he's awake and on his phone but don't say anything and just walk by.

I take a quick shower, then wrap a towel around myself to do my make-up. As I'm starting my eyeshadow Jake walks in and stands behind me expectedly. Normally this is where I would break and say something. What's worse is he knows it and it's what he's waiting for, but I refuse to give in. It truly breaks my heart. I hate it when we fight and in all honesty, it's just easier to give in and do things his way. I just don't know how much more of it I can take without completely losing my mind. It's time to make my stand regardless of my discomfort. I want my old husband back, the one without his devil of a mother on his shoulder whispering in his ear.

"So…" He finally says.

"So what?" I ask in return.

"So you're getting ready to go to Joy's?"

"That depends on you. If you're going to stop your stubborn bullshit and agree to come with us to the cabin then yes. If not then I'm getting ready to drive the kids up there." I tell him calmly.

"Are you really going to keep pushing this?" He asks as if I'm being a child. Maybe I am, but I'm done being told what to do and when.

I put my eye shadow brush down, having gone for a half green, half red look in the spirit of Christmas, and picked up my eyeliner to begin applying it. " I'm not pushing anything Jake. I'm sick of you and your mother making all of our plans, this marriage is supposed to be me and you. Not me, you and your mother with me acting as the role of a child being told where to go and when. I need a break and I need to get out of the city. It's really as simple as that, and being your wife, what I need should actually matter to you."

"It does matter. How can you think it doesn't?" He asks in blatant outrage.

Oh let me count the ways mother fucker. "Simple your actions show differently than your words. I'm not getting into this Jake it's Christmas eve and I refuse to let your bullheadedness ruin it for me. You know the options you have until I'm finished getting ready to make your choice. The balls in your court figure it out."

He stands there staring at me as I finish the holly's I decided to draw at the end of my eyeliner. Doing makeup is something I've always found cathartic as weird as that sounds. I've never been sure of why but hey it's helping me not get worked up at the moment.

"Fine we'll go up north but can we leave early tomorrow morning? I'd rather not drive after and who knows how late we'll be. They want us there at noon."

"No well go tonight and you'll grow a spine and tell them we aren't staying all night." I tell him firmly.

"But you said we could leave in the morning."

"True I did, but now my dad and brother will be up there tonight and I don't want to leave them up there all night waiting for us." I leave out the fact that we did plan for that possibility. It's petty I know but his whole we don't know how late we'll be bothering me way more than it should at the moment. Besides I don't want him to pull some shit and decide to back out in the morning. It's not like he hasn't done it before.

"What if I don't want to drive after?" He asks, it's clear he's trying to play on mys sympathy. Problem is right now I don't have any.

"Then I will. Like I said Jake I'm sick of my life being nothing more than a damn dictation of everyone else's will." I point out, knowing he's probably pissed now that I have my license he's lost that excuse.

"Fuck, fine." He says defeatedly.

"Good, it's settled. I'll be ready soon go tell the kids to get ready. They already have their clothes. Also, tell them to throw their PJs and anything they wanna bring into a bag and put them in my car."

"Why are we taking your car? We don't have to leave this early."

"We're taking my car because it's already packed and we're leaving this early because every time your mother says noon we don't eat forever and then I listen to the kids whine for hours about how hungry they are skipping lunch. To your mom, eating at noon means eating at six and I'm not playing that game so we're stopping for food."

"Then the kids won't eat and mom will get offended and pissed off and I'll have to hear about it."

"Then tell her to actually serve at noon if she says noon. However sorry you don't know your kids if you think they won't be hungry again they're pigs. They don't eat much over there because they don't like it, it's that simple. Just go Jake before I change my mind." I explain in exasperation.

With that, he goes and I finish my lips with a moron red eye shadow. Sounds weird I know but try it, it stays better and doesn't rub off, especially when you use finishing powder and spray. After finishing my make up I throw on my long sleeve red V-neck shirt and black jeans. I add my leather jacket and grab my boots opting to wait to put them on because I hate driving in shoes.

I head out to the car hollering on my way. "I'll be in the car hurry up! Don't forget Kyra." Grab my purse and keys as I pass them by the front door. As I get in my car I see my security detail get into their SUV. I'd discussed with my uncle how to go about this and he'd said they won't come into the property but would park across the street and walk over to stay outside the gate just in case. I didn't bother telling Jake because I don't want to give him another reason to whine. I see Jake and the kids coming out with Kyra. Jake looks upset to see me behind the wheel to bad shouldn't have made the comment about not wanting to drive. They throw a few bags in the back and get Kyra in the back seat. Wisely Jake said nothing, so we left peacefully enough.

The drive to his grandma's was quiet and tense with all the kids playing on their phones. Jake of course had forgotten to tell me we had to stop and get things for his mom so I got to fight the rush in the store to come out and find him in the driver's seat. I decided to let it go and not make a big deal about it mainly because I lacked the energy at the moment. We'd stopped and grabbed food at McDonald's which Jake insisted we eat before getting there.

Due to the unexpected stop, we ended up being thirty minutes late as also Rachele was outside waiting. " You're late." She said the second we stepped out of the car.

"Yeah sorry, mom it takes the girls a bit to get ready," Jake says.

Oh hell no he's not blaming us. "Jake forgot to mention we had to stop at the store," I say and watch him cringe and her sneer.

She basically ignores it. "Yeah well, I've never understood wasting all that time putting all that gunk on your face. Sure it's pretty but it's just a mask." She says with so much ire.

I choose to just ignore it and walk inside to see Joy and wish her a merry Christmas and a happy birthday. Her birthday is the only reason I'd ever let Jake take this day. It used to be spent at aunt Jes's house with all my extended family. It was the only time we really saw each other and when I stopped going was when the drift started. They were furious. I let a man dictate where I spent the holidays while they weren't fully wrong. That actually came much later. I only did this for Joy. I tried to get them to come to see us on Christmas or even do theirs earlier since Joys were always at night but they absolutely refused to meet me halfway. I'm a bitch sure but not so much I'd deprive his grandma off a birthday.

As always Rachele put Jake to work almost immediately and he was busy fixing things on this decrepit old land. It's nice, yes the main house is a one bedroom with an office, living room, kitchen and two dining rooms with a bar. It reeks of money and privilege. Literally, everywhere you go there are breakable collectibles, china cabinets filled with more, a glass case with a leather jacket that belonged to some singer I'd never heard of. It's got two bathrooms which is nice since we don't have to awkwardly use the one in the bedroom. There's a strange adobe feel to it with the built-in entertainment center and the alcoves towards the ceiling filled with more collectibles. I swear the collectibles here alone are worth millions. However, it's got a modern look that kills the nice Adobe-like feel. It's a forty-acre property in downtown Phoenix with a guest house that's smaller but has two bedrooms. An eight-car garage, a boat garage, and a pool and hot tub. Of course, we can't forget the yard full of rose bushes and the orchard. Like I said, reeks of money, don't get me wrong I'm all for a big house but I'm more for comfort which is why I want my compound so I can be comfortable and rarely have to deal with people if I don't want to. Yes, I'm that bitch sorry but 99% of the world's population are complete idiots and I can't handle day-to-day contact with them on my compound I wouldn't have to. That said, it will be cozy. I used to hate bringing the kids here, always terrified they'd break something, hell I still am.

As I'd told Jake this morning it took hours for the food to be ready. For whatever twacked-out reason Christmas Eve dinner is tamales like really who the hell has tamales for Christmas Eve? They didn't even start dinner until around five, which shows how ridiculous it was to insist we get here at noon. I declined wine at dinner for two reasons. One I'm not sure if I'll have to drive and unlike anyone here I won't drive after drinking. Two I'm a stubborn contrary bitch and I didn't like how Rachele said 'we all know Angelika wants some wine' like it's some cardinal sin. The look on her face was worth it turning it down. Besides, I'll drink one of the ten bottles I'm taking with us once we get to the cabin. Of course one of the first things Rachele does after dinner is tell Jake about two more damn projects she has for him. So while she's in the office with Joy I head out to smoke where Jake is.

"No," I say simply as I walk up to him. He looks at me in confusion. "We don't have time for this and you know it, Jake. The answer is no. We need to do your grandma's cake, open presents, visit for a SHORT while, and leave."

"We'll have the time, it's just a couple of small things." He replies meekly.

"No Jake. One, you know they are going to take longer than you think. Two, you have been working ever since we've gotten here and I've told you how pissed off that makes me. This is your family. I shouldn't be stuck with them on holidays while you're working your ass off. Hell, your cousin didn't even come today so he's not even here to buffer and I'm done with your mom's comments. Three, you are not backing out even if I have to drive and I'm not driving dead tired because you don't know the word no."

"I'll drive you won't have to and I won't back out."

"No Jake…" I start as Rachele walks up and interrupts.

"So let's go look at that lawn mower." She says to Jake and he looks completely torn.

"He can't. We are going to Payson after we leave here and we still want to do cake, presents, and visit a bit. We don't have time tonight." I say as sweetly as I can muster.

"It won't take long and I need the lawn mower and pump fixed so I can do work after the new year."

"Then I will pay for someone to come fix them for you, but we don't have time for it tonight and Jake needs to spend time with Joy on her birthday before we go." I offer up a solution.

Jake looks completely beside himself torn between pleasing his mom and not pissing me off more. Rachele is caught in the fact that she can't argue with Jake about spending time with his grandma because she's not dumb and knows I will tell her.

"Fine, I guess that'll have to work. I have to say I don't like you making decisions for my son like this. It's not right." Rachele informs me.

"You may be right, you may be wrong, whose to say? However, I'm making this decision for my family and to make sure nobody takes away from Joy's day. You can take it how you want. Jake, let's go back inside."

He actually follows still looking torn and his mom behind him muttering some bullshit I choose not to even try and hear.

Once we're inside Rachele announces. " I guess we should do dessert then open presents. Apparently Angelika has made other plans tonight."

"I know the kids already told me. A cabin in the woods for Christmas is so exciting! I was just getting dessert out now!" Joy says as cheerful as ever.

She's completely oblivious to her daughter's allegations that I'm trying to ruin her day. Either that or she's chosen to ignore it.

The dessert was a delicious ice cream cake that you can tell Joy made. The only thing Rachele can make taste good is apple pie and that's her mom's recipe. So we sang happy birthday and had the cake. Jake and his mom were in their own little conversation God only knows what about since they went and sat at the bar to eat leaving the rest of us to converse. Joy was really interested in everything going on and even asked where in her words my hunky uncle was. The woman is amazing truthfully. It's just like with Brian I have no clue how she birthed and raised a demon like her daughter.

We went and opened presents and I can tell that Joy actually had a hand in them this year. Normally Rachele gets me utter bullshit and everyone but Jake gets stuff they don't care much for, have, or like but had no interest in. Hell, she got them a basketball carnival-type game one year which would be great if we didn't live in an apartment and had to keep it in a box. Or my personal favorite is the gifts they can't take home. Like what?

Oh my God, this woman makes me sound like a selfish ungrateful bitch but I promise I'm not. Every year she gets me gifts with the intent of pissing me off and every year it doesn't work. One year she got me a pink tool set after finding out I hate the color pink. I was still okay with it though I was sick of either having to search for Jake's tools or getting him mad because I actually put them up and he couldn't find them because heaven forbid we check where they belong. Another year she bought me a "Cooking For Dummies" cookbook after making a comment about my cooking. The fact is I don't need her fluffing my ego because I know I can cook. However, that book has some amazing information like what to use instead of eggs, different measurements, and the like. I'd wanted one forever, she was pissed to find that out.

This year she bought me some weird ass thing to put strawberries you grow in. I'll just give it to Fy. She's been wanting to grow them so it works out. The rest of the gifts though I got shelves which I know we're Joy we'd talked about them. No, they weren't bookshelves but still, they are cute little wall shelves. I got picture frames, dishes, and a bunch of stuff for the house. I know that's all Joy. Fy even got a couple of horror movies and Tasia got make-up. Neither of which Rachele would buy if you had a gun pointed to her thick head. Jake of course got the best gifts and the most as always.

Rachele never understood why I made sure everyone had the same amount of gifts. The fact with kids if their sister got four more they get upset, and my kids even get upset when they notice I didn't get as much. What can I say? I raised good fair kids. However, as they got older they accepted their grandma for who she was and stopped getting upset about it thankfully. Oh but that first Christmas, when they were old enough to understand, was a nightmare. They were only three, five, and seven but Tasia got 14 gifts while the other two only got six. If you had kids you'd understand the nightmare of that night.

After we were finished Joy said she was going to box up some leftovers for us but that she wouldn't send us any cake since it would melt. I told her not to worry about it but she said she'd make Rachele bring us our own when we're back home. I don't even bother objecting because well hey as rude as it is I don't think I care about Rachele's inconvenience. At the last minute Joy remembers Kyra's present but says she'll just send it with us to give to Kyra tomorrow but requests pictures which I promise to get to her.

Surprisingly we are actually out of there by eight which is an utter miracle. Apparently, the secret is telling his grandma we need to leave and she makes sure it happens. Thankfully she didn't even seem upset but excited for the kids saying we all could use some time away and hoping she can come next time. If it can happen without Rachele I'm totally down. Rachele on the other hand is furious and keeps going on about how Jake needs to stop letting me push him around and make decisions for him. Especially since I don't work, seriously? She's spiteful that now I don't have to work something she's been pushing for since my surgery when my Dr told me I couldn't work. She only works two days a week and lives with only electricity and water. She used to have a phone bill but Jake added her to ours and has been paying it since. Everything else she uses Joy's money which I find a complete joke considering she has four hundred thousand just sitting in the bank and turned down a full-time job because she didn't need it to get by. Yet she acts superior?

She finally leaves off telling Jake to call her tomorrow, so grateful the place has no cell service, something he'll find out. "So where are we going?" Jake asks from the driver's seat. I text him the address my uncle gave me. "You know I'm never going to hear the end of that right?" he asks.

"Not to be a bitch but I don't really care. Time to cut the apron strings. I'm your wife, not her. You need to start taking my wants and feelings into consideration. I'm done coming in second to everything."

"As long as you're happy." He mumbles and I just ignore him and settle in for the drive.

CHAPTER 14

At six in the morning, I'm the only one up. I've always gotten up super early on Christmas, my mom used to hate it. My kids never got that trait the earliest they've gotten up on Christmas without my waking them up is nine. My brother and Darlene will sleep all day if I let them. Sadly they've trained my little sweet niece to be the same. My Dad to be honest is probably awake but waiting to hear people moving to get out of bed.

When we got in last night only my brother, Darlene and Ro were awake, so we tried to be quiet. I wasn't happy to hear that not only did Bella come with my uncle, so did Tala. Apparently, she gave some sob story about not being able to go see her family, Sierra informed me she does it every holiday. So now I got to play nice with her and Jake who I'm still annoyed with. So much for my stress-free Christmas. I'd originally planned on staying through the new year but we will actually be heading back out on the twenty-seventh, so only two days.

I decided to go for a walk in the woods. I've always loved walking through the woods. Hell, even the desert. I truly just love nature but there's something extra peaceful about being surrounded by trees especially if there's a spring, streams, or even a lake. My Uncle had told me there was a waterfall nearby and if I'd followed the stream from the cabin towards the south

I'd find it. So obviously I decided that's what I'm going to do. First, however, I have to throw on a jacket and some boots, the cold and snow is the only reason I would never live up north. I absolutely hate the cold. It's nice for a visit but nothing more. If I use this cabin more I will have to come up and get some better winter clothes. They just don't have good enough ones in the valley.

"Where ya off too?" Sierra asks as I head for the door.

"I was gonna go for a walk and see if I can find the waterfall," I reply.

"It's probably frozen right now." She informs me.

"Probably but I want to walk anyway."

"Okay let me get my coat and shoes."

"You don't have to come. Really. I just wanted a peaceful quiet walk." I assure her.

"I won't say a word but you know my not coming isn't an option. Maybe when we don't have the Vampyr over our heads but until then? Sorry one of us has to always shadow you. Your uncle will use our hides for a new wolf skin rug if we don't."

I could swear I heard someone upstairs when she said that but when I glance up I don't see anyone. "Okay fine you can come. I don't want you to get in trouble. I won't demand you be quiet so you can talk if you want it'll still be peaceful either way."

After she gets her stuff we head out and follow the trail along the stream heading south as Edward said. As we're walking a thought occurs to me.

"Do you know if Bella did the protection wards?" I ask.

"She did yes. Your uncle insisted as soon as they arrived according to the guard that was here. You don't have to worry it was done before your family arrived. Your uncle says your property extends past the waterfall, but Bella was only able to do the wards for the cabins and a little further into the woods with such a short amount of time. Our people are patrolling out here though."

"That's good. I was worried about bringing my family up here, but I really needed this." She nods at me in sympathy.

Ever since Ian's freak out Sierra has been a lot more cordial with me. I'm not sure what happened but whatever they talked about that night seems to have taken away her bite towards me. It's always kind of amazed me how even when she didn't care for me she was pretty observant and intuitive about what I was thinking or feeling. When we were talking about coming up here she noticed I was skirting around asking if Ian would be coming and informed me he would not be. Something I was extremely grateful for.

"It's beautiful," I say as we reach the falls.

"It is." She replies.

The water that should be flowing freely has frozen into icicles. It strangely looks like a mouth in which the ice forms the teeth, albeit sharp glacier teeth but teeth nonetheless. Behind it is a cave, it doesn't appear to go in too deep. Granted my eyesight in the dark is abysmal so what do I know? The falls aren't extremely tall I'd say maybe eight feet max but beautiful all the same. It doesn't go directly into the stream like I'd thought but rather into a gorgeous pool of water well it would be anyway if that too wasn't frozen over. The pool narrows off into the stream we followed here. I go sit on a large rock hanging over the edge of the pool, probably not smart with the rock being slick but it's where I want to be. Sierra follows silently and sits next to me.

I couldn't say how long we sat there, hell I didn't even know how long it took us to get there really. It didn't matter, it was the most relaxing experience ever. Just sitting there looking at this remarkable waterfall, the rocks, and trails surrounding it from a distance leave a white sandy beach still slightly visible through patches of snow. It was truly the most tranquil experience ever.

Of course, all good things must come to an end. Out of nowhere, we heard the most heart-jerking canine cry, I'd have to assume has ever been made. Due to the rock formations, it echoes like nothing I've ever heard before. Sierra and I look at each other. I can see her intent to stop me from what she knows I'm about to do just as clearly as I can see her desire to run toward the animal. Before she can even act I get up and run slipping on the stupid frost-glazed rock and scraping up my hands and knees in the process. I don't let it stop me, I refuse to let it stop me. I stand back up and dart off. You'd think with still getting over my prior injuries while yes they are mostly gone they still hurt like hell, I'd be slowed down much more easily. Adrenaline though is a powerful thing.

I'm not certain how far I've run but I can hear Sierra closing in behind me. Sadly I don't think my quick acting gave me as much of a head start as I thought it would. The pain-filled howl we'd originally heard has now turned into whines and yips, the good news is the sounds coming from just ahead, the bad news? I don't know if I'll get there before Sierra stops me slowing me down, to help whatever caninoid is making that dreadful sound.

My luck for once holds out, well sort of. I make it to the origins of the cry only to enter a clearing. That in and of itself is no problem, what is a problem is the six Vampyrs I see surrounding the most gorgeous and wolf-like husky I've ever seen in my life. Even under the blood and dirt, I can see his white cover with black splotches and markings so similar to a wolf it easily is mistaken for one. I can't tell where the blood is coming from but the vampyrs surrounding it seem eager to feast. All the Vampyrs have Dark hair and glowing red eyes, a trait Nick has taught me only happens during certain times like feedings. A very powerful Vampyr can prevent the eyes from changing but not many are strong enough. The blood sucker's intentions are clear, to bleed this poor baby dry. What isn't clear is why they are waiting.

I only let the thought pass my mind before I scream. "Hey, blood whores! What the fuck are you doing on my land?"

Truth is I don't even know if we are still on my land but at this point I'm pissed and don't care. I hear Sierra pull up behind me and gasp at the same sight that has enraged me. I'm a serious animal lover, it took me years to come to terms with the circle of life and the necessity of using animals for things like food. This though? This is needless violence. The most unnecessary thing anyone can do. I understand hunting helps keep the ecosystem balanced when done right, but senseless torture even a hunter would be horrified by. These psychos need to be killed and STAT. The problem is I may be impulsive and bullheaded but it doesn't mean I'm actually stupid. This is a fight I know I would never win even with Sierra, but it doesn't mean I won't give it my best effort.

I step forward. " Hey, assholes, why don't you pick on someone who can fight back instead of a half-dead animal?" I demand hoping to draw their attention. Turn to Sierra and tell her. " You need to go get help! It's the only chance you have at keeping me alive, which I know is your goal. Go get anyone I don't care. Fuck get Ian. Just go and hurry." She stares at me with what I can only assume is reluctance and sorrow. She knows she has no choice, I gave her none, but she doesn't want to run, it's the last thing she wants. She however is forced to and so she does.

"The master was right. She's soft, she comes to save the pitiful creature." Lead goon says with a disgusting look of glee.

"Okay you *children of the corn* rejects. Get the fucking hell off my property, NOW!" I demand.

Goon two and three giggle while goon one replies. "Of course, we will go. You come with us and we go to the master."

"Sorry bro, not sure what kool-aid you're drinking but I'm not going anywhere." God I wish I had my weapons right now!

Before I can blink one of them charges me and grabs me. I thrash and kick, fight with everything I have. I realize blind fury is useless so I take a few calming breaths and try to remember what I was taught. While Ian's training never prepared me for this, my childhood did. I had an unconventional childhood, knowing what I do now I'm not sure that was accidental. However, various family members used to put me in weird situations to make me learn to get out. Like duct taped to a chair, or in the trunk of a car. As such I throw my head back as hard as I can and feel their hold loosen just a little bit as it slams into their nose. I then side step and lift my right foot like I'm about to stomp down. As they move their foot I fling my hand back and wrap my fingers around their balls as tight as I can and yank!

Since they had expected me to stomp on their foot the change shocked them so much that they couldn't even try to stop it. Now I'm loose and they're I guess I should say he curled in the fetal position crying like a toddler who just got their lollipop stolen. I jump away as fast as I can.

"Next," I say sarcastically while doing a bring it motion with my hand. Dated I know but sue me nineties I dare you.

For a few minutes I think I might have stunned them into stone, no such luck medusa I am not. Hmm, I need to ask if Medusa is real. Damn it Angel focus, you're already gonna die don't look stupid while you do it, huh? The head dick hole finally recovers and charges at me. I brace for impact while trying desperately to think of my next move. The problem with saying whatever is on your mind is, that you're too stupid to truly consider consequences which I'd just started to as I closed my eyes and waited to be hit.

Instead of a hit I hear an umph and look up to see what happened. I merely see a blur of motion dropping the vampyrs so quickly I can't even begin to register what's happening. Hell, I can't even tell if the vampyrs are alive or dead when they hit the ground. After what feels like an eternity once the final Vampyr falls the blur stops. Before me is standing a very angry, very red-eyed Nick. Not gonna lie I just got hit with a mixture of fear and arousal. One thing I always wished Nick would be was angry. I don't know if it was the copious amount of weed he smoked or what but I'd never seen him truly angry. If it is the weed he needs to teach Jake how to smoke because he's doing it wrong. Very very wrong.

"What the hell were you thinking Angel?" He snarls at me.

Yep, that's enough to snap me out of my lust-filled fantasy daze. "Excuse me, Nicky? What was I thinking? Fuck you I was thinking about a helpless dog being tortured!" I scream running over to the pup.

Nick takes a few very deep breaths. "I get that part! Why didn't you come and have one of us go? You had to know it was a trap, you aren't stupid don't act like you are!"

"I didn't think there was time. I sent Sierra for someone. I couldn't let them hurt him anymore!" I yell more in desperate worry then anger.

"Shit." He says. I see the uncertainty in his eyes, he doesn't know whether to chastise me or help me. "You can't act so foolishly Angel. You're playing into their hands. I know how this bothers you. I don't like it either but they could have killed you. Don't you get that."

The problem wasn't that I didn't know that, hell I did. I also knew those in charge of protecting me would've had a reckoning if I died. Problem was, at that moment, that time I simply didn't care. I couldn't bring myself to care if I wanted to. Animals were one of my true weaknesses, family, and friends were my other. My running stupidly into this wasn't what bothered me, no I'm used to my ridiculous fight or fight harder response. What bothered me was how did they know? We're they just guessing and got lucky? If it was something else do they know my weakness with my family too? What will they do next?

These were the most pressing issues going through my mind as I walked over and rubbed the poor baby as softly as I could, reassuring him he was safe and wouldn't be hurt. There was so much blood I was afraid to move him but knew I needed to. I gently placed my arms under him making soothing sounds as I did and tried to pick him up. I say I tried not because while he was not necessarily heavy I couldn't get my arms in a position around him that would guarantee I wouldn't drop the poor guy.

After struggling for a bit, Nick comes over. "Let me do it." He says anger and frustration bleeding into his voice. "We need to get out of here."

He grabs the pup more gently than I expected but with such quickness that didn't match. He began walking back and I had to fight my rebellious urge to refuse to follow. I wanted to be there. I wanted to know what was happening to the pup. I'm praying to every god, every angel I can think of to let him live. This is most definitely not at all how I expected to spend Christmas! We get towards the clearing that leads to the house and Sierra and the patrols circle us. Seeing what was happening they merely followed us making sure to keep a protective perimeter. Doubtful we're in danger at the point but still, I feel a bit safer.

As we approach the house Nick stops. "You have kids in there right?" He asks me and I mutely nod my head. "Someone put your jacket over the dog." He commands and I start taking off my jacket. "Not you Angel, you need it. " Sierra already had hers off and is covering the pup. "Okay Angel I'm taking the dog straight into the downstairs spare bedroom, Sierra will come with and keep people's focus off me. You need to find your uncle and that witch and get to us immediately." Again I stupidly nod. I'm so worried I can't even form words. I want to kick myself.

We head inside and I hear noises in the kitchen, I can only pray none of the kids are in there. I separate from Sierra and Nick who have to walk through the kitchen to get to the bedroom. Instead I run upstairs to my uncle's room and knock as loud and incessantly as I can.

Finally, the door cracks open and I see my uncle's shocked and worried face. "What is it, Angel? Are you okay? What happened?"

You can see his worry increase the longer I go without answering. Once I've finally mustered up a voice. "There was a hurt dog....woods....vampyrs... I need Belladonna!"

"Woah, calm down, take a breath and tell me what's happened?" He instructs as he exits his room and heads down the hall towards what I assume is Belladonna's room.

I follow trying to untie my stupid ass tongue which only works when I don't fucking want it too. After quite a few deep breaths and word searching I muster to ramble out the story of what happened by the time we reach her door.

"Okay so you went for a walk, and heard a hurt dog. Went to save it and found Vampyrs. You were then saved by Nick, a vampyr and the dogs downstairs needing help?" when I nod in reply he finally knocks.

Bella opens the door. "Why hello Edward." She says in an extremely creepily flirty voice.

After my uncle explains the situation we all run down stairs. Bella of course grabbed a bag first. Thankfully as we pass the kitchen we see Jake and my brother utterly confused, my dad confused and I think angry not sure what to make of that. The good news though is that there's no kids. Once we get in the room Bella gasps and starts mumbling "Poor baby, poor, poor baby." Over and over.

"Can you do anything?" Sierra asks. Which earns a shush.

After several agonizing minutes. "I can keep him alive, but you will have to get a Dr here quickly, Angelika I would ask you to stay here to help keep him calm. He seems to like you and it will make it easier. You will do this, yes?" She says as a command more than a question.

Of course I agree, what more can I do? My Uncle leaves to call in a helicopter with the pack dock on it. I merely sit here talking to the sweet dog, while letting Bella work her Magick. I have no real brain power at the moment so I couldn't say how long we were out there but the clock says it's nine forty-five meaning my day has only started.

The Doc managed to arrive in just under an hour. He actually apologized for taking so long, personally, I was impressed at how quick he'd gotten here. Bella had eventually kicked everyone out of the room but she gave up when I refused to leave. The Doc however wasn't as willing to let it go he said he needed a sterile environment to work and no distractions. So I headed out to the kitchen to wait. Everyone was wise enough to leave me alone except Jake. I swear God forgot to give that man a brain. He'd tried to start in on and to be honest, he wasn't entirely wrong he wanted to know why I hadn't told him Nick was here, let alone that I'd seen him. I actually intended to tell him but when we'd gotten in that fight I ended up completely forgetting and I hadn't actually seen Nick up here. Yes, he'd told me he'd have to come but, I figured he'd changed his mind since he was nowhere to be seen. Unfortunately for Jake no matter how justifiable his quarry was, I'm not in the mood. I'd ended up telling him as nicely as I could that we'd discuss it once the dog was okay.

I'm too sensitive, that's my biggest downfall if I'm being honest.

Yes sensitivity can be good but it's what's led to my family walking all over me, and my almost getting killed by Vamps on more than one occasion. If I could be as selfish as my mother in-law thinks I am, well I'd never have to worry about being suckered into a trap and I wouldn't need all these fucking guards. I know it's been driving Jake crazy having our every move watched but it's not like it's a picnic for me. Granted I do at least know the real threat. Fuck I'm going to have to tell him soon no matter how crazy he ends up thinking I am.

"He's going to be okay." The Doc says coming out the door only an hour after going in.

I immediately stand. "Can I go back in?" I ask.

"You can if you want he's still under sedation. It should wear off soon. Huskies are very resilient and have a high pain tolerance so he'll probably be up and moving soon after but we do want to keep his activity limited. He has a chip. I've already reached out to the owners who were trying to get rid of him and said if you want to keep him he's yours, otherwise take him to the nearest shelter. What do you want to do?"

"I'll have to talk to Jake, but personally I want to keep him."

"Okay, well let me know. They have the paperwork on him and they said they would send it to me. I will have them do it either way. I'm going to stay if that's okay to keep an eye on him and I'll head back with you guys. Is there a place down stairs I can sleep? I want to stay close to him."

"You can stay of course but are you sure you want to? It's Christmas, what about your family?"

"I only have a daughter and a granddaughter and I was already getting ready to leave their house when Edward called." He explains.

"Okay well there's the office. It does have a pull out couch. We can move the dog in there so you can have the bed?"

"No-no leave him. I'll be fine."

"That's good. I really didn't want to move the dog. What's his name?" I ask.

"They said it was Rex, but I don't think they had him very long so I'm sure changing it won't be hard."

"Okay," I say and head into the room.

I pet the poor boy's head, trying to give him what little comfort I can. He's still asleep as the doc said. I can't let go of how this is all my fault. They tortured him to get to me. I want to keep him like I told the doc but maybe that's not for the best with everything going on. I don't know if I would forgive myself if he got hurt again and it was my fault. Hell, I don't know if I will this time. So I sit there silently sobbing as I contemplate what's best for the dog rather than myself.

"Hey, how is he?" I hear Nick ask as he comes in.

"Doc says he's going to be okay. Apparently, his asshat owners were already getting rid of him so he's mine if I want him." I say with a sneer. I hate people who just dump their pets like they're nothing.

"Are you going to keep him?"

" I don't know. I gotta talk to Jake first. I just don't know if I should."

"What do you mean?" He asks in confusion.

"Well, he was hurt to get to me. What if I keep him and he gets hurt again or worse? Maybe keeping him is selfish?"

"Angel, even if you're right and they did hurt him to get to you. We didn't know he was out there. Hell, I don't even know how you heard him, Sierra said she barely heard him and only because she was trying after you'd obviously heard something. If we knew he was there this would have never happened."

"Still, Nick, I'm a target! Nothing around me is safe. You should all leave everyone and let's see if fate decides I win or lose!"

"Angel, stop that bullshit. It's ridiculous and you know it. Even if people weren't with you they'd be used to getting to you. It's safer together. Besides, we don't know this was done to get you." He explains hopeful to alleviate my guilt.

"Bullshit Nick! You're not stupid you know this was targeted. What's worse is it means someone who knows me is giving them information, it is someone who knows me, or they're watching me closer than anyone thought."

"Okay, you're right it probably was targeted at you, but how many people would risk their lives for a dog that means nothing to them personally?"

"Anyone who is a decent human being deserving of living. The torture of a helpless, trusting animal is bullshit. On that everyone should agree. Those who don't should be thrown into a volcano!" I exclaim angrily.

He chuckles at that. Then I feel a wet tongue licking my cheek. "I don't know Angel, he seems to agree with me.."

I look into the beautiful cobalt eyes of the husky and decide then and there he's mine.

CHAPTER 15

I went to find Jake to talk to him about the dog and of course, he was in the room playing call of duty. Like seriously it's fucking Christmas and that's what you do? I was surprised my brother noticed the commotion and everything happening and took all the kids outside to play. I swear I've seen DJ play outside a total of four times his entire life and he's usually oblivious to the world around him. Though he was a tremendous help with Tasia when she was a baby. Jake had gone off to basic and I was basically a single mother it was torture! DJ would feed her in the mornings and put her down before school or take her on the weekends and let me sleep in, turning off my alarm. He was a real godsend. Even when Jake got back he never got up and did the feedings, it was always babe the baby's crying. I love the man but good with children under ten he is not.

DJ however is amazing with little kids it's the older ones he's not so great with. This is surprising since everyone always thought he'd be the next Unabomber. He's the creepy quiet kid in the corner everyone is worried about, but I love him. The funniest part is everyone was always afraid of him when I was the one who would probably lose it and go on a rampage. It took years to get my anger and mood swings under control. Bipolar is not manageable without meds they told me! Ha! Proved them wrong. It's been years since a real freak-out.

"Hey?" I say tentatively. It seems ridiculous but he's hit or miss when he's playing that damn game. He can get pissed cause you come to talk to him or totally be fine. Yeah and I'm the one with problems?

He takes his headset off and exits the loading screen which shocks me. He probably is eager to hear about Nick which isn't why I came up here. "What?" He says with a heavy tinge of anger.

"So, the dog I brought in. Its owners were getting rid of it anyway. They said if we want it, to keep it. If not, give it to a shelter." I replied.

"Really? That's what you came in here for?"

"Yes." I reply tentatively.

"Oh, so you just want to ignore your ex-boyfriend being here on our vacation?" He accuses, his anger fully on display.

"No Jake, I don't want to ignore it. I just want to wait until tonight after we've done all the Christmas stuff to get into it." I tell him hoping he'll understand and drop it. No such luck of course.

"Of course you do! Let me guess you think avoidance is best. My mom's right! You think you walk on water don't you?"

"Jake, DO NOT bring your mother into this. You won't like the direction of this conversation if you do!"

"Oh really? Now you have a problem with my mother?" He asks in disbelief.

"Dude are you dumb? I've had an issue with your mother since she's decided she's had an issue with me."

"Yet, you choose to have no issue with your family?"

"Oh fuck you Jake you know that's not true. I've had plenty of issues with my family. Most caused by you I might add. However,

I've always stood my ground when it's come to you! They say what they want about me, but they don't talk about you, or the kids. I don't tolerate it. That's my line and you know that better than anyone. You let your mom walk all over me, and treat me like shit!"

"No, you use me and you don't like her pointing it out."

"Oh really? I use you for what? Working and wasting your money on video games and booze because you need an escape like nobody else does?" I ask sarcastically.

"You use me so you don't have to work!"

"Come off it Jake. You were the one who didn't want me to work. Then when I physically couldn't you wanted me to, because mommy came back in and told you I should be working!"

"That's just your excuse. Things changed, we weren't making enough. She went back to work after her surgery!"

"Yeah sure after her WRIST surgery I would have been more than happy to return to work after wrist surgery. However, I had full spinal surgery, you moron. One is not like the other! Not to mention you made way more than enough, you chose to spend all your money on bullshit, and even without my job I managed to make sure bills, you couldn't pay cause it went to bullshit, got paid. I made excuses why you didn't get up in the morning like today for your kids who would hate you otherwise. I made sure they got what they needed because you weren't paying attention. This is not a fight you want to get into Jake because for once you will not come out on top. I love you more than anything but I'm sick of this shit. Grow up and be a father be MY husband or go fuck yourself I don't care at the moment I can't do this. " He's quiet. I'm not sure if he's thinking or had already made up his mind and is too much of a bitch to say it but at this point, I don't know if I even care. " As for Nick you dumb ass. I didn't have a choice in his hiring and I fully intended to tell you, but you threw a fifteen-year-old girl temper tantrum over this trip and I didn't get a chance!"

He doesn't say anything for quite some time when he finally does with a look of confusion he asks. "Wait, so he didn't work for you the whole time?"

"No you fucking idiot! He just started the day we had the fight and it wasn't my choice. I'd already explained I'm not fully in charge yet! Hell, I haven't even really had much say in the company yet!"

"We thought you'd hired him." He says as if it explains everything.

"Who the fuck is we? Got some multiple personalities like your aunt? Gonna start calling yourself Elon musk now?"

"Do you have to be such a bitch?"

"When I come up to ask a simple question and tell you we should do presents now and you turn this into some bullshit? Yes, yes I do and I won't apologize for it. Maybe you should grow the fuck up and not start bull shit fights! Who the fuck are we?"

"I was talking to mom and…" He admits.

"Oh fuck no! This is what I'm talking about! It seems like I'm a sister wife with your mom!"

"You talk to your friends."

"Yes, friends moron! Not my parents, friends. Not people who fucking hate you for breathing! People who actually like you, who call me on my bullshit and tell me when I'm wrong!"

"Well, I gave up all my friends." He whines.

"No, your friends were gang bangers and drug users who I refused to have around my family. Or ex-girlfriends who claimed to be lesbian to try and fuck you. Get real friends. Try starting with people who act like adults, hell ones who have kids even better!" I point out.

"I'm not arguing about this. Fine, I was wrong you didn't bring him in."

"Yeah, you were. Maybe try talking to me once in a while, not your mother! She's a conniving bitch who hates me and you know this!"

"I'm sorry for that okay? Maybe I should have talked to you. I was just so pissed off about how you were changing our plans. We do the same thing every year."

"Only because you never care about what I want to do! This isn't even what we used to do. It's only been since your mother decided to talk to you again! Ever since you jump when she says jump, rollover when she says rollover. I didn't marry a pussy ass momma's boy!"

"Jesus, Angel I said I was sorry." Again his voice turns whiny while his face takes on a toddler like expression.

"Yeah, and while nobody else realizes it because I have better control I'm meaner than you'll ever be. It just takes longer to get me there and you know it. So think about how much I am suppressing myself to be this furious and why are you still breathing?" I stop and take some deep breaths. Maybe he's right maybe I'm being way too much of a fucking bitch right now. I don't really know but Fuck I can't take the guilt I feel now this is what I worked so hard to learn to control. I always feel bad, always feel guilty " Look I need to know what to tell the doc about the dog. I really didn't come up here to fight."

"Yes, we can keep the dog. Of course, we can keep the dog. Hello, puppy! Did you even have to ask? "He says with a sadder than a normal chuckle.

"I just wanted to include you before I say yes. You should come to meet him."

"Does he have a name?"

"The Doc said the owners called him Rex but didn't have him long so renaming him should be easy. I'm thinking about Koda?"

"Koda, I like it. Let's go see Koda." He agrees.

Like always that's how our fight ends. Not a true ending. We didn't accomplish much more than just scream frustrations at each other. While I always try to take what he says to heart and make changes where truly needed, he usually acts better for a few weeks, months at most then poof right back to normal. This time though maybe it'll be different. One can hope. So not wanting to fight more, we head down to see the pup. As the doc said he's already up and moving around. He's extremely happy to see me, but even more excited to meet Jake. All animals love Jake. I've never fully understood it. People naturally steer clear but animals? They flock to him. After seeing Koda I found the doc and let him know our choice. By this point, it's already after one.

Going to look for the kids I found out my brother brought them in and got them lunch but then he'd taken them back out for a hike. Instantly my heart lurches, that's exactly how this all happened. I went for a hike and now my kids are out there. However, my dad stops my mini freak out by telling me that he was not sure why other than maybe my brother not being "woods savvy" but that he'd asked Nick and Sierra to go with him. It makes me feel a little better but I'm still freaked out and Jake, of course, doesn't understand why I want to go find them rather than wait.

Apparently, the story was that the dog got attacked by wild wolves, ironic in my opinion but okay. Either way, I play up my paranoia about that. It didn't take us long to find them, when we did I told them it was time for presents and how sorry I was that it was delayed. Not surprisingly they all take it well but Tasia mentioned how if she were late she'd be in trouble. Even baby Ro doesn't seem to mind though she is a baby I suppose. We get back to the cabin and my brother asks me to wait outside for a minute which of course I do, after all, he's never asked much of me. He goes to take Ro inside and is back out quicker than I'd expected.

"Hey, um let's go for a quick walk." He says. Noticing my impatient face he adds. "Just past the tree line away from prying ears in the house."

I nod and follow him. He didn't lie, we barely went far enough to avoid being overheard, by humans at least.

"So, what's up bro?" I ask.

"You tell me?" He replies.

"Umm, I don't follow. You wanted to talk?"

"So, Vampyrs and wolves huh?" He says casually.

I stumble, knowing how dangerous this knowledge is. "What?" I squeak.

"Don't try and play dumb sis, I heard you all this morning, I saw your ex's eyes when you came in. I'm not stupid you know!" He demands.

"I don't think you're stupid, idiot! Unobservant one hundred and ten percent, stupid no!" I deny.

"Tell me. Now!" He demands.

So I do. He's my brother. I've never kept secrets from him. No, we aren't one of those sweet movie brothers and sisters who talk every day. We are definitely not *Monica and Ross*, but I've never lied or kept secrets from him. Nor has he from me. We've always been there for each other and truth be told these secrets have been killing me. So I unload everything on him.

When I'm finished he doesn't speak for a few minutes then

finally. " So you've been dealing with this all on your own with basic strangers?"

"Pretty much yeah."

"Why the fuck didn't you tell me? I would've helped you!" He asks in sympathy.

"I didn't want you to think I'm crazy."

"You're many things. Including crazy but not hallucinations type crazy." He points out.

"You're the only person who would think that. Hell at least hallucinating I could get a vacation in a nice padded cell with lots of drugs."

This of course makes him laugh. "Don't ever hide shit again. You shouldn't deal with this on your own. Look I know Jake and dad may not take this well, but you have some amazing friends and you have me. We are here for you, so stop bottling. We both know how bad that is for you. Yes anyone but you specifically should never do that. Talk to us damn it."

"So you don't hate me?" I ask timidly.

"Hate you? For what?" He asks confused.

"For inviting you up here with Ro with all this going on?"

"If I only let Ro see her aunt when life was safe you'd never see her. I wish you'd told me, but I'm not mad at you. I know you, she's safer with you than anyone no matter what's happening. You would give your life for anyone around you."

His words alleviate so much stress I didn't realize I'd been holding. "I love you!" I tell him as I give him a bone-crushing hug

"I love you too sis. So am I gonna sprout fur or something I need to know about?" He asks as he hugs me back.

I slap him in the arm. "No, you idiot!" I say laughing. "It's on my father's side. Unless dads got a secret he hasn't told us though I don't see grandma hiding it well. Maybe you should not try rhyming anytime soon though. The witch is on mom's side."

"Well shit there goes my poetry career! We better get inside before those gremlins destroy the house in search of presents!". He says in mirth.

I laugh at that and we head inside. This is why I wouldn't trade my brother for anything in the world! Seriously, he's amazing.

After we got inside we opened presents, since it wasn't super early Jake actually stayed out with the family for it. He used to always open presents with us but that was another thing to change since his mom came back in the picture. She gave him this deluded idea that he doesn't need to participate in such things. So I do the best I can with it saying they can wait for him to get up or open them without him and we'll take him, his later. Yeah, the kids don't get up really early but Jake usually is asleep until noon on Christmas which I don't get since I'm the one up all night wrapping any final things and setting up gifts.

The kids all love what they got, Tasia mainly got make-up, jewelry, and clothes. My dad and brother got her some art stuff. Fy of course got a bunch of hoodies, basketball shorts, and horror T-shirts. She also got a few horror movies and games from my dad and brother and I did get her a pennywise figurine. Remi just got games and toys from everyone which made his day. Ro got completely spoiled as all of my kids got her gifts. Lots and lots of unicorn blankets, night lights, and toys she was tickled pink. Darlene actually likes the spa set and foot massaging bath I got her. DJ got swords to add to his collection and I got my dad some seat covers, with a warmer and massager. As well as floor mats and a stealing wheel cover. I got Jake some tools and Ohio state stuff. I got him a toolbox too but it's at home.

My dad got me a new coffee maker, and my brother got me a Reese's coffee mug. What really surprised me though was that my uncle gave everyone, including each of the kids a card with a thousand dollars. I told him it was too much, but he simply said nonsense. This whole having money thing is going to take some getting used to, if handing out almost ten grand just for Christmas is normal. My brother's face though when little Ro opened hers was priceless. More surprising though was that Bella had gifts too, she gave all the girls a necklace that she told them to wear at all times because they'd keep them safe. They were all amethysts but in different type settings. She also gave the guys a weird-looking coin, but not like any coin I've ever seen, they looked like amethysts just coin-shaped.. They almost looked handmade and had triquetra on them. She told them to keep them in their wallets. What wasn't surprising was the jealous look on Tala's face. I'd actually feel bad if she hadn't forced her way in.

I actually did get gifts for all the guards, nothing really big, just a few gift cards. Bella however, we'd stopped at a small shop on our way up here to get drinks and I found a decorative crystal ball that made me think of her. So after she gave out her gifts I ran upstairs to get it for her. I had planned to give it to her when we got back, but I decided not to wait. Jake of course gave me an envelope with twenty dollars in it, no card, just the money. I really can't remember the last time he went out and bought me a gift, it's sadly disappointing, to be honest.

After everyone had finished I had an announcement. "Kids, I've got one last present for you." They all stare at me, then start looking towards the tree I'm sure trying to figure it out. I'd worked this out with the Doc already, so he walks over to me with Koda. He'd said the small walk would do him good but we had to get him to lay down and not strain himself and get him back to bed quickly. I'd had Nick take Kyra out to play with her while we did presents for that very reason. When he handed me the leash I say. "Kids, this is Koda. He's coming home with us. You've got to be gentle though he'd hurt right now."

The kids squeal louder than I've ever heard even Fy who isn't a squealer. I'm pretty sure it's safe to say their favorite gift was the puppy. I let them spend some time with him and then return him to bed. My Uncle had already said he'd take him and the Doc back home when we leave. Afterward, I have Nick bring Kyra back in and give her, her Christmas gifts. Yes, I'm that pathetic, and worse I'll have to go get something for Koda when we get back. I already have stuff for the cats in the closets to give them when I'm home. What can I say? I spoil my pets. I sit back and relax, hoping the day will continue being calm and the rest of our stay ends up uneventful.

CHAPTER 16

Later that night Jake and I headed up to bed after the kids went down. Ro wanted to sleep with Tasia and no one really wanted to fight that, especially because of how cute she was when she asked. I'd planned on taking a bath once I got to my room, but Jake of course had other plans.

"So why the hell is Nick here and why didn't you tell me about him?" Jake demands almost immediately after I've closed the bedroom door.

I sigh. I thought we were done with this, but apparently, that was just making sure it wasn't my choice, not the end of it. How am I going to explain this without looking crazy and without him thinking I just want Nick around? "Nick was asked to consult with the security company. He works with a different company but has knowledge that can help find the person who's been doing this. I had nothing to do with it and didn't even know he was involved until I saw him myself. You know I haven't really stepped up to starting to run the company yet, not with everything going on and my uncle didn't know we knew each other. He is qualified, uniquely qualified for this. As for not telling you I fully planned to and if you'd have shut your damn mouth, when I wanted to come up here you would have known."

"Okay, fine I can see that. Why is he here though, right now with us for Christmas."

"Like I said, he knows about the person after me. He's here to protect us, which in case you forgot he already has. I might have died trying to save that dog."

"Right, he protected you from wolves but didn't even get a scratch." He says with his skepticism unhidden. I'd forgotten that was the story everyone was told that wolves were attacking the dog and I stupidly placed myself in the middle of it.

"He's got a way with them. What do you want here Jake? What do you want me to say?"

"I want to know why you left the bed to go out with your ex-boyfriend."

"Oh my god, you're jealous!" I say with laughter. I probably should point out I didn't even leave with Nick but damn his condescending tone pisses me off so fuck it. "Really? Do you want to lecture me about my ex? What about Beth? I didn't spend all night at the bar with him and then go back to his house until the next morning. I didn't constantly see him while lying to your face. I didn't help him pay the insurance on his car so he can get an Uber license then go out to dinner for two and to the point! The point of all places. The whole time claiming he's gay and we're just friends. Stop pushing your guilty conscience on me, Jake! He is here to help protect my family, not to try and cause our divorce, end of discussion. While we're on the topic, when's the last time you talked to Beth?"

"What? It's been years you know that!" He deflects.

"Oh really? So was it someone else using her Facebook to message on your birthday?" I ask with amusement.

"I don't know what you're talking about. You're crazy always seeing stuff that's not there."

"Of course Jake I'm the crazy one. I'm the one freaking out over an ex who has never done anything to cause problems for our marriage. Oh, wait no that's you. Beth has always been an issue and tried to sleep with you multiple times, which you claim never happened and against my better judgment, I chose to believe you over her. She's tried to get me to leave you for years. Worse, she isn't the only damn woman. Yet every time I talk to a man you act like I can't help but fall on their dicks. What about me has ever once suggested that's an issue? You know what Jake I'm not doing this shit anymore. You're not pawning your guilt off on me, I'm done cutting out friends because you can't handle other guys around and I'm finished walking on eggshells. So grow the fuck up!" I walk over to my bags to pull out some clothes.

"What are you doing?" Jake demands.

"I'm taking a shower you dick!" I respond and walk into the adjoining bathroom slamming the door behind me. Shit, I hope I didn't wake the kids!

I quickly undress and hop in, standing under the stream of hot water I merely brace my hands against the wall and hang my head letting the water cascade down. I hear the door open and close, but choose to ignore it. Usually ignoring Jake is the best way to get him to leave me alone.

Instead, I get lost in my thoughts so lost I'm not sure how long I've been standing here. I never heard the door again but figured he must have left. He's not one for being quiet long when he's mad and he hates my throwing Beth at him. I get it. I do they were friends since junior high, but I'm his wife damn it and I left most of the friends I had behind because they were guys and he couldn't handle it whether I'd dated them or not.

I finish lathering my hair and squirt some body wash onto my loofah when I hear the glass door click open, and then closed after he stepped in. I know it's Jake, you can't be with a man for seventeen years and not be able to tell when he's the one behind you. Anyone who says otherwise lies or wasn't paying attention.

He reaches around me and takes the loofah out of my hand, before I can tell him to fuck off, he starts running it over my body. Any woman who ever had a man wash them would understand my current dilemma. On one hand I'm pissed, but on the other having your man wash you makes you feel pampered in a way I can't even put into words. After he washes my back and neck he shuffles closer so he can reach around and wash the front of me. I can feel his erection along the small of my back.

He takes his time once he reaches my breasts, they were never really big but they have increased in size since I'd put on a little weight, they've always been extremely sensitive though. That has only increased, I immediately start to feel the pressure built in my core. After several long torturous minutes of him caressing my chest, he moves down towards my belly and begins kissing the crease of my neck. I let out the softest moan.

By this point, I'd literally forgotten why I was mad at him altogether. I'd always loved how people act as though women aren't in the least bit sexual, we can and do get distracted by sex just as often as men do, the problem is getting close enough to try and distract us when we're mad. He slowly moves his hand lower and just when he reaches my soft mound and I think I'm about to find some release, he moves to my thighs.

I can't help it, I whimper. Slightly disappointed he didn't stop where he was. He backs away a little and crotches down washing my lower legs and feet though doing so much more quickly than he had anywhere else. When he finishes he stands again, pressing himself into my back once more. He began suckling on my earlobe which sends an irresistible tingling sensation straight to my center which I can feel is now drenched.

When he puts his hands back on me I realize he's left the loofah behind altogether, he again finds my breasts and starts to gently massage them with both hands, causing another soft moan to slip out. I can feel his erection twitch in response to the sound.

Ever so slowly he moves his right hand lower, until it finally finds the mound of my clit.

Rubbing his thumb in a circular motion he returned to placing soft kisses along my neck. I can't help but to bow my body pressing my clit more firmly against his thumb encouraging him to give me more. My breaths have become irregular by this point and I can't help but continue to make the soft whimpers of approval mixed with begging for him to keep going.

He adjusts himself just a bit so he can press two of his long digits inside my now throbbing canal while still keeping his thumb circling my clit. My legs start to shake as I feel my orgasm begin to build to ridiculous heights as he pumps his fingers in and out at a torturous pace. I cry out and my knees start to buckle, he holds me up keeping his punishing rhythm.

Then he withdraws his fingers and I whimper at the loss, but I don't have to worry. He spins me around, lifts me up and slams his hard cock right into my center and I gasp. He begins pounding me and not slowly, but fast and hard right against the shower wall. With all the build-up it doesn't take long before we both reach our release. I cum clawing his back crying out his name, he lets go at the same time with a grunt.

After a few minutes of just staying there, he gently sets me down, giving me a kiss. "I'm sorry Angel, I've been an ass and unfair about everything. I'm not even certain why but I want to figure this out together. I love you."

"I love you too," I say back breathlessly. "Let's go to bed."

The rest of our stay went by quickly, too quickly in my opinion. Now that there was a bit less tension between Jake and me, it was a lot more enjoyable, so the leaving was bitter-sweet. Like I said I love nature, and being in the middle of the forest is amazing. If Idaho weren't so cold I'd have stayed there for that reason alone. Jake and I did talk a bit more the next morning and thankfully this time it was a lot more relaxed and calm, no more fighting and screaming. He agreed to be a bit more understanding and even engaged with the kids and me, and I agreed to be more open and honest. Unfortunately again I'm stuck with how open and honest I can truly be with him which makes me feel like a horrible hypocrite, but I'm not sure what to do really.

I'm going to have to work out how to tell him everything and very soon I don't see us getting past our issues until I'm honest about everything. I mean yes we do have other issues to be sure but currently, this is a big one. I'm actually starting to wonder if my lack of trust in him is a huge part of the reason I'm finding being completely honest such a problem. Don't get me wrong he doesn't believe in the supernatural and has a tendency to think people who do belong in psych wards, but I'm sure I can make him believe if I really was willing to put forth the effort.

Tonight is New Year's, we've been back home for days now. I'd let Maggie come pick up the kids this morning. She wanted them last night but new years eve is always something we spent doing together playing games and waiting for midnight. New years day however we've never really done anything special. Apparently though Jake's mom wanted him and the kids to go to his grandma's today to make up for leaving early Christmas Eve as if we'd done something wrong. Aside from her attitude, the biggest problem is Jake didn't tell me so I'd let the kids go with Maggie. He was still sleeping when she picked them up so they were gone by the time he got out of bed.

I thought for certain that was going to ruin the peace we'd acquired, but he surprised me by saying it was his fault for not telling me and that he'd explain it to his mom. He'd asked me if I wanted to come but I opted to stay home, I wasn't invited and I know how she gets when I come and she only wanted him and the kids I really would prefer not to deal with that at the moment. Instead, he'd promised to bring home a movie and dinner so we can spend the evening together. Since it's already six at night I'm not holding my breath.

My phone rings showing a restricted number. The only reason I even bother answering it, is because I know Joy's home phone shows up restricted and I want to make sure nothing happened to Jake. **"Hello?"**

"Hello, little wolf. I believe we have something that belongs to you." I freeze at the words the male voice says.

I tried racking my brain thinking of what anyone could have of mine and can't think of anything. Jake and the kids both have security. All my animals are in the house except the new husky who's still staying with the Doc at my uncle's.
Not being able to think of a thing I reply bluntly. **"Oh ya and what might that be?"**

"Mom?" I hear my sweet girl's voice through the phone.

"Tasia? Sweetie, are you okay?" I'm going to kill this mother fucker!

"I'm sorry little wolf, your pup can't talk right now. Tell me would you like her back?"

"Where are you, you fucking coward! Take me let her go!" I ask frantically.

"Well yes, that is the goal after all. We just couldn't get to you with all the security you hide behind, so we had to improvise. I'm more than willing to trade her for you."

"Where, you sick fuck?" I say as I grab my keys from my dresser and head out my bedroom door.

"Hmm, how about the crossroads of ChuiChui and Battalia? Say ten minutes. Oh and this should be obvious but lose your bloodhounds who bark at your command, or lose your daughter."

"I'll be there," I say and hang up. I stop for just a minute to call Maggie as a thought occurs to me. To be honest all I heard was mom what if they don't have her? That's what I would do if I were them and who knows how smart they really are? Unfortunately, Maggie isn't answering, that's not a good sign. I leave her a message and head through the garage door. I freaked for just a second momentarily forgetting I was tired when I drove last night so I parked in the driveway instead of the garage.

I want to check with Sierra about the team that followed the kids, but I can't risk Tasia's life doing that. He said to lose them which will be hard enough or so I'd thought until I stepped out of my garage. I see a bunch of wolves and even a few vampyrs rushing over to my uncle's which leaves my escape wide open. It's a bad sign, and of course, I'm worried about my uncle but I have to block that out at the moment. Instead, I hop in my car and drive off.

It only takes a few minutes to get there and when I do I see a black car with tinted windows. So dark I can't see inside. My phone rings again. **"Where is she?"**

"Get out and step away from your car and we will get out."

"I want to see her first!"

"If you don't get out right now, I will drive off and you'll never see her alive again." He demands.

Fuck I have no choice I'm not risking it, I can't it's not in me. So I do what they say, leaving my door open and the car running, hoping like hell I can grab her, get in the car, and drive off. Stepping on the hot dirt I suddenly realized in my haste I'd forgotten my shoes. As I begin walking to the other car my phone rings again and I look at it seeing Maggie's name. **"Maggie, what happened? Where are the other kids, are they okay?"**

"Angel, are you okay? The kids are fine. Tasia and Fy are making cookies, Remis on the Xbox." Fuck! I knew I was being stupid. **"What's going on hon? Why did you leave a message**

about Tasia being kidnapped? She's right here."

"It must have been a sick joke. I'm sorry, I gotta go." I say backing up.

"Are you sure? You sound weird. What's going on?" Asks clearly concerned.

"I can't talk about it right now if you don't hear from me in twenty minutes, call Jake. Tell everyone I'm sorry and I love them." I say and hang up. My only chance is to reach my car and I'm almost there, no one's even tried getting out of the black car. I back into a solid chest and now I know why it was only to keep my attention.

"Hello, little wolf." A sadistic voice whispers in my ear right before my entire world goes black!

Nick

The attack on Edwards came completely out of the blue. What was even weirder is they hit right after dark. They weren't even trying to do real damage, it felt like a distraction. I found Sierra, Angel's guard, and told her when the thought struck me. She wasn't too worried though because Angel had her own team it wasn't until she realized Grant who was supposed to be guarding her was here that she began to worry. She'd told me to help with the Vamps she'd go check on Angel and as much as I hated it she was right, I was more needed here. She'd been gone for twenty minutes when all the Vamps as if on cue just turned and left. I'd gone inside to check on everyone. They were all thankfully fine.

As I was getting ready to head out, Sierra ran through the door. "Edward, Angel's gone!" She announces fear clear in her voice.

The look on Edwards's face is filled with concern and regret. "What do you mean gone? Who was on guard duty?"

"I was sir, Tala called and said we were needed here immediately and she would be fine since the attack was here. I didn't like it but she made it sound like it was your orders, sir." Grant says, looking terrified. I'm not sure if he's afraid of Edwards' coming reaction or what happened to Angel.

"I never said he ordered it," Tala interjects.

"But you did call and tell them to come?" Edward asks sternly.

"We needed the help sir, I thought she'd be okay their attention was here," I swear the girl is about to cry.

Edwards's face is flush with anger. He looks at Sierra, "What did you find?"

"I searched the whole house, there was no struggle so she left willingly and I think in a hurry. Her shoes and purse are all still there. Her garage door is open and her car is gone." Sierra answers.

"Go, all of you! Find her now! I swear to God if she's not brought back I will end every one of you who had anything to do with her guards leaving!" He screams.

Both Grant and Tala gulped at the threat. I was already heading to the door when Sierra stops me. "Ride with me. The only other person here I'd be willing to work with is Grant and right now I'll kill him for his stupidity."

I simply nod and follow her to the car. It doesn't take us long at all to find Angel's car pulled off to the side of the intersection. We both hop out and walk over to it, the driver's door is open and the car is still running. This must have been where she went, but why and where is she now?

"I smell Vamps, at least five but I don't recognize any of them. Do you?" She asks me.

I take a deep breath. "Only one. Amon was here. The one that attacked us on the side of the road."

I hear a phone ringing over by the car and go back, I crouch down and find Angel's phone just far enough under for us to miss seeing it. It stops ringing and I look at it, noticing a ton of missed calls and texts from Maggie and Jake. I'd met Maggie once, she's not one to hound someone so this can't be good. It rings again.

"Hello," I answered, seeing Jake's name on the screen.

"Why do you have my wife's phone? Where is she?" He says angrily.

"That's what we're trying to find out. Something happened. She ditched security and we just found her car and phone on the side of the road." I explain a lot more calmly then I feel.

"Fuck! Where are you? I'm almost home?" He demands.

I tell him where we are and he says he'll be there in a few seconds. I didn't put much stock in it because he was an hour away and it's only been maybe a half hour since she went missing but true to his word he was there in seconds. He walks right up to me and punches me square in the jaw.

"You mother fucker! You were supposed to protect her, that's why you're here. Where the fuck we're you?" He accuses.

"Where was I? Where were you? You're her husband not me, I would not be disappearing all the time if I were." I demand.

"Why you…." He began before Sierra cut him off.

"Enough both of you measure your dicks later, will you? This isn't important right now! Jake, do you know anything? Even the smallest thing might help. Why did you even know there was a problem?"

He takes a few deep breaths, then says." Maggie called me. She said Angel had called, leaving a strange voicemail, something about Tasia being kidnapped and she hoped they were okay, if the other kids were okay. Maggie was completely confused since Tasia was standing right there making cookies so she called Angel back. Angel answers still worried about the kids, she said she sounded kind of frantic. Once Maggie told her the kids were all fine, she said Angel got really strange, saying it must have been a joke and she had to go. What worried Maggie the most was she said Angel basically said to tell us goodbye and that she's sorry, and loves us if Maggie didn't hear from her in the next twenty minutes. When she tried calling back after Angel hung up she got voicemail and called me immediately so I left and floored it here."

As if to emphasize how fast he was driving his security team finally pulled in behind us. Of course, they'd used her kids to get to her. It's smart there's nothing she wouldn't do for them including handing herself over. Fuck!

"Shit! She's preparing to die!" I say to no one in particular.

"No, she's preparing to fight but making sure to say her goodbyes in case she does. She won't go down easy, especially now she knows the kids are safe. They only took her because she was caught off guard thinking they had her child. They probably grabbed her before she could react to knowing they didn't have the kid and the lack of signs of a struggle says she probably wasn't conscious. My guess is they knocked her out. When she comes to I have no doubt she's going to be spitting mad. We need to get back to Edwards and try and find her. I'm more worried about her hurting herself at this point. Jake, will Maggie keep the kids longer? Would she be okay with the security being inside the house? I plan to send some more. They might try to grab the kids when they realize she's not going to cooperate."

"I'm sure she will. I'll call."

CHAPTER 17

Angelika

I wake up feeling completely disorientated. Why does my head hurt so fucking bad? Shit, what the hell did I do last night? It hurts to open my eyes so I just let them stay closed for a little bit trying desperately to remember what happened. Hell trying to remember why I'm standing with my hands bound above my head?

"So you're finally awake little wolf." I hear a deep voice rumble. "Don't bother pretending I heard it when your breathing changed."

"I'm not pretending anything dick hole. Where the fuck am I?" I say with my eyes still closed. It's starting to come back to me, the phone call, Tasia, Maggie, the vampyrs. Fuck I'm a god, damned idiot! This is what Jake always worried about. It was never that I couldn't defend myself, it's that my emotions overwhelm my logical thinking, and I react irrationally sometimes.

"Oh don't worry little wolf, you're hidden safely where no one will ever find you." He laughs maniacally. "Why don't you open your eyes, little wolf and meet our other guest?"

Fuck, who the hell else do they have? I force my eyes open and immediately find a girl. She can't be more than twelve, she's so dirty I can't make out many details. I can see her eyes though they're the most unusual shade of green, almost like emeralds, and they look to be glowing. Her hair is so filthy I can't even make out the color. Her clothes are completely caked with dirt and grime. I'm horrified they have this girl, but can't help being grateful it's not Tasia.

"Who is she?" I demand.

"Oh nobody really, just someone to keep you in line. Don't trouble yourself my little wolf, she wasn't taken because of you. She'll just be useful to you. Well now, I best be going people to speak to, threats to be made you understand." He then turns around and leaves.

Only when he's out of the room do I take the time to look around and see my surroundings. It looks like a basement but I can't be certain, definitely underground. There's only one light in the room and it's one of those old-fashioned dangling single light bulbs that doesn't really help you see much. I don't see any windows and the only thing really in the room is the hook I'm attached to a chair in the corner, and the bed the girls are on with a chain bolted to the ground.

"Hey sweetie, what's your name?" I ask her. I heard her whisper a reply but didn't make it out. "I'm sorry sweetie, I couldn't hear that?"

"My name is Kora." She replies quietly.

"How long have you been here? Where are your parents? How old are you?" I pepper her with questions knowing I might not have much time.

"I don't know, a long time?" She says questioning her own reply. "My parents were killed when they took me. I'm eleven. I think?"

"Well, Kora I'm gonna get us out of here okay? It will all be okay."

I assure her.

"Don't. Don't fight them! It will only be worse." She says quietly.

I don't know what she's been through but they are going to pay for it. If it's the last thing I fucking do.

Nick

We're at Angel's house in her kitchen. Moved over here because it was getting too cramped over at Edwards. With Grant, Sierra, Jake, Edward, Talla, and even Ian who'd returned as soon as he heard always here not to mention the other security who keeps coming in and out constantly. Jake also wanted to be here in case she made it home, it's unrealistic as hell but I think he's trying to cope. The kids are still at her friend Maggie's who I swear has called every few hours checking in. She says she hasn't told the kids, but Fy keeps asking what's going on. Ian and Sierra said she's smart.

At first, I wasn't too worried, but it's been three days now and nothing. Jake's been saying we need to call the police but Edward assures him it's been reported but we can do what they can't. He's skeptical and I can't really blame him after all we did lose her in the first place. We have wolves and Vamps trying to pick up her trail, and IT trying to find her electronically. Nothing though and they can be anywhere. Sierra comes flying in the door. Running towards the office.

"Edward, we just got an email with a link. The subject merely says... Do you want her back?" She yells as she passes.

All of us drop what we're doing and follow, Jake pushes his way to the front understandably so. The Doc's the last one to come in, Edward called him in yesterday unsure of what we are going to get if we find her at this point.

"Pull it up and face the screen this way," Edward says. His voice is calm but you can see the worry on his face.

"I am, one second." She replies.

She types a few more things, a couple of clicks then turns the screen. At first, all we see is what looks like a blank movie screen. Then a picture comes through. Sierra and the Doc both gasp. Ian just curses under his breath, and Jake, well he puts his fist through the wall.

On the screen we see Angel, she's standing upright but I don't know if she could if it was of her own volition. Her hands are bound above her head wrapped around a hook, dangling from the ceiling. She has a black eye and a deep bruise on her cheek the side opposite the black eye. Her lips busted and I'm pretty sure there's blood draining from her nose. Her shirt is torn and it looks like electrical burns are on her stomach. Thankfully her pants and bra are still on. Sierra must have been right about her not grabbing shoes because she's barefoot.

She's not crying, and she doesn't even look scared. No, her eyes are burning with hatred and anger. She's fucking pissed I would really hate to be these guys if she gets loose. She's not staring at the camera though, she's staring at the corner.

There's a mattress and what appears to be a bundle of clothes but then I see it, it's a girl. Not one of Angel's thank God this girl has green eyes not Angel's blue ones but she's young. This isn't good. She'll do whatever she has to, to keep that girl safe.

"Oh my God! Is that a fucking child?" Sierra says, noticing what I did.

"Get the IT guy we had brought in, here now Grant, let's see if he can trace this signal," Edward demands.

Another figure steps into the frame, fucking Amon. This is really not good that fuck is sadistic as they come. He's the very definition of psychotic. I'm pretty sure he's been on a supernatural watch list for years.

He walks over to the little girl. "Come on sugar, we're gonna give Angels friends on camera a show. Give them a preview of what I'm gonna do to their precious little wolf." He says in a sick attempt at a seductive tone. Angel immediately starts struggling with that.

"Leave her alone you cock sucker! What's the matter, can't take on a real woman? You gotta go after little girls." Angel says it with a strength I don't think any of us expected.

The door behind me opens and I don't even pay attention until I hear Maggie's voice. "Hey, Jake. Fy was going to walk if…"

She's cut off. "Mom?" I hear Fys voice.

"Oh my god, Angel?" Maggie says.

Sierra turns the screen away. Jake looks over, "Shit Maggie you and Fy need to go to the living room."

"Like hell, that's my mom!" Fy says and rushes around to see the screen before anyone can stop her. "Why didn't you tell us?" she looks accusingly at Jake and Maggie as she pulls the screen back to us.

"No little wolf, we tried that last time look at the outcome?" Amon says holding up his arms which are bitten and bruised to hell. Shit, even tied up she did a number on the asshole. I look more closely and see he has a black eye as well.

"What happened to beating me into submission, teaching me my place? Too cowardly to complete your goal bitch?" Angel hollers. "Come on pussy, give it your best shot!"

"God damn it, Angel! Shut your mouth!" Ian sneers angrily.

"She's not going to. Not with that girl there." Jake, Maggie and I all say at once. "She couldn't live with herself if that girl got hurt instead of her and she did nothing." Jake continues.

"Now, now are you trying to make me angry little wolf? One normally learns their lesson when they've been beaten as bad as you've been." Amon says amused at himself.

She literally shrugs her shoulders. "What? This? This is nothing, you think beating up a tied-up woman is going to make me cower?" She laughs. "Damn your pathetic master should have picked a real man for the job! Hell if Nick were anywhere near as sadistic as you he would at least be able to get the job done."

That does it, he's pissed we can see his eyes flash red. He flashes over to her and smacks her so hard that her head slams to the side. Maggie and Sierra both gasp.

Fy, her eyes flash just as angrily as her mother's and I swear to God they just glowed blue. "I'm going to kill him!" she says. "You!" She points at me. "How do I kill that man?"

I'll give the girl one thing: she's feisty as hell. I wonder if Angel knows, hell anyone, but I'm pretty damn sure the girls a potential. "A stake to the heart, rip off his head, light him on fire." I reply as evenly as I can.

"You make him sound like a Vampyr." Jake says with a laugh. So, Angel was right he'll deny the supernatural at all costs. Fy knows you can see it.

Angel turns her head back and blood is dripping down her mouth; she spits it right in his face. He hisses and jumps backward. "You fucking bitch!" He takes another swing.

Jake loses it then. He's screaming incoherently, kicking shit. I watch the Doc come up behind him, I don't see what happens but he drops out cold.

"What you do to my dad?" Fy asks the Doc.

"Just a sedative dear. Your mom will lose it if he destroys the house or hurts anyone." The Doc tells her. She just nods her head in return.

Edward has Grant take Jake upstairs. The rest of us turn back to the screen. Angel and Amon are staring each other down. It's almost like they're daring the other to do something. Amon breaks first and turns to start walking towards the girl.

"Stop!" Angel yells.

"No, not this time. You fight too much and a man has needs he has to scratch." He calmly replies.

"He's not…" Maggie says but can't finish.

I don't have the heart to tell her what she's thinking is exactly what he's planning. He's done it before, that's probably why the girl is there in the first place. You can tell she's been there way longer than Angel has. I see the desperation in Angel's eyes and I see her struggling. Then all of a sudden she just stops, I watch her look up to the ropes binding her and see it in her eyes when she notices that she can get out if she can get leverage to lift herself up. I think I know what she's about to do, but then her words floor me.

"I won't fight." She says softly. Never mind guess I was wrong.

"What was that little wolf?" Amon stops turning back to her. His voice taking on a husky tone.

"I won't fight you, just leave the girl alone." She says again a little louder. I see the girl shaking her head and begin to cry. As Amon starts to walk back to Angel.

"I can't watch this. Fy you should come with me." Maggie says.

"I'm not going anywhere," Fy replies. "You should go, but I'm not leaving mom."

"No, I'll stay." Maggie says defeatedly.

Amon gets close to Angel, right in her face really. "So you're going to finally give yourself to me, little wolf? In front of all your little friends even?" He asks, pointing to the camera.

"Oh yeah, I'm going to give you something." She says with a smirk.

I see the move seconds before she does it. She swings backward and slams into him so hard he starts to tumble. Before he can completely go down though she wraps her thighs around his neck and pulls him back towards her. He's fighting to catch himself and does straighten not realizing what she just forced him to do. As soon as her wrists are high enough to pull the rope out of the hook she does. Then she grabs the hook with her hands and kicks him back again with her feet.

He must have slammed into the camera and knocked it over because we don't see them anymore. We can still hear them though, which is why we can still hear Angel. "What you gonna do now mother fucker? Did you like to beat on tied-up little girls and women? What about women who can fight back?"

"We got it!" The IT guy yells.

"Do you have her location?" Edward asks.

"Yes, She's not too far from here."

"Sierra, Ian, Nick, grab Grant and the rest of the team. Get there now!" He demands.

On the way out I see that Tala chick pulls her phone from her pocket. I pull Sierra aside. "You need to have someone watch Tala closely and keep her off the phone." At first, she looks like she's going to defend the girl, but then she looks at her then glances at me, and nods.

Angelika

That idiot Vampyr is just staring at me stunned. He honestly thought he'd keep me here? How weak do these morons think I am? I walk right up to him and kick him square in the jaw.

"Come on little wolf I thought we were becoming friends." He says with his hands up in mock surrender.

"Fuck you!" I shout and kick him again. He falls back and I hear a crack. I've seen a few others so I know I have to move. I run over to Kora. "Sweetie I need you to untie me so I can undo your chain." The poor thing is traumatized but she does what I ask. "Okay, I need you to follow me. You need to listen to everything I say when I say it. If I say get down you get down. If I say run, run like the devil himself is chasing you! Can you do that?" I ask as I'm unchaining her. She nods at me quite enthusiastically too. "Okay let's go, stay close."

I slowly make my way to the stairs. I'm not sure if that Amon guy is dead or not but I know I don't have time to check. I've got to move if either of us is going to make it. I grab her hand and pull her after me skirting the side giving him a wide berth. Hell no, not gonna be one of those dumb-ass horror movie bitches who step right over the body.

I pull her halfway up the stairs and hold my hand up slightly. "Stay here, let me check." She nods.

I continue creeping up the stairs and get to the door. As soon as I begin opening it, it creeks because why the fuck wouldn't it? I stop and glance back downstairs. Amon is still motionless. So I listen at the door. When I'm reasonably sure no one's reacted I start opening the door again only a lot more carefully. I get it open and see that we aren't in a basement at all. It's almost like a bunker, there's a house nearby but far enough away that I don't even think a vampyr will see us. It opens up to the woods, it's a risk to head in there but our only chance. We'll have to take it. I rush back to Kora.

"Okay Kora. You're going to go ahead of me, no one's out there, don't worry. As soon as we're outside, that door run. Even if we get separated, you run and don't stop. I'll find you." She shakes her head no. "Sweetie, you have to do it. Don't worry I will be right behind you, just go." I'm afraid she'll say no again but she softly nods as tears form in her eyes. I give her a quick hug and push her forward.

We're almost to the top, god I've never been so grateful to get to the end of anything in my life. Kora steps out the door a few steps then turns to me and waits. I'm a few steps behind her so it doesn't take long. I take a step outside and see her eyes widen, right before strong arms wrap around my middle and lift me up. Fuck!

In a split-second decision I look at Kora and scream." Run!!!" Just as I brace my legs on the door jam and shove myself backward. We tumble down the stairs in a tight bundle. I feel my head slam against the step hard. Then my hip hits, and my knee. By the time I hit the bottom, I think my body is covered in more bruises than anything else. I know I'm screwed, I can't move, anything. This is the first time I actually believe I'm going to actually die here.

It takes everything I have in me to roll on my belly and start trying to drag myself away from the approaching footsteps. "Damn little wolf. Look what you've gone and done? Vampyr, remember? Did you think that would stop me?" He says.

"She… got out…at least…" I force out.

"Oh, you think so? No, you see I'm going to go get her, bring her back and rip her throat out right In front of you. Then we'll have some fun." He says and starts laughing.

That's when I feel it. It's just like what they described to me and I realized I've felt it before, many times before. I've always fought against it afraid it was the inner demons I hide but know are there. The tingling starts in my toes and fingers. Gradually moving towards the middle to meet I know what this might mean. I may never walk again but Fuck it, I might live. Instead of fighting I welcome it, embrace it. I see my hands start to change into paws covered in pure snow white fur, the tingling becomes unbelievable pain but I decide to scream through it and embrace the pain. My scream turns to a howl before I know it.

Slowly I stand, Amon has stopped laughing and is gawking at me in disbelief. "They said you can't change! You can't change!"

The deepest, most terrifying growl comes out of my throat. I swear to God this vamp just pissed itself. I'd be scared too if I were him, the problem is I don't know what the hell I'm doing.

"Trust me!" A musical voice in my head says. That's it I've finally fucking cracked, cuckoo goodbye, crayon box is broken fucking great!

"You're not crazy Angel," The voice says with a giggle great the voices in my head even think I'm a joke. *"I'm your wolf. You've kept me locked away."*

Am I being chastised by the damn voices in my head? *"You know what, I don't even care. I'll deal with my declining mental state later. You say you can help? Help!"*

"As you wish." The voice assures me.

I feel something push my consciousness aside. Well, not exactly but it's the closest description I can think of. Thankfully, numb nuts is still telling himself what's happened isn't possible. My wolf body flies at him going for his throat but at the last minute, he moves. I hit his shoulder but my jaws still clamp down and shake, tearing the flesh as I do. He punches me hard in the one leg and I feel the bone snap but my jaw doesn't release.

"Fuck you! You psycho bitch let go!" He screams as he grabs my jaw and rips me off flinging me.

My body hit the wall but as soon as I landed my body was up again. I almost fall, too much pressure going on my bad leg, but my body quickly readjusts so I'm standing on only three. I charge him steadier than I'd have thought. He's too distracted and I'm sure doesn't expect me to be up this time my lunge is flawless and his neck is in my strong jaws. He hit the ground with me on top of him and I started tugging, jerking, and shaking my head until his head came off. Once that's accomplished my body collapses. I try to regain control.

"No, you can't shift back! If you do, you will be paralyzed. You handled the change and might even handle it now. You won't handle the new damage from the throw though." The voice says.

"Why should I trust you?"

"Because I am you."

I'm not going to say I trust her but I hurt too much right now and need to wait a bit before I can even do anything. I'd like to at least move off this dead body at least but not having control I can't do much. Next thing I know my body gets up and moves to a bit cleaner spot. The move isn't easy and it's super slow but at least I'm not on a dead guy. I guess she can hear me.

"Yes, I can."

Footsteps come down the stairs and I smell a vampyr. I instantly jump to my three good legs and turn towards the sound, growling.

"Wow, easy." I see it's Nick and stop growling but still stand tensely. "Doc, I got her, come quick!" He yells up the stairs.

I turn my head and see the Doc, but not the normal Doc I'm used to. This is the Doc who put the damn metal in my back! "Well, I'll be damned." Doc U says. I can't pronounce the man's name to save my life never could. "Angel sweet girl. What on earth did you do to yourself? Let's get you fixed up hmm?" he says as he kneels next to me.

The last thing I hear before my eyes close is Nick say,
"Damn Angel you're a beautiful wolf. You're gonna be okay,
you're safe now. Not that we actually saved you, you did that."

EPILOGUE

I would really love it if I could wake up without a massive headache, just once you know. I'm not sure how long I've been out, well out isn't really correct exactly, I've come to a few times so I've more been in and out of consciousness. Just not sure for how long. Plenty of people have come in to see me and have been talking to me, I've caught bits and pieces of what people have been saying to me.

Fy has been demanding I stop this and wake up already. Tasia has been in to tell me about her days. Remi mainly just cries. He's always been a sweet and sensitive boy like that. Maggie's been in too saying we have a lot to talk about and I need to wake up so we can. The fact that she sounds angry makes me figure we won't actually talk once I wake up. She's never been big on confrontation.

Ian, Sierra, and Grant have all told me to wake up because if I don't my uncle might kill them. My uncle however has begged me to wake up because he can't have found his niece only to lose her. Tala on the other hand I've caught saying she hopes I never wake up because I've ruined her life. As far as I'm concerned she can screw herself, my life wasn't great but I was doing just fine before all this crap came into it. No, I wouldn't change it since I can now give the kids financial security, a car, hell a college education I never could have before. Still though to say I ruined her life? Bitch, please?

Jake on the other hand has tried everything. Threatening to move his mother in. Demanding I get up right now because the kids need me, heaven forbid he admit he actually needs me. Telling me Sara, and Vivi, are about to fly out here if I don't wake up right now. Those two are truly more like family than any of mine. To begging, he's actually resorted to begging. The problem is I've been trying to fully wake up and just haven't been able to. Hell, when I am conscious I don't even think anyone noticed it.

The first few times I regained consciousness, I was still a wolf. The voice in my head told me it was okay but my body needed to heal a bit more. The last time I came to as a wolf I'm not certain what happened but the Doc told someone in the room he had to do it now. Not sure what it was, but after I felt a sharp pinch in my neck and lost consciousness again. When I came to the next time I was back in my human body, that was the first time Jake, the kids, or Maggie was ever in the room. So I'm assuming someone kept them out while I was still in wolf form.

The visit that really jarred me was Nick, I know he only said what he said because he thought I couldn't hear him. Admitting he's still in love with me though? Not at all what I was expecting. Last we'd spoken about relationship stuff was after we had split up and decided to be friends. He told me he still cared deeply for me as a friend but that he didn't think he ever really loved me even though he had said he did. It stung, of course, it did but he was always such a good friend I didn't care I'd rather have him as a friend than nothing at all. Now of all times, he's going to say that to me? I'd already made the decision to ignore it and act like it never happened unless he brings it up again of course at which point I will have to face it.

Not sure who's here now and lacking the energy to actually look, I simply croak out. "Drink." I hear rustling and then…

"Angel?" Jake whispers. "Angel, are you awake?"

"Drink?" I repeat.

"Of course, I'll be right back. One second." He says quickly.

I hear him rush out the door. While he's gone I open my eyes. The light streaming in from the window stings so I blink a few times to let my eyes adjust to the harsh rays. Once they finally feel less painful I look around and see I'm in the downstairs guest bedroom of my house. Turning my head slightly I find Solas curled up on my pillow next to my head. Of course, my little protector kitty is doing his job.

When Jake comes back in he has Doc U with him. The man and I will have to have a discussion at some point but now isn't going to be the time. Jake looks completely disheveled, he's shirtless as he usually is at home, and of course, is wearing basketball shorts. His hair, however, is grown out longer than he usually lets it, as is his beard, it's sticking up in all directions as well. Of course, with the speed his hair grows it's no indication of how long I've been out. It doesn't look like he's taken a shower in at least a week. Not to mention the circles under his eyes are horrible.

"Here Angel." He says holding a cup with a straw out for me. I try to sit, but find I can't. My arms are fine. I can move my feet a little but I can't sit up. Jake notices the struggle and holds the cup closer straw right at my lips. I'm torn of course. I want to do this on my own but at the same time, I desperately need a drink. My throat is so dry, raw, and sore I won't be able to say much until I drink. So I do.

After a few long sips. "What the hell? Why can't I sit up?" I ask Jake, his face flushing like he's nervous. He looks to the Doc.

"Angel, remember how we'd discussed the metal? What damaging it might do? Or even removing it?" The Doc asks.

"I do, and I swear to everything I know if you're about to tell me I'm paralyzed I'm going to resurrect that fuck and kill him again!"

"We're not sure. I believe this is only temporary but we will have to prepare for the worst. The fall twisted the metal up something awful. The rest only added to it." He means my shifting I'm sure. "I had to go and remove all the metal. If there had been no problems you'd already have your mobility unfortunately we weren't that lucky. I had to fish around and gather a lot of the pieces. We won't know the full extent of the damage for a little while now. We may get lucky and in the end, there may be no damage. Your nerves just may have suffered a shock and need time to recover. This is of course what we're hoping for."

"So is this like after my surgery the sooner I get up walking the better?"

"That will probably help but I'm not sure you can right this second. The sedation I don't think has fully passed. Remember how you handled sedation last time, we had to use a lot more this time. "

"Yeah and not one of them would listen to me, and take you to the hospital!" Jake interjected.

"I told you Jake there was no reason to. After what she's been through the last thing I wanted was to take her there and have the cops breathing down her neck the second she regained consciousness." Doc U explains.

"Jake, it's fine. He's right, I'm not up to dealing with cops." I tell him mainly to calm him. "I will have to speak with them at some point though I figure?"

"Not anytime soon, no. Your uncle has basically told them they will wait until you're ready or have to kill him to get to you." The Doc explains. "Well, I will be back shortly to check on you. Let's give it a day before you start trying to walk and this time listen to me." I simply nod.

Of course, he'd add that last time I barely followed any of the rules he gave me. Not smart I know but Jake was gone for work all the time and with three younger kids there's a lot to be done. I didn't have the time or luxury to sit around. Hell three months after my surgery I did the cancer walk for Jake's grandma. Hell, I went to the lake and even tried to swim to the buoy. Well more than tried I did make it but thought I might drown. I was supposed to use my walker for a year and ditched it at two months. Was only supposed to walk twenty feet without resting for the first year which lasted only a month. I'm not very good at following directions not because I don't understand them, but because I don't want to be helpless and pathetic.

I look at Jake. "Jake baby I'm okay," I say as enthusiastically as I can. I'm not in the least okay, I'm scared, in pain, and tired. However I want to calm him, he looks like he's about to jump out of his skin.

He doesn't say anything, he just stares at me. He stares for the longest time and I'm starting to think the man's broken or some shit! Just as I'm about to say something he leaps forwards and grabs my shoulders firmly. Then he captures my mouth in his for a bruising almost painful kiss. The kiss doesn't last long, it's fast and hard, but the emotions behind it are enough to shatter worlds.

When he finally pulls away he looks into my eyes and demands. "Don't ever fucking do that again. Do you hear me? Don't ever be that stupid again. I love you damn it I can't fucking lose you. Don't do it again." He takes a few deep breaths. "I'm going to go tell the kids you're awake, they've been very worried about you. I love you." This is why I'm still with him. Why I've put up with all the bullshit. No matter what, when I'm hurt or in trouble, everything always stops. That's when he puts me first. True I shouldn't have to wait for it, but it's how I know he really loves me. We can be in the middle of a knock-down drag-out fight and it all disappears.

With that, he simply walks out. He didn't wait for my response which is good cause I don't know that I could've responded if I'd wanted to. It's not like being kidnapped and tortured was my plan. I certainly can't promise I won't do it again because in the same circumstances I know I would.

It's not only that though, I'm terrified. I'm more afraid now than I ever have been in my entire life. The reality is I'd already known I may never walk again when I made the choice to shift, but I didn't really even have a choice. It basically was to shift and risk paralyzation or death. I chose the only option with a chance of living. Now I'm going to have to keep my head up and pretend I'm perfectly okay with everything. I have no choice here either, I won't let this break me!

ACKNOWLEDGEMENT

Thank you to JS for all your support and opinions as well as your help with editing. I could never say enough how much your friendship has meant to me. You are my calm in the storm.

Thank you to AG for all your opinions and help with brainstorming. For your imput and guidance. Your support has been amazing, and I am forever grateful for your friendship. For always responding with when and where. You are my safe haven.

Thank you, AL for your never ending encouragement with all of my stupid endeavors in life. You are the cheerleader I never knew I needed

Thank you SF and CR you have both been incredible and I appreciate your input more than you will ever know. You taught me the true meaning of being there for a friend. Even though we hadn't talked in years you both stepped up when I needed people most no questions asked.

You all are forever in my heart!

BOOKS IN THIS SERIES

Angelika has lived her whole life ignorant of the supernatural heritage. That all changes one day when a man shows up at her door looking for her using a name she hasn't heard since she was a child.

Having just moved into her first house with her husband and children, leaving the pain of her past behind she believes her life will now change for the better. It definitely changes just not in the white picket fence, quiet and peaceful way she'd imagined. Nope instead she is introduced into a world of fantasy that she had only ever dared dreamed might exist.

Witch new friends and connections, the return of old ones she never thought she would see again and most especially the involvement of some blood thirsty creatures her worlds been flipped on its axis.

Can she face the new challenges put before her? Can she keep her family safe from the demons hunting her? Can she even survive? Find out how this mouthy Momma copes with the changes forcing their way into her life. How she faces down ever threat with sarcasm and a mouth that would make a sailor blush.

She proves that even moms can stand their ground when faced with an unbelievable life change!

Her Secret Chaos

Angelika is still recovering from her run in with Amon. Even though she is not yet back to normal she already has the Were council breathing down her neck, a new child to take care of,

yet another blast from the past, and top it all off, her child is missing.
She is facing the most challenging moment of her life and her mental limits will be tested to the max. Will she be able to come of this with all her senses intact or will the hidden deception in her family finally do her in?